THE THREE KINGS OF COLOGNE

THE THREE KINGS OF COLOGNE

Kate Sedley

Severn House Large Print
London & New York

This first large print edition published 2008
in Great Britain and the USA by
SEVERN HOUSE PUBLISHERS of
9-15 High Street, Sutton, Surrey, SM1 1DF.
First world regular print edition published 2007 by
Severn House Publishers, London and New York.

British Library Cataloguing in Publication Data

Sedley, Kate
  The three kings of Cologne. - Large print ed. - (Roger the
  Chapman mysteries)
  1. Roger the Chapman (Fictitious character) - Fiction
  2. Peddlers and peddling - England - Fiction 3. Great
  Britain - History - Edward IV, 1461-1483 - Fiction
  4. Detective and mystery stories 5. Large type books
  I. Title
  823.9'14[F]

  ISBN-13: 978-0-7278-7666-9

Printed and bound in Great Britain by
MPG Books Ltd, Bodmin, Cornwall.

One

The workmen found the body on the fourth day.

The first two days had been spent clearing the thickets of brambles, struggling saplings and carpet of weeds that had overrun the site for the past ten years, ever since the Magdalen nuns had abandoned it as a burial ground. Indeed, the plot had never, to anyone's knowledge, been used for that purpose, the number of Sisters who comprised the cell having gradually dwindled until, in this early spring of the Year of Our Lord, 1481, there were only three of them left.

The digging proper – turning the soil and removing the larger stones – was begun at dawn on the third working day; but it was not until halfway through the following morning that three of the labourers, trying between them to prise loose a particularly solid and obdurate boulder, dug down far enough to uncover what was obviously the skeletal remains of a human foot and leg.

Further investigation revealed the rest of what had undoubtedly once been a woman, with some strands of the long, dark, waist-length hair still clinging to the scalp. As I understood matters later, the workmen at first assumed that a mistake had been made; that at some time or another one of the nuns had been buried in the intended graveyard and the interment had subsequently gone unrecorded. But when the scandalized Sisters had pointed out that no nun would be buried wearing several fine gold finger rings, a gold and amber necklace and a girdle of gold and silver links, boasting an amethyst clasp, this idea was swiftly dispelled. Furthermore, the head man of the gang and two of his subordinates attested to the fact that a swathe of some rich emerald-green material, possibly velvet or silk, had been visible for several seconds after the body was uncovered and before it crumbled to dust as it came into contact with the air.

So! If this was not the skeleton of some long-dead Magdalen nun, whose body was it?

This story, as far as I was concerned, had begun some weeks earlier, when Bristol and the surrounding countryside had still been in the grip of winter; when fingers and noses were still nipped red-raw by the sleet and wind blowing up the River Avon from the sea. To some extent, the city was protected from the worst of the weather by the high ground to the north. But when the snow and frosts of January eventually gave way to the icy rains of February, there was little let-up either in the epidemic of coughs, sore throats and running noses, or in the general depression endemic to short, cold days and long, dark, even colder nights.

It was the time of year, too, when tempers also grew shorter, when domestic tiffs flared into serious quarrels and the constant herding together indoors caused rows out of all proportion to any provocation that might have been offered. I got out and about with my pack and dog as much as I could. But that left Adela cooped up all day with the children; and when I returned at dusk, tired, freezing and hungry, the loving wife I had parted from in the morning had turned into a nagging scold, exhausted as much in mind as in body, and ready to fly out at me over every little thing. The two elder children – my stepson, Nicholas, and my daughter, Elizabeth – were sulky and bored as only six-year-olds know how to be, while two-and-a-half-year-old Adam toddled around getting under everyone's feet, screaming in frustration each time he was prevented from getting his own way, and endearing himself to no one.

'Think yourselves lucky that you have a whole house to play in and not a one-roomed cottage, you ungrateful little brute!' I roared at Nicholas one evening when his whinging had irked me more than usual.

Now, however much you might think you have become one family, it only needs a harsh word from the step-parent to the child that isn't his (or hers) to prove what a mistaken idea this is.

'Don't call my son a brute,' Adela reprimanded me sharply, ladling out portions of dried fish and lentil broth into our respective bowls.

The day had been an exceptionally long one; a cold, tiring slog the five miles to Keynsham and back, and with not much in my purse to show for such a journey at the end of it. I was in no mood to be taken to task.

7

'Oh, *your* son is he now?' I retorted nastily. 'Well, my love, I'd remind you that it's *my* efforts that clothe and feed him.'

I watched Adela's face assume that blank mask it wears when she is deeply hurt or offended.

'Don't call me your love when you don't mean it,' she snapped. 'And at the moment, you plainly don't.'

Elizabeth startled us both at this juncture by bursting into tears. Guiltily, I had half-risen from my stool to go to her, when she sniffed, 'Why do you quarrel so much?' She glared accusingly at me. 'It's not like this when you're away and Uncle Richard's here.'

'Uncle Richard?' I asked blankly, thinking fleetingly of my self-avowed friend and occasional employer, the Duke of Gloucester, before rightly dismissing the notion as absurd.

'Onken Dick! Onken Dick!' Adam shouted, banging the table with his little spoon.

I glanced at Adela for enlightenment.

Stooping over Elizabeth, murmuring words of comfort, she raised a flushed and defiant face to mine.

'Bess means Richard. Richard Manifold,' she said.

'You invite that man here when I'm away from home?' I was outraged.

'Sometimes. I get lonely in your absence,' she pleaded. 'Our neighbours, as you know, have never been very friendly towards us, and it's not always convenient for Margaret –' my former mother-in-law and Adela's cousin – 'to come all the way from Redcliffe. And Richard is such an

8

old friend. I've known him for years.'

There was reason in what she said, but I was in no mood to be appeased.

'Well, my dear, you'll antagonize the neighbours even more if you entertain men while I'm gone.'

'What are you implying, Roger?' she asked, dangerously quiet.

We both knew what I was implying, and we both knew – or, at least, I hoped I knew – that the implication was unfounded. But I was not prepared, at the moment, to discuss the matter.

'And I will not have my children calling Richard Manifold "uncle".' I banged my fist on the table and then wished that I hadn't as Hercules started barking and Adam began to thump in emulation. 'Whose suggestion was it?'

'Richard's.'

'I see.'

By now, a cold fury had me in its grip, and although I knew it to be unreasonable, I was too exhausted to fight it. I had never liked Richard Manifold and clearly perceived that the Sergeant now felt himself so assured of Adela's friendship, had managed to get his feet so securely under my table, that he was ready to claim a spurious kinship with our children.

I swallowed a mouthful of broth and said thickly, 'Understand me, Adela! I will not have that man eating here when I'm absent. Nor will I allow either Elizabeth or Adam to call him uncle.'

I deliberately omitted any mention of my stepson. She could make of that what she liked.

9

What she liked was to resume her seat at the kitchen table without a word and finish eating her supper. But I couldn't let matters rest.

'Is that understood?' I persisted.

'Perfectly. And I shall, of course, obey your commands to the letter.' Her tone would have made Hell itself freeze over.

Such obedience was, it goes without saying, due to the head of a household from his dependants; but I had never been the sort of man to expect submissive behaviour from his family. This was just as well as I rarely received it and, as now, was uncomfortable when I did. Normally, I would have made haste to mend fences, but on this occasion I lapsed into a sulky silence, the reason being Richard Manifold and my simmering jealousy of him.

He had once, many years ago and before she married her first husband, Owen Juett, been a pretender to Adela's hand, but she had preferred her swain from Hereford. And since her return to her native Bristol, she had made it quite plain that she loved me and not him. Yet since our wedding day, he had become a constant presence in our life, which, as a Sheriff's man I suppose was in some ways understandable, considering my interest in crime. But it was more than that. Richard Manifold had never married and, as a single man, was always open to any invitation from friends for a free meal and company other than his own. Adela, much to my annoyance, had frequently taken pity on him, and allowed him a seat at our table and fireside far too often for my peace of mind.

10

She told me and showed me that she loved me, but I was a man. I wanted total adoration from my chosen woman, while retaining for myself the freedom to ogle and flirt with any female who caught my fancy. Not that I had ever been unfaithful to Adela, but there was always a chance that one day I might succumb to temptation. But then, as anyone with any sense knows, it's different for a man.

The meal proceeded in silence, broken only by the two elder children's mutterings to one another, and by Adam's discovery that if he hummed loudly and tunelessly – he had inherited my inability to carry a tune – he could ignore the rest of us. Adela and I said nothing, she refilling my bowl with stew and cup with ale without being asked, until the atmosphere between us had become so tense that only an explosion could clear the air.

But I was suddenly too tired to quarrel: it would have to wait for another time.

'I'm going out,' I said.

It was dark by now, the short February day having ended in a steady rain that drummed against the shutters. The city gates were long since closed and locked, but the alehouses would be open for honest citizens who wanted to make merry or, like myself, drown their sorrows. I pulled on my boots again, wrapped myself in my cloak with the hood well up, and made my way up Small Street to the warmth and comfort of the Green Lattis, my regular drinking den in the shadow of All Saints Church. (There were other inns in Bristol, and plenty of them, but I had

11

grown accustomed to the Lattis – or Abyngdon's or the New Inn, whichever you liked to call it – and felt at home there.)

Not being in the mood for convivial conversation, I squeezed on to a stool at a corner table, well back in the shadows, buried my nose in my beaker and prepared to brood on my wrongs as a husband and father. I had just reached the maudlin stage of feeling extremely sorry for myself when my comfortable wallow in self-pity was disturbed by the arrival of a noisy crowd at the central table, among whom I recognized the ship owner, John Jay, and his captain, the Welshman, Thomas Lloyd. The previous summer, these two men and their crew had set sail from Bristol in an attempt to find the Island of Brazil, believed to lie somewhere to the west of Ireland. They had been lost at sea for nine weeks, while relatives, friends and the city's population in general gave them up for dead. And now, it seemed – for their loud, jovial tones made the whole inn a party to their discussion – they were planning to do it all over again this coming summer. To a confirmed landlubber like me, it was incredible that these fools could be serious in wishing to endanger their lives and everyone else's peace of mind by setting off a second time to look for an island no one was even sure existed.

I was still staring at them in utter fascination when the man sitting beside me got up and left, and I barely noticed when another customer took his place. It was not until a pleasant voice said, 'Good evening, Master Chapman,' that I turned my head and recognized a neighbour of ours,

Alderman John Foster.

Now, normally, our neighbours in Small Street avoided recognition of me and my family as keenly as they would have avoided acknowledging a parcel of tinkers, and had never quite forgiven Cicely Ford for leaving her house to me when she died. (Had she not been well known in Bristol for her sweetness and goodness, her generosity might have been more widely misinterpreted. As it was, a few false and scurrilous rumours still persisted concerning my relationship with her.) I had had dealings, however, with Alderman Foster the preceding year when the mystery I had been trying to solve involved a distant kinswoman of his. I had found him not only polite, but friendly; an unusual state of affairs considering the difference in our social standing. I was an indigent pedlar. He was a former Bailiff and Sheriff of the city; a wealthy merchant importing tons of salt each year from the Rhineland (and with a passion for Cologne Cathedral). Moreover, he was Bristol's Mayor-elect and would shortly take up the reins of that prestigious office. He was not the man I would have expected to encounter in a common alehouse; nor, having done so, would I have expected him to take the trouble to speak to me. Which goes to show, you never can tell.

'You appear very interested in our friends over there,' he remarked when I had returned his greeting.

Never shy of stating an opinion, I expressed myself forcibly on the subject of the projected expedition.

'They've already given folk one nasty fright. Now they want to do it again. And for what? Does this so-called Island of Brazil even exist? Most people I've ever spoken to seem to believe it's a myth.'

The Alderman sipped thoughtfully from the beaker of ale that an obsequious potboy, prompted by the landlord, had just placed before him in double-quick time.

'As far as this island goes, I think you may be right,' he admitted. 'But although I'm no sea-farer myself – I own no ships and merely hire the vessels bringing my salt from the Rhineland – I still believe there might be territory somewhere beyond Ireland. There are certain accounts of sightings that I find hard to dismiss completely. My own feeling, however, shared by some others, is that this land, whatever it is, lies much further west than has previously been thought. But if it does exist, we, as a trading port, need to find it.'

'Why?' My tone was blunt.

My companion chuckled. 'I could give you a high-flown answer and say that it is our God-given duty to discover all we can about His creation; to extend our knowledge of His world and to spread His message to all who have not yet heard it. But the more prosaic truth, my friend, is that Bristol needs new markets if we are to maintain our prosperity and position as the foremost port outside of London.'

I was sceptical. 'I should have thought that Bristol was rich enough and busy enough for that not to be in doubt. There are ships from all

14

over Europe and beyond in and out of the city every hour of the day, six days a week. Sometimes the Backs are so crowded you can barely squeeze your hand between the prow of one ship and the stern of the next.'

The Alderman took another sip of ale.

'That's as maybe, Master Chapman,' he said, wiping his mouth on his sleeve in a homely fashion. 'Some days no doubt it is so, but not always. Not now. In the past, yes. Wine was among the chief of our imports. But thirty years ago we lost Bordeaux and Gascony to the French, and the great wine fleets disappeared almost overnight. It's true that the trade is reviving a little with our imports from Spain and Portugal, but not in sufficient quantities. And, besides, to the discerning palate Spanish wine can never be a substitute for French. But the wine trade is not the only one in danger of decline. Fish,' he added, beckoning to a passing potboy to refill his beaker and mine.

'Fish?' I queried doubtfully. It sometimes seemed to me that more fish were landed on Bristol's quays than there could possibly be in the entire ocean. There were days when the whole city reeked of them.

'Fish,' the Alderman repeated. 'In particular, stockfish – or cod if you want to give them their new-fangled name. For over a century, we have had a thriving trade with Iceland. In return for our soap and woollen cloth, the Icelanders have sent us all the dried stockfish that we could handle, enabling us to supply our own wants and sell the surplus on over an area stretching as far east as London, south to Salisbury and north to Worcester. But now that trade, too, is in jeopardy. So, you see, we want new markets. And if there is indeed a land west of Ireland, we urgently need to know about it and establish trading links before it's discovered by anyone else.'

'Why is the stockfish trade in danger?' I asked.

'Because members of the Hanseatic League are offering the Icelanders higher prices for their fish; prices that Bristol merchants can't afford, either in goods or money.' My companion heaved a regretful sigh. 'Unfortunately, the city of Cologne is a part of the League.'

'Why unfortunately?'

I thought for a moment that John Foster was not going to answer. Then he asked,

'Can you keep a secret, Master Chapman?'

'I think so,' I replied cautiously, not sure what was coming.

The Alderman smiled. 'In any case, it won't be a secret for long.' He continued with apparent irrelevance and an endearing modesty, 'You may know that I am shortly to become Mayor.' I nodded. 'I have therefore come to the conclusion that it is high time I did something for my native city. After talking the matter over with my wife, I have decided to build a chapel and almshouses on a piece of land outside the walls, at the top of Steep Street, which I have recently acquired from the Magdalen nuns. They rented it some years ago from the Abbot of Tewkesbury – a ninety-nine-year lease – intending to use it as a graveyard. But no one has ever been buried

16

there, and the Sisters eventually decided to rid themselves of what has become an encumbrance. So, after some negotiations, the land is now mine. Oh, I know what you're thinking!' He didn't: at that moment, my mind was a total blank. 'You're thinking – and you'd be right – that Bristol is already blessed with a number of excellent almshouses, amongst them those founded by my good friends, William Spencer and Robert Strange, not to mention the ancient Gaunts' Hospital. But we all have the arrogance to want our names to live on after we have gone to meet our Maker.'

'A...a very noble enterprise,' I agreed somewhat stiffly. 'But...but, forgive me, what has this to do with our previous conversation? With the fact that Cologne is a member of the Hanseatic League?'

Alderman Foster chuckled. 'Of course, I was forgetting. I mentioned, I think, that I mean to have a chapel built as well as the almshouses. When it is finished – and who knows when that might be? Our English stonemasons are not noted for their swiftness.'

'But splendid craftsmen,' I put in with what I hoped was a twinkle in my eye.

'Of course,' he concurred gravely, but with an answering twinkle. 'That goes without saying. So! When my chapel is finally completed, I shall have it dedicated to the Three Kings of Cologne. If there is still trouble with the League, I anticipate some opposition, but I am determined to have my way.'

'The Three Kings of Cologne,' I murmured.

17

'The Magi? The Three Wise Men?'

'Indeed. In the twelfth century, their remains were taken from Milan to Cologne by the Holy Roman Emperor, Frederick Barbarossa himself. Melchior, King of Nubia and Arabia, gave gold to the Christ Child as a symbol of His kingship. Caspar, King of Tarsus and Egypt, gave frankincense, as a tribute to His godhead. And Balthazar, King of Godolu and Seba, gave myrrh, which presaged His death. In the east, myrrh is used for embalming corpses.'

'It will certainly be unusual,' I said. 'To the best of my knowledge, there is no other church or chapel with such a dedication.'

'I know of none,' he answered cheerfully. 'It will certainly stir up some controversy. But, as I say, that's for the future. The land itself has to be cleared first; it's very overgrown. I shall set the workmen to start on that as soon as the better weather comes. Mid-April or early May. Perhaps a little earlier if we should have a clement spring. Who can tell? Now, let me buy you another beaker of ale and then I'll bid you goodnight. You must be wanting to get home to your family.'

I suppressed a grimace and thanked him, but could not forbear from asking, 'Why have you chosen me for these confidences, Alderman?'

He didn't pretend not to understand me, but replied frankly, 'I like you. I was impressed by the way you solved that little mystery down at Wells last year. My kinswoman has informed me of the outcome – in the strictest confidence, of course. And I hear rumours that you have a

18

reputation for that sort of thing. You have, I believe, worked for His Grace, the Duke of Gloucester, on occasions. You are not quite the simple pedlar you pretend to be. And who knows? I might have need of your services myself one day.'

It was almost as if the Alderman had been granted second sight. For, two months later, when the woman's body was discovered in the ground at the top of Steep Street, and the nuns had disowned it, John Foster felt himself to be responsible for it. The land was now his, and the poor creature had most certainly never received a Christian burial, for when the skull was lifted, it was found to have a great hole at the back, plainly indicating that its owner had been battered to death by some blunt instrument. Whoever the woman was, there was no doubt whatsoever that she had been murdered.

Two

It was another two days after the discovery of the body that I received a request from Alderman Foster to visit him at home. The messenger was a scruffy urchin whom I recognized as a regular scavenger in the central drain that ran along the middle of the roadway.

'Oi! Master Foster wants t' see you.'

The April weather had turned cold again after several days of springlike warmth, a chill wind sweeping the streets, sending dust and bits of dried onion skin skimming along the ground, whistling up through cracks in the floorboards and under doors and making me reluctant to get out of bed in the morning. Fortunately for the state of my finances, Adela and the children made it impossible for me to turn over and snatch another half hour's sleep, the former shaking me vigorously before getting out of bed herself, and the latter jumping all over me. That particular morning I had been roused not only to wakefulness but to fury by Adam's instructions to his siblings to 'kick him in the nuts!'

'Adam!' I roared, heaving myself into a sitting position and thereby dislodging both Nicholas and Elizabeth from the bed, so that they tumbled on to the floor. All three immediately set up a wail that brought Adela hotfoot back into the room, anxious to know the cause of the disturbance.

I repeated Adam's remark and demanded to know where he'd got hold of such expressions. 'He's only two!'

'He'll be three in a couple of months' time,' my wife pointed out, but could hardly speak for laughing, which she tried valiantly but unsuccessfully to turn into a fit of coughing.

In the end, I could see the funny side of things myself, swung my feet out of bed and kissed all three children soundly before shooing them from the bedchamber while I dressed.

With the coming of the lighter nights and warmer days, life had eased considerably and, as a family, we were again on friendly terms, the children able to play out of doors in the tiny yard at the back of the house, or upstairs during the day without freezing to death. And until this particular morning, when, in typically English fashion, winter had once more interrupted spring, I had been content to be out on the road shortly after sunrise and the opening of the city gates, hawking my wares in the hamlets and villages around Bristol, sometimes going as far as Bath or Gloucester and staying a night, sometimes two as necessity demanded, away from home. This morning, however, with the suspicion that I had a rheum coming on, judging by a sore throat and runny nose, I had loitered over breakfast and was only just filling my pack with a new stock of goods, purchased the previous day from various ships along the Backs, by the time Adela was ready to teach the two elder children their numbers and letters. Their hornbooks were laid ready on the kitchen table and she was obviously growing impatient with my continued presence.

The knock on the street door diverted her attention, and she rose from her stool to answer it. She returned a few moments later, the young boy at her heels. Before she could enlighten me, the lad had delivered his message.

I straightened my back and glared at him.

'*Alderman* Foster to you, my lad. And what did he really say?'

'I jus' told you, didn' I? 'E wants t' see you.'

I gave up. 'What about, did he mention?'

'Nah! Why should 'e? None o' my business. But 'e gave I a half a groat.' He opened his dirty palm to show me the coin, then bit it with his sharp, surprisingly good little teeth. 'It's genuine.'

'I should suppose it is,' I said. 'I can't imagine the Alderman would ever deal in counterfeit coins. And you'd better take care of it. That's half a day's wage for a field labourer.' I looked at Adela. 'I ought to go at once.'

She nodded resignedly. 'No doubt it'll be about this body they've dug up at the top of Steep Street. Everyone's talking about it.'

'Perhaps,' I answered cautiously. 'Although what the Alderman thinks I can do about it, I don't know.'

She sighed. 'Well, you'd better go and see. And you,' she added, addressing the boy, 'you'd better get off home before you lose that money.'

'It's safe with me, mother,' he retorted cheekily, then stuck his tongue out at the children, who were regarding him open-mouthed, and disappeared, banging the street door noisily in his wake.

I followed him, kissing Adela a hurried goodbye before she had time to remind me that I had a family to clothe and feed and should really be out on the road, selling my wares, not allowing myself to get involved with mysterious deaths that didn't concern me.

The wind had dropped slightly as I walked up Small Street amidst all the bustle of a new day. The muckrakers were out, trying to clear the drains, piling the refuse on to carts before driving it out of the city, either to dump it in the river somewhere a good way upstream, or to bury it in pits a few miles distant from the town. But it was a never-ending battle. Already, as fast as they were emptied, the drains were being filled up again. And the stench from the Shambles, where butchers were carving up the freshly killed carcasses of sheep, cows and pigs was overpowering enough this morning to make me retch. Normally, I didn't notice it. I must be sickening for something.

Alderman Foster's house was basically like my own; a hall, parlour, buttery, kitchen and, upstairs, three bedchambers. Beneath street level were cellars where he stored his salt. The difference lay in the richness of the furnishings; tapestries on the walls, silver candelabra, a profusion of velvet-covered cushions on window seats and chairs, decorated wall cupboards displaying contents of pewter, silver and gold plates and drinking vessels, rugs scattered among rushes which were freshly laid and sprinkled with dried flowers. There were no children's toys left lying around for the unwary to trip over and no noise as the little darlings themselves pounded around, screaming, overhead. And there was no scruff of a dog scratching for fleas, only two well-behaved hounds stretched out beside a fire of logs and sea coal burning steadily in the grate.

A rosy-faced, neatly dressed young maid opened the door to me.

'Master's in the parlour,' she said, bobbing a curtsey. 'He said I'm to take you straight in.'

I was unused to such deferential treatment, and felt uncomfortable. Even in royal palaces, servants treated me for what I was; a nobody, like themselves.

John Foster rose to greet me, as I was ushered into the parlour, from a carved armchair near the window whose panes, I noticed, were oiled parchment, unlike those in the hall. (Those, to impress visitors, were made of the rarer and very expensive glass.)

'Master Chapman, thank you for coming so promptly. Please, sit down.' And he indicated another lavishly carved armchair, pulled close to his own. Yellow brocaded cushions covered the seat and cradled my back as I sank into it.

'How can I be of use, sir?'

For a moment, having sat down again, he seemed at a loss as to how to begin. Then he leaned forward, elbows on knees, and said, 'I'm sure you've heard about this body that has

24

recently been found?' My nod encouraged him to go on. 'Of course you have. A silly question. There's been little talk of anything else for the past two days. You are aware, naturally, that it was buried on the land I've acquired from the Magdalen nuns? Forgive me. Another unnecessary question. After our conversation in the Lattis in February, you would probably have realized that fact sooner than most, although I think that the majority of my fellow citizens know by now of my intentions. But have you been told that the identity of the poor victim has been established?'

This was news to me. 'No, I didn't know,' I said shaking my head vigorously. 'Who...Who is she? Did you know her?' In my eagerness, I even forgot to address him as 'sir'.

'I knew of her. And of her parents,' the Alderman admitted. 'But only by hearsay. From friends of friends or acquaintances, so to speak. It's all a long time ago. It must be getting on for twenty years since Isabella Linkinhorne disappeared.'

'Twenty years!' I echoed, astonished, not having seen the state of the body, nor having had it described to me. But now I could guess, which made my next question inevitable. 'How, in that case, has it been possible to establish who she is? Or, rather, was?'

'By a gold and amber necklace, and by a girdle of gold and silver links with an amethyst clasp that the corpse was still wearing. One of the nuns, who had known the lady well, was able to identify them almost immediately. And her father – Isabella's father, that is – who is now a very old man of eighty-five, was able to confirm Sister Walburga's story when they were shown to him.'

'The parents are still alive, then?'

'Not the mother. Mistress Linkinhorne, so I'm told, was found drowned in the Avon a year after her daughter's disappearance. A terrible accident. I don't know the details, but possibly distress of mind at not knowing what had happened to her child might have been a cause. Who can say? But Jonathan Linkinhorne is still alive and lives now in the Gaunts' Hospital.'

'How old was this Isabella Linkinhorne when she vanished?' I wanted to know. 'And when you say disappeared...?'

The Alderman pursed his lips. 'My understanding, from the enquiries I have made, is that she was about twenty, the only child of elderly parents, born when they had given up all hope of having children. Those in the know say that as a consequence, Isabella grew up over-indulged, spoiled and wilful, just as you might expect of one allowed to run wild from an early age.'

'And she just disappeared?'

'Apparently. One day she went out riding, as was her daily custom, and never came home.'

I frowned. 'Was she not looked for? Weren't enquiries made as to what might have become of her?'

At this point, the little maid re-entered the parlour, carrying a tray on which reposed a flask of wine, two beakers and a silver dish of sweet oatmeal biscuits. She placed it on a small table near the Alderman's chair.

'Sorry to take so long, Master,' she said, giving him a fleeting, conspiratorial grin. 'Trouble in the kitchen.'

'Again?' he murmured with a rueful smile. 'All right, my dear, and thank you. You'd better get back and see if there's anything you can do.'

She departed with a giggle, leaving me relieved to know that things could go wrong in the most well-run establishment as well as in the chaos of my family kitchen.

Alderman Foster poured and handed me a beaker of wine, then sipped his own. 'Now, what was it you were asking me, Master Chapman?'

'I was asking, sir, what efforts were made to find the girl at the time of her disappearance.'

'That I don't know. The impression I get from the various people I spoke to yesterday – people who were acquainted with Jonathan and Amorette Linkinhorne – is not perhaps as much as one would expect. For the simple reason, I gather, that the idea of Isabella having come to any harm never entered her parents' heads. They assumed she had run away with one of her many admirers. She was known to have at least three. Anyway, you will be able to find out more when you make your enquiries.'

'When I...?' At last, we had come to the nub of the matter; the reason for my urgent summons which, I had to admit, had escaped me until now. I should have guessed.

Alderman Foster lowered his beaker, looking guilty. 'Forgive me, Master Chapman, but I was hoping that...well, that you could be persuaded

27

to discover the circumstances surrounding Isabella Linkinhorne's death. Her body has been found on land that now belongs to me and, foolish though it may seem, I feel responsible for uncovering the facts of the crime and bringing the murderer to justice if I can. You're the only person I know who might be able to do this.'

Oh, thank you, God! You've taken over my life again!

'But...but, Alderman,' I managed to stammer before he raised a finger, enjoining my silence.

'Master Chapman, believe me, I know what you're going to say. You have a wife and family to support. I understand that. Therefore you must allow me to be your paymaster during such time as you are working at my behest.'

He rose and crossed the room to where a small chest, beautifully carved with acanthus leaves, stood on top of another, larger one. The former had a wrought-iron lock that the Alderman opened with a key, taken from the pocket of his velvet gown, and lifted out a leather drawstring purse which he brought back and placed in my lap. As he did so there was a satisfactory chink of coin on coin.

I made a half-hearted protest. 'Sir, I have never taken money for any of the mysteries that I've solved. I've always regarded the ability to do so as a God-given talent; something to be shared freely with other people.' All the same, I could just imagine Adela's anger if she learned that I had refused the proffered assistance.

My companion seemed to read my thoughts

and chuckled.

'If your conscience troubles you, Master Chapman, give the purse to your goodwife as a present from me. You needn't touch a penny of its contents. Well, what do you say? Will you take on this search for me? Will you try to discover what really happened to this poor young woman, even though she was murdered twenty years ago? I feel sure it's within your powers of deduction.'

I hesitated, but more for effect than any other reason. I could already feel the prickles of curiosity, the need to know the answer to any problem with which I was presented, nudging me towards acceptance of John Foster's proposal.

'And if I'm unable to discover the truth?' I queried.

'I shall still be satisfied that you have done your best.' Nevertheless, his tone implied that he would be disappointed.

I sighed. That was my constant fear; that one day someone would present me with a mystery I would find impossible to unravel. My self-esteem would be trampled in the dust.

'Very well,' I said, 'but only if my wife agrees.' The Alderman inclined his head. 'So, tell me,' I went on, 'who are the people I should speak to? Is there anything further that you, yourself, know about the Linkinhornes?'

The Alderman resumed his seat, reaching out to lay a hand on my arm.

'First, accept my thanks. I'm deeply grateful to you for your willingness to undertake this investigation for me. I could not go ahead and build a chapel on this land at the top of Steep Street if I felt that I had not done everything in my power to let this poor girl's spirit lie easy; to bring her murderer to book.'

I doubted that the killer, supposing I could unmask him, would share the same sentiments. Whoever he was, the discovery of Isabella Linkinhorne's body – if, that is, he had yet heard about it – must have come as a nasty shock. He would surely have thought himself safe after twenty years or more. All the same, he would probably consider it unlikely that anyone would bother to search for him, or that his identity would be uncovered even if anyone tried. It would be almost impossible to prove a man was in a certain place at a certain time two decades earlier. I began to feel very uneasy, wondering what I had taken on.

I realized that Alderman Foster was speaking, answering my question.

'I can only advise you, my dear young man, to visit Jonathan Linkinhorne at the Gaunts' Hospital as soon as possible. As I told you, he is a very old man now, eighty-five or thereabouts, unable to look after himself and with no woman to care for him and tend to his needs. Only he can give you the true facts of his daughter's disappearance, so I would suggest that you talk to him without delay.'

I nodded, picking up the purse and making preparations to rise. 'Are – were – the Linkinhornes a Bristol family?' I asked.

'I believe they lived in the manor of Clifton. Indeed, my information is that Jonathan Linkinhorne continued to live there until he grew too weak to fend for himself. But he will tell you all you need to know. He may be frail in body, but it seems his mind and understanding are as good as ever. Although I am only repeating what friends and mutual acquaintances have told me.'

I got to my feet. The Alderman rose with me. 'Let me say again how grateful I am to you, Master Chapman. I am in your debt.'

I smiled wryly. 'Save your thanks, sir, until I'm able to tell you what you want to know. I promise nothing.'

He patted my arm once more. 'I feel certain you won't fail me.' I wished I could share his certainty.

Adela was not best pleased when I reported my conversation with Alderman Foster, but her feelings underwent a change when I produced the purse. She emptied its contents on to the kitchen table and drew a deep breath as the coins ran in all directions. The children, always interested spectators, whooped with excitement and chased those that fell off the edge and clattered across the stone-flagged floor.

'That's very generous of the Alderman,' she said, rescuing the groat that Adam was trying to stuff into his mouth, and instructing the other two to put their booty back on the table. She was beset by sudden doubts. 'Should you really be willing to accept so much, Roger? I daresay that altogether there's the value of at least two or three nobles here.'

Her sentiments found an echo in my own

mind, but how could I tell how long this enquiry might take me?

'I didn't solicit the money,' I answered quietly. 'Nor did I expect it. Alderman Foster offered it entirely of his own accord. He's very anxious that the mystery of this Isabella Linkinhorne's death should be cleared up and the person responsible brought to justice.'

'Why, do you suppose? You say he didn't even know her or her family.'

I shrugged. 'If he were only intending to build the almshouses on the site, perhaps he wouldn't worry. But, as I understand it, he is reluctant to raise a chapel on ground that has been contaminated by murder. If the criminal can be brought to book and made to pay the penalty for his misdeeds, then I think the Alderman will feel that he can safely have the graveyard re-consecrated.'

My wife carefully gathered up the coins, dropping them one by one back into the purse. 'You must do your very best, Roger.'

I suppressed a grin at her change of tune and merely replied that I always did; whereupon she put her arms around my neck, kissed me soundly, apologized and said she knew that without being told.

'When do you intend to start? If you are going to the Gaunts' Hospital right away...'

I shook my head. 'Master Linkinhorne can wait. First, I need to talk to the workmen who found the body. But before even that, I shall walk over to Redcliffe and have a word with Margaret.'

'In heaven's name, why?'

I grinned. 'My love, there's precious little that's gone on in this city for the past fifty years that either Margaret or one of her cronies doesn't know about. I'll own myself extremely surprised if one of them can't tell me more about the Linkinhornes than the family even knew about themselves.'

Adela laughed. 'You're probably right. If my cousin or Bess Simnel or Maria Watkins have nothing to say, there's most likely nothing to tell.' She added, 'Take the dog with you. He needs the exercise.'

Hercules was stretched out by the fire and I stirred him with my toe. He opened a bleary eye, farted loudly, rolled over and went back to sleep once more. My wife, however, was having none of that. She fetched the rough leather collar I had made for him and the length of rope we used as a leading string and handed them both to me with an imperious gesture. Ten minutes later, while she and the two elder children settled down with their hornbooks for an hour of lessons, I trudged up Small Street yet again, at my heels a reluctant hound who was making his displeasure plain by dragging at the rope and stopping to investigate every smell that caught his fancy. In the end, exasperated, I picked him up, tucked him under one arm and carried him the rest of the way, down High Street, across the Backs and Bristol Bridge and into Redcliffe.

I was in luck.

My former mother-in-law was not only at

home, but was enlivening a dull April morning by entertaining Bess Simnel and Maria Watkins to small beer and oatcakes, the three of them sat around the table, their heads close together, emitting sudden snorts and cackles of laughter as they busily tore some poor neighbour's character to shreds. Indeed, they were so busy gossiping that they didn't even hear me knock, and only glanced up when the draught of my entry into the little room fluttered their caps.

'Dear Lord,' Maria Watkins grumbled, flashing her toothless gums, 'look what the cat's dragged in.'

'Don't you mean the dog?' giggled Bess Simnel and promptly doubled up at her own witticism.

Margaret Walker demanded suspiciously, 'What's wrong? Is Adela or one of the children ill?' With a mixture of pride and ill-usage, she added to her friends, 'They can't get along without me, you know.'

The other two exchanged fleeting grins and made to rise from their stools.

'We'll be off then,' Goody Watkins said. 'Come along, Bess.'

'No, no!' I expostulated. 'I need all three of you. There's nothing wrong at home, Mother-in-law. I just need some information.' At the magic word, the two elder women resumed their seats with alacrity, fixing me with their bright, beady blue eyes. 'It's about the girl whose body was found in the old Magdalen nuns' graveyard a few days ago. Isabella Linkinhorne, I'm told her name was. I'm wondering if you know anything of her, or her parents' history. If you know any-thing at all, that is.'

If they knew anything! The mere suggestion that they might not was an insult that made them grow pink with indignation.

Maria Watkins gnashed her gums and declared that she'd always known that that girl would come to a bad end. She appealed to her friends. Hadn't she always said so?

The others nodded solemnly. 'We all did,' Bess Simnel amended, unwilling to let one of them take credit over the other two.

'But did you know her well?' I asked, frown-ing and stooping to untie the rope from around Hercules's collar. 'I was told she and her parents lived in the manor of Clifton.'

'True enough,' Margaret admitted. 'And she was some years younger than any of us.'

'Four or five, at least,' Goody Watkins agreed.

'Oh, really, Maria!' Bess Simnel was scathing. 'In your case, ten or eleven, surely. Isabella would be over forty now, if she'd lived. And you can't pretend to me that you're a day younger than fifty-five!'

Margaret Walker intervened hurriedly. 'Let's just say that Isabella Linkinhorne was younger than the three of us and leave it at that. And yes, the family did live in the manor of Clifton. But that didn't prevent us hearing about her and her wild goings-on.'

'An only child, Alderman Foster tells me, and very spoiled,' I said.

But mentioning the Alderman was a mistake, and they insisted I inform them of his and my involvement in the search for the murdered woman's killer. They were, of course, thrilled. They would be first with this news throughout Redcliffe and then the city. They were immediately willing to tell me everything they knew.

Disappointingly, this varied little from what John Foster had already told me, except that they remembered Isabella visiting the city on occasions with her parents.

'And not just with Master and Mistress Linkinhorne,' Bess Simnel said, nodding her head and pulling down the corners of her mouth. 'I recall times when she arrived entirely on her own, without even a maid in attendance.'

'That's true enough,' Maria Watkins agreed, mashing one of the oatcakes to pulp with the back of a horn spoon, then feeding her toothless mouth with the crumbs. 'Hard-faced hussy she was, in spite of her youth.'

'She was very beautiful, as I remember,' objected Bess.

'Didn't say she wasn't,' her friend retorted, spluttering through a mouthful of crumbs and spitting most of them out over the table. 'Jus' said she was hard-faced. And so she was.'

'You're both right,' Margaret said, keeping the peace. 'Lovely to look at, but wilful with it.'

'Men,' Goody Watkins opined darkly. 'They were her weakness. And her downfall, mark my words.'

'They're most poor women's downfall,' Bess Simnel agreed gloomily.

They all three nodded and glared reproachfully at me. I knew better than to try defending my

reprehensible sex, and looked suitably con-
science-stricken. Even Hercules raised his head
and gave me an accusing stare.

'Was there a particular man in Isabella's life?'
I asked.

Margaret sniffed, Maria Watkins let rip with a
raucous laugh and Bess Simnel looked down her
nose.

'More than one, if all the rumours were true,'
my former mother-in-law said disapprovingly.
'The story was that one of 'em was a Bristol
man.'

I was puzzled. 'Why was it only a story?' I
asked. 'Wasn't she ever seen with him?'

Goody Watkins guzzled some beer, then
smacked her lips together. 'She was a crafty
piece, that Isabella Linkinhorne. She was never
actually seen by anyone with any of her lovers.
Leastways, not up close, so's they were recog-
nizable. And if she'd a man in Bristol, she kept
him pretty dark.'

'It sounds to me,' I said severely, 'as if this
poor girl's reputation was undeserved. If no one
ever saw her with a man...'

'Oh, she was seen all right!' Margaret protested. 'From the time she could get astride a
horse...'

'Or a fellow,' cackled Goody Watkins, then
laughed so heartily she choked on a crumb.

'Be quiet, Maria,' Margaret admonished her
and turned back to me. 'From the moment
Isabella could sit astride a horse, she was out
nearly every day, in all weathers, riding across
the downs. And as she grew older, not always

37

alone. Very often there was somebody with her, thought to be a man.'

'And not necessarily the same one every time,' Bess Simnel added. 'As I recall, there were reports of two or three.'

All this while I had been helping myself, unbidden, to Margaret's oatcakes, but now cleared my mouth to say reprovingly, 'Isabella's lovers were nothing but hearsay, in fact. A case of give a dog a bad name and hang him. Or, in this case, her.'

The three women exchanged indignant glances.

'If that's going to be your attitude,' Margaret said, 'you might as well leave now – and while there are still some oatcakes left for the rest of us,' she added waspishly.

'We know what we know,' Bess Simnel snapped. 'And we stand by every word of what we've said.'

'Danged impudence!' shouted Maria, banging her spoon on the table, just the way Adam did when he was angry.

I rose meekly from my stool and fastened the rope leading string around Hercules's collar.

'We'd better go, my lad,' I whispered. 'I think we've offended the ladies.'

We both beat a strategic retreat.

Three

I walked back to the bridge, pausing only for a
brief chat with Burl Hodge, on his way home to
dinner from the tenting fields where he worked.
We had once been firm friends, but my good
fortune in being left the old Herepath house by
Cicely Ford had soured our relationship; and
even the fact that, two years earlier, I had proved
him innocent of a charge of murder and saved
him from the hangman's noose, had not been
enough to assuage his envy. Nowadays, it was
true, he treated me politely and no longer sub-
jected me to the jibes and barbed comments
which had, on more than one occasion in the
past, nearly brought us to blows; but the old free
and easy manner had been lost for good. His
wife, Jenny, and his two sons, Jack and Dick,
might show me the same courteous affection
they had always done, but I had forced myself to
accept that Burl would always begrudge me my
luck.

After a minute or so, the conversation floun-
dered, and more to keep it afloat than for any
other reason, I enquired after his mate and
fellow tenter, Hob Jarrett.

'Oh, him!' Burl shrugged dismissively. 'He's
given up tenting. Too cold in the winter, he says,

39

what with the wind and all them ells of wet cloth.' Burl displayed his raw, chilblained hands with their swollen knuckles and other painful-looking joints. 'He's with a labouring gang now. Out all weathers just the same, but he reckons it's warmer work than tenting.'

Acting on a sudden hunch, I asked, 'Hob's not by any chance one of the gang clearing the ground at the top of Steep Street?'

'You mean what's now Alderman Foster's land and used to be the nuns' graveyard? Strange you should ask. He was round at our cottage night before last telling me and Jenny and the boys about the woman's body they've found there. Hob was the one who uncovered it.'

'Ah! Do you think he'd be willing to talk to me, then?'

Burl's eyes narrowed. 'What's your interest, Roger?'

I told him, and saw again the flash of malice before he blinked it away and smoothed out his features.

'Friends with the Mayor-elect, are we? Of course! I forgot. Alderman Foster's a neighbour of yours.'

I let this go. 'Remember me to Jenny,' was all I said.

I tugged on Hercules's rope and walked on, stopping only once more to use the public latrine on Bristol Bridge before making my own way home to dinner.

It was yesterday's fish stew warmed up, but with some fresh cabbage and a fistful of chopped leeks added to the boiled cod and lentils that had comprised our suitably abstemious Friday fare.

'Sunday tomorrow. Meat,' Adela promised me, smiling at my unhappy grimace as I swallowed the first spoonful of broth. 'How was Margaret? Was she able to give you any information about the Linkinhornes that you hadn't been told already?'

'Goody Watkins and Bess Simnel were there as well,' I said. 'They all three remember the daughter, and all three agree that she was spoiled and wilful. "A crafty piece" was the way Maria described her. Overly fond of the men was the general opinion, although there seemed precious little direct evidence, at least as far as I could gather, to uphold the claim. Only hearsay. One of them – I forget which – reckoned Isabella had an admirer among the Bristol men. Mind you, it all happened twenty years or more ago.'

'Twenty years! I'd have been ten.' And Adela heaved a sigh for the lost innocence of childhood. 'So I'm afraid I can't help you,' she added. 'I don't even recollect hearing the girl's name... What will you do next?'

'First, I'm going to pay a visit to the workmen who found the body. I understand they're still clearing the ground. Afterwards, I'll go to the Gaunts' Hospital and speak with Jonathan Linkinhorne. He's well into his eighties according to Alderman Foster – eighty-five I think he said – so I'm praying he's still in possession of all his faculties. Oh, and while I'm at Steep Street I must go to the Magdalen nunnery and have a word with Sister Walburga. You don't happen to know her, by any chance?'

Adela pursed her lips. 'I have very little to do with the Sisters, but I fancy Walburga's the timid, retiring one.'

I finished my stew, drained my beaker and stood up, shrugging myself into my jerkin and arming myself with my cudgel.

'In any case, there should be no problem in identifying her,' I remarked. 'There are only three nuns.' I hesitated. 'Do – 'er – do you want me to take Hercules?'

My wife eyed the dog unfavourably, but he was sleeping – or pretending to sleep – so soundly that she hadn't the heart to wake him.

'You can leave him here,' she agreed grudgingly. 'I don't suppose either the workmen or the sisters will welcome his disruptive presence.'

As though aware of this slur cast on his character, the dog emitted a faint growl, but his eyes remained fast shut. Probably just a touch of indigestion.

I kissed my children a fond farewell, all three demonstrating their usual indifference to my departure, hugged Adela, who showed a more flattering inclination to linger in my embrace, left the hound to his slumbers and went out again into the chilly morning air.

It was still cold and the thin April sun struggled to make itself felt as it emerged fitfully from behind the clouds. The Frome Gate was crowded with traffic as people from the surrounding districts poured into the city to do their Saturday shopping for the Sabbath. Edgar Capgrave was the gatekeeper on duty, but we had no chance to

42

exchange greetings as my arrival coincided with that of a swineherd driving his pigs to market and violently disputing the amount of toll he was required to pay.

'Daylight robbery!' he was shouting as I passed. 'How are honest men expected to make a decent living?'

I left him to it. He'd get no joy, and no reduction, from Edgar Capgrave, who, in spite of his lack of inches, was quite capable of taking on any malcontent in the kingdom, and winning.

I turned into Horse Street and made my way along the Frome Backs to where the piles of wood for the city's fires were stored beside the river. From there I began the ascent to the top of Steep Street, not forgetting to make my obeisance to the statue of the Virgin, set in the wall of the Carmelite Friary, on my left. (I reckoned I could probably do with all the goodwill I could get from the Lady.) As I neared the top, where the stone cross and well mark the convergence of Saint Michael's Hill with the long, eastward-bound track to the manor of Clifton and Ghyston Cliff, I could hear the sounds of men at work; the intermittent thud of picks and spades and the non-stop flow of cursing.

Half the graveyard was now more or less cleared, the other half, even after the greater part of a week, still matted with weeds and brambles. A cart stood in the roadway, laden with stones and uprooted foliage of one kind or another, while the sorry-looking nag that pulled it, having been released from the shafts, was ambling around, either getting in the workmen's way or wandering off, up and down the hill, on little expeditions of its own.

I recognized Hob Jarrett at once; a smallish man with wisps of greasy brown hair curling out from beneath his equally greasy hood, a thin, chapped mouth and sharp brown eyes peering from beneath a pair of bushy eyebrows that almost met above a broken nose. He failed to notice my approach as he leaned on the handle of his spade, deep in conversation with his two fellow workers.

'Hard work, eh, Hob?' I clapped him on the back.

He jumped violently and swung round, a guilty expression on his face. When he saw who it was, alarm was replaced by anger.

'Sod me, Chapman, you fair gave me a start! Consider yourself lucky I didn't lay you out with this spade. What do you mean by creeping up on a fellow when he's working?'

I grinned. 'Is that what you were doing? All right! All right!' I raised my hands in a placatory gesture. 'No offence meant!' Well, not much. 'I was talking to Burl. He says you're the one who uncovered the body that's been found.'

'Oho! That's it, is it? Trust you to be poking your long nose into what doesn't concern you.'

But I could see that he wasn't exactly displeased by my interest. He was already puffing out his chest preparatory to embarking on an account of his gruesome discovery.

'As a matter of fact,' I corrected him, 'my enquiries are at the behest of Alderman Foster.' I told him the story.

Hob was impressed, although, in honour bound, he pretended not to be.

'Working for the Mayor now, eh? Foster's being sworn in next week, did you know? Mean to say you haven't been invited? No? Well, well! Come over here, then, and I'll show you where I found the body.'

He led me across the cleared ground to a low stone wall which marked the boundary of the former graveyard.

'There were some gert big stones hereabouts that had to be dug out, and a tangle o' weeds with roots that seemingly stretched right down to Hades. Together, they meant a good deal of digging and some damned back-breaking work. Ain't that so, lads? You tell 'n!'

Both the other men nodded in unison.

'Ar, that's right,' agreed the taller of the two.

'I had blisters on my hands the size of apricots,' complained the other one. 'My goody said she'd never seen nothing like 'em.'

Hob glared at this second man and waved him to silence. *He* was the hero of the tale, and resented any attempt to deflect attention from his central role.

'As I was telling you, Chapman, I was digging away and had got a fair few feet down, when I came across what I thought at first must be a dog's bone. But I was just thinking to myself that dogs don't bury their bones that deep when I saw that what I'd uncovered was a bit of a leg with a foot on the end. Lots o' little bones in what remained of a leather shoe. A woman's shoe,' he added.

'I said as 'ow it were a woman's shoe,' the shorter fellow put in. 'You said as 'ow it looked like a man's.'

'I did not!' was the hot rejoinder. 'You're a liar, Colin!'

'But you eventually found the whole skeleton,' I interrupted hurriedly in order to prevent the termination of a beautiful friendship.

The tall man shuddered. 'Ain't that the truth! It was a shock, I can tell 'ee. There was still some hair attached to the scalp...'

'Long, black hair,' the one called Colin amplified.

'...and a strip of green material that I guess was all that remained of whatever gown she'd been wearing. But it just crumbled into dust as soon as Hob here touched it.'

'I did not touch it!' Hob disclaimed furiously. 'It was the air. A breath of wind caught it and it were gone to nothing in a trice. Anyway, who's telling this story? Me or you?' He glared belligerently at the other two, then turned back to me. 'We thought it must be one o' the Sisters who'd been buried there and then forgotten about. Because we were given to understand quite definitely that this place had never been used as a burial ground, even though that's what it'd been meant for. But then, o' course, when I fetched the Sisters down to look at it – the body that is – they said as how it couldn't possibly be one o' them on account of the jewellery the corpse was wearing. Gold rings, gold and amber necklace and what I could see was a girdle made o' gold and silver links with a jewelled clasp.'

'What happened next?' I asked, although I could guess without being told.

The notifying of authority, the ponderous grinding of the law into action, the lifting of the body from its long resting place, the removal of the bones to the city charnel house and the slow process of trying to identify to whom they had once belonged... Then I recollected that identification had followed almost at once.

'Who recognized the remains as those of Isabella Linkinhorne, and how?' And although I already knew the answer to my question, it's always as well to get confirmation of a story when one can.

'Sister Walburga said it were her,' Hob told me, sucking his teeth, trying to locate any odd, uneaten bits of dinner that might have got lodged between them. He found a shred of meat and spat it out. (Well, he was lucky. Some of us had dined on yesterday's fish stew.) 'Seems this Isabella what's-her-name was a kinswoman of sorts. Sister Walburga knew the jewellery at once. Seen the girl wearing it, she said. And when Colin –' Hob nodded towards his friend – 'mentioned the strip o' green cloth, she knew, or pretended she knew, the dress as well.'

'A green brocade gown is how she described it,' Colin nodded.

'And, of course,' the tall man whose name still eluded me chimed in, 'Sister Walburga also knew that this girl had disappeared without trace twenty years ago. Shocked, she was, I can tell you, Chapman.'

'Stunned, more like,' Hob amended.

47

'I think perhaps I'd better go and speak to Sister Walburga myself,' I said.

I glanced up at the sky where the sun was still struggling to break through the scudding clouds. When it did finally reveal itself for a moment or two, I could see from its position in the heavens that it was not yet noon. If I went to the convent now, I would not be interrupting any service, only disturbing the nuns at their private devotions or going about their daily tasks.

I thanked Hob and his two companions, adding with a sly grin, 'I'm sorry to have held you up. You must be anxious to get on with your work.'

'Oh... Oh, ah!' said Hob, gripping his spade with renewed vigour and attempting to look like a man whose chief pleasure in life was a good, full day's hard work. Colin, too, swung his pick to the imminent peril of his fellow labourers, though without, I noticed, actually managing to strike the ground. Only the tall man gave a snort of laughter and made no immediate move to resume his digging.

I walked the short distance from the former graveyard to the Magdalen nunnery, which stood at the bottom of Saint Michael's Hill, opposite the church of Saint Michael-on-the-Mount-Without. Further up the hill was one of the city's boundary stones and the gallows, which, mercifully, was at present empty of any executed felons whose bodies had been left to the attentions of ravens and crows, as a warning to other would-be criminals.

The Magdalen nunnery had originally been

founded as a house of retreat and a seminary for wealthy young women, but had long since dwindled from a thriving community to the three sisters who inhabited it at that time. Fewer women in the modern world seemed to feel the need for a period of quiet reflection on their own and the world's sins: they were far too busy enjoying themselves and spending their husbands' or their fathers' money. The hedonistic example of the court – which I had witnessed more than once at first hand – had permeated all walks of life in all but the remotest corners of the kingdom. And as for learning, girls were increasingly being educated at home, where a private tutor was seen as a badge of affluence.

The Magdalen nuns had never been an enclosed order. (Indeed, there was a story told that during the Great Death of the previous century, several of their number had rowed themselves across the River Avon to take food and medicine to the inhabitants of Saint Bede's Minster; or Be'minster as the locals always called it.) So the middle-aged Sister who answered my knock and inspected me through the grille of the door had little hesitation in letting me in when I expressed a wish to speak to Sister Walburga.

I was shown into a small, whitewashed room, boasting no furniture of any kind, and illuminated only by a single barred window set high in one wall.

'Wait here while I find out if Sister Walburga is willing to speak to you,' the nun instructed me, before going out and shutting the door noiselessly behind her.

Only a few moments had passed when I heard a light footfall in the passageway outside; then the latch was lifted and Sister Walburga came in.

Adela had been wrong about her. She was not the shy, retiring one. I could tell that at once by her face which was strong, almost masculine in feature. She was old and her sallow skin was deeply furrowed. Heavily incised lines ran from the outside of each nostril to the corners of her thin, nearly bloodless mouth, giving her a stern, forbidding expression. But the hazel eyes were bright and full of intelligence, and when she smiled it was easy to see that, in her youth, she had probably been a very handsome woman. Not pretty; I doubted she had ever been that, but with the stern good looks that frighten a lot of men.

She paused just inside the door, eyeing me up and down.

'Who are you and what do you want with me?' she demanded, wasting no time on formal greetings.

I answered both her questions as briefly as I could, guessing that she was the sort of woman to appreciate a concise, bare-boned narrative. When I finished, she said nothing for a moment or two, then gave a decisive nod of her head.

'I'm grateful,' she remarked at last, 'that someone is taking it upon himself to discover what really happened to my cousin's daughter. I have found the Sheriff's officer, Sergeant Manifold, reluctant to pursue any investigation of the facts. I suppose I don't altogether blame him. It's twenty years since Isabella disappeared, and for all that time, we – myself, my cousin and, in the beginning, his wife – have assumed that she simply ran away with some man or other. She always had two or three dangling at her apron strings. But to my mind that is no excuse for not trying to find the culprit now that we know she was murdered. I shall write to Alderman Foster – Mayor Foster, I should say – and express my sincere obligation to him. As to you, my son, please accept my gratitude for being the instrument of this investigation.' I thought she was looking a little dubious, so I gave her my best smile. She took a deep breath and continued, 'So what is it you want from me?'

'Whatever you can tell me concerning your... your cousin's daughter, did you say?'

Sister Walburga inclined her head. 'Jonathan Linkinhorne's father and mine were brothers. Jon and I were never in each other's pockets, as the saying is, but we played together as children and kept in touch when we were adults.'

'And how well did you know Isabella? Well enough, obviously, to recognize the jewellery and girdle found with the body.'

'Oh, they were all favourite pieces – the rings, the gold and amber necklace, the gold and silver girdle with its amethyst clasp. And as for the strip of cloth the workmen described seeing just before it crumbled into dust, Isabella had a green silk brocade gown she was very fond of and frequently wore.'

'You saw her often?'

'Often enough. My cousin and I were both only children. I never married, so Isabella was the only child of the family. Until I became a postulant here twenty years ago, I lived near Westbury village. Isabella would sometimes call on me when she rode that way.'

'Your cousin seems to have had some expensive jewellery for so young a woman,' I said. 'Is Master Linkinhorne a rich man?' If so, it seemed strange to me that he was now living in the Gaunts' Hospital and not in the comfort of his own home, surrounded by his servants.

'Cousin Jonathan? A rich man?' Sister Walburga smiled. 'Our family has never been a wealthy one, Master Chapman. We're of solid yeoman stock, and proud of it. No, the jewellery came from one of Isabella's admirers who was a goldsmith. A fact she let slip one day when I caught her off-guard.'

'She was secretive?'

'Oh, very! At least, where her various swains were concerned. And perhaps in other respects, as well. She appeared open and friendly enough, but I doubt if anyone, especially those closest to her, really knew what she was thinking, not even as a child. Mind you,' my companion went on, suddenly moving away from the door and beginning to pace about the room, 'it was easy to understand why. My cousin and his wife were both elderly when Isabella was born – Amorette, I think, must have been over forty, Jonathan even older – and they smothered her with love. The poor child was stifled with it from the moment of her birth. They watched over her every movement, supervised her every action until Isabella must have felt she couldn't breathe. The only place she could hide was inside her own head, so the need for secrecy was probably engendered in her from a very young age. And when rebellion finally came, and Isabella defied her parents to go out riding every day, sometimes all day, she would never tell them where she'd been or who she'd seen. The habit of silence was too inbred in her by then.'

'Surely her father could have enforced her obedience?'

Sister Walburga shook her head.

'My cousin would never have lifted a finger against Isabella. He and Amorette doted too much on her. Along with the all-embracing love went a desire to give first the child and then the girl everything she wanted; everything her heart desired. Isabella grew up spoiled, wilful and wild.' My informant paused, chewing her bottom lip and looking pensive. 'You know, Master Chapman,' she continued after a minute, 'love can be ugly and destructive as well as beautiful and life-giving. If you have children of your own, never forget that.'

'I'll try not to,' I promised. 'I've been told that Master Linkinhorne and his family lived in the manor of Clifton.'

'Yes. He and his wife ran, very successfully, a smallholding which they held in tenure from the lord of the manor, Lord Cobham. It was a quarter of a mile or so from Ghyston Cliff, above Rownham Passage. The place is derelict now. It was gutted by fire some years ago. An accident, my cousin said, when a candle flame caught the edge of his bed hangings. Jonathan was old and lonely by then – Amorette had been found drowned in the Avon a year after Isabella's disappearance – and growing careless. Lord Cobham used his influence to obtain a place for my cousin in the Gaunts' Hospital, but he never rebuilt the house.'

I thought over all she'd told me, then asked, 'Did it never cross Master Linkinhorne's or his wife's minds that any harm might have befallen their daughter? Was no sort of effort made to find her?'

'Half-hearted ones. Oh, I realize it must seem very reprehensible to you now, now that we all know the truth of what really happened. But everyone, including myself – I take equal blame – was convinced that Isabella had run off with a man.'

'But who were these men?' I demanded impatiently. 'I've heard talk from other sources of three. Surely enquiries could have been put afoot to discover if Isabella had indeed run off with one of them.'

Sister Walburga gave her thin-lipped smile. 'Easier said than done, my friend. No one knew their names. You find that incredible?' I certainly did, and let it show. A note of defiance entered my companion's voice as she continued, 'So do I – now! Now that I can look back on events from a distance and with my present awareness of what really became of Isabella. But the sad fact is that her parents' knowledge of these clandestine meetings came to them second-hand, through neighbours' gossip or anonymous notes slipped under their door or from well-meaning busybodies who thought they ought to know, and so on and so on. Whenever Jonathan or Amorette tried to find out the truth of the rumours, Isabella flatly refused to answer their questions. She vowed it was all malicious lies, an attempt to tarnish her good name by people who were jealous of her. She swore there were no men. When she went out riding, she did so alone. My cousin didn't believe her, of course. The stories were too rife. But what could he or Amorette do in the face of such flat denials? And now, I really must return to my duties.' Sister Walburga moved back to the door, laying her hand on the latch. 'I have already spent far too much time talking to you. Go and see my cousin at the Gaunts' Hospital, that's my advice. He will be able to explain matters to you far better than I can. I was at best an observer.'

I felt this remark to be disingenuous, but said nothing. Sister Walburga gave me a brief inclination of the head and was gone.

Four

The Gaunts' Hospital, as I have already explained in one of my earlier chronicles, stands close
by Saint Augustine's Abbey, in the lee of the
steeply rising ground to the north of the city. (A
series of heart-stopping hills leads eventually to
the plateau above the great gorge – whose bed is
that of the River Avon – and the manor of Clifton.) The hospital was founded in the thirteenth
century by Maurice and Henry de Gaunt, and
further endowed by their nephew, Robert de
Gourney. Its function is to nurse the sick, feed
the poor and educate children, and is large
enough to accommodate twenty to thirty inmates. Run by a master and three chaplains, all
belonging to the order of the Bons-Hommes, it
comprises the church of Saint Mark, surrounded
by hall, kitchen, buttery, dormitories, outbuild-
ings, a pigeon loft and an orchard that, to the
east, abuts the land of the Carmelite Friars
(whose huge cistern has supplied Bristol with
water for several centuries, piped as it is across
the Frome Bridge to the conduit by Saint John-
on-the-Arch).

From Steep Street, I approached the hospital
along Frog Lane. The apple trees, already in bud,
and soon to be a sea of foaming blossom, raised

their tossing heads above the grey stone wall, their branches whispering to the tune of a gentle breeze blowing up from the river.

The porter made no demur when I expressed a wish to speak to Jonathan Linkinhorne, and conducted me to the main hall, where most of the elderly residents were to be found at that time of day. A fire, far too hot for me, burned on the hearth and spread its warmth around the stone benches that lined the other three walls. There were also stools and trestle tables scattered about to provide more comfortable seating and arm support for the frail and very old. The man pointed out to me as Master Linkinhorne was sitting at a trestle as close to the fire as he could get, his chin propped in his cupped hands, staring sightlessly at a half-full beaker of ale in front of him.

Before I could approach my quarry, however, I was intercepted by two old acquaintances, Miles Huckbody and Henry Dando. Like all old people herded together with no one but their own generation for company they were desperate for news of the wider world and the stimulation of younger minds.

'What you doing here, Roger?' Miles asked, his long, wrinkled face alight with curiosity beneath the white hair. He slipped one bony hand into the crook of my elbow and stroked the sleeve of my jerkin with the other. 'You remember Henry, here,' he went on, when his friend's attempts to attract my attention became too importunate to ignore.

'Master Dando,' I said, smiling into the faded,

rheumy blue eyes and wishing their owner at the devil.

Miles Huckbody let out a squawk of protest. 'You've no cause to go a-"master"-ing him, Chapman. Henry ain't of any importance.'

'I'm just naturally polite,' I said; a claim that provoked another cackle of derision from my companion.

'Who you come to see?' Miles demanded. 'Is it one of us?' He stared up at me hopefully.

'I'm afraid not,' I apologized. 'I want to speak to Master Linkinhorne.' And I nodded towards the silent figure, hunched over his drink.

'Oh, 'im!' Henry Dando sniffed. 'You won't get a lot of joy outta him. Miserable old sod, 'e is. Don't talk to anyone much.'

This was bad news. But then I asked myself what would Jonathan Linkinhorne – provided he was anything like his cousin, Sister Walburga – have in common with Miles Huckbody and Henry Dando, with their constant stream of old men's chatter? Besides which, at present, he must be suffering from a deep sense of shock, and possibly self-reproach, to think that his daughter had been dead, brutally murdered, for all these years when he had thought her alive somewhere, well and happy.

'You're here about that body they dug up in the nuns' graveyard, ain't you?' Miles poked me sharply in the ribs. 'Jonathan's daughter, weren't it? That Sergeant Manifold was here yesterday and spoke to him in private. Old Linkinhorne, he didn't tell us nothing. But gossip soon leaks out in a place like this. Bound to.'

58

'You can't keep nothing secret in here,' Henry Dando confirmed, trying to look regretful and failing miserably.

I guessed that such a morsel of news had generated enough excitement to keep the Gaunts' inhabitants in a ferment for months to come.

There was no point in denying my mission. 'You're right. I do want to speak to Master Linkinhorne about his daughter,' I agreed, disengaging my arm from Miles's clawlike grip. 'But alone,' I added firmly. 'I'll wish you both goodday. It's been a pleasure seeing you again.' (As I've remarked before, we all have to tell untruths from time to time.)

'We'll introduce you,' Miles offered.

'He knows us, you see,' Henry added.

'I'll introduce myself,' I said in a tone of voice that left them in no doubt that I was refusing their very kind offices.

They sheered off, muttering together in offended whispers. I took no notice, seating myself at the opposite side of the trestle to Jonathan Linkinhorne and folding my arms in front of me. He glanced up briefly, registered the fact that my face was unfamiliar and looked down again at his beaker, but without making any serious attempt to finish his ale.

'Master Linkinhorne,' I said.

He raised his head once more, this time frowning. 'Do I know you?'

In his youth, he must have been a heavy-jowled man, but the flesh now hung slackly around the jawline, running into his neck and making him appear almost chinless. Like Henry

59

Dando, indeed like a lot of blue-eyed people, the colour of the irises had faded with age, but in his case they were also milky, hinting at incipient blindness. He had pushed back his hood to reveal a bald head, with a few wisps and tufts of white hair growing low down around the ears. I suspected that he had once been an imposing, powerfully built man who found the indignities of ageing more trying than most. When he spoke, his voice rasped with resentment.

I had a sudden vision of him in his middle years; a man used to being in command, used to being obeyed by everyone with whom he came into contact, lording it over wife and servants, confident in all his dealings with the world around him. Then, suddenly, he had found himself confronting a will-o'-the-wisp of a girl, lovely to look at, physically fragile, but with a will of iron, a determination to dominate matched only by his own. He, who all his adult life had known nothing but subservience, would have been confused, bedazzled by this glorious, unpredictable creature he had fathered and blinded by his love...

Jonathan Linkinhorne repeated impatiently, giving equal emphasis to every word, 'Do I know you?'

I pulled my wandering thoughts together and plunged into my explanation.

When I had finished, there was a lengthy and unnerving silence while my companion drummed with his fingers on the tabletop, a sign of agitation that was in no way reflected on his face, which remained an expressionless mask. At

60

least, so I thought until I was shocked to see tears gathering in the corners of his eyes, then trickling unchecked down his lined and weathered cheeks.

The silence continued to stretch while I gave us both time to recover our composure. I disliked intruding into anyone's private grief, and silently deplored John Foster's desire to uncover the truth of past events. The past was dead: let it lie.

This uncharacteristic state of mind did not last long, however, and I was immediately all ears when Master Linkinhorne suddenly roused himself, blinking rapidly like a man coming out of darkness into light – or like a man reaching a decision after a long period of uncertainty.

'It's extremely kind of our new Mayor to interest himself in my affairs,' he said grudgingly, 'but I doubt if he – or, rather, you, as his instrument – will be able to find out much after all this time. The year that Isabella disappeared was the year in which King Edward won the battle of Mortimer's Cross and seized the crown from King Henry...It seems like another life.'

And so it did. My lord of Gloucester and I had both been eight years old – nine at the beginning of that October – and Edward of York, now growing ill and bloated from an excess of food, wine and women, had been regarded as the handsomest man in the whole of Europe; over six feet tall and as dazzling as the sun. His badge, the Sun in Splendour, had then reflected his glory: nowadays it was nothing but an empty mockery of what he had once been.

I said gently, 'The discovery of your daughter's body must have been a terrible shock for you, Master Linkinhorne. But surely you must have some desire to know what happened to her? Who murdered her?' He made no response. I hesitated, then went on, 'Did...forgive me, but did neither you nor your wife ever consider the possibility that some harm might have befallen Isabella?'

He was silent for a moment or two longer, then slowly shook his head.

'I daresay you think we should have done,' he said at last, 'but I'm ashamed to say that it never so much as crossed our minds.'

'Can you...? Do you know why not?'

Again there was a protracted pause as though he were struggling to come to terms with something that was almost too painful to contemplate.

'Isabella,' he murmured at length, 'was always threatening to run away from home.' He drew a long, ragged breath. 'My wife, Master Chapman, was over forty when our daughter was born. I was five years older. We had given up all hope of having a child, so Isabella was...was like a miracle sent by God. And we knew that we should have no more children. Foolishly, we indulged her every whim, both when she was a little girl and as she grew older. Everything she wanted, she had.'

Except her freedom, I thought. Except her freedom! I could see that Sister Walburga had been in the right of it when she'd said that an old couple's overwhelming love had stifled an eager, high-spirited girl. And when that girl had become a woman, she had rebelled.

Almost as an echo to my thoughts, Jonathan Linkinhorne went on, 'Suddenly Amorette, my wife, and I didn't know her any more. Looking back, of course I can see that even when she was small, riding her pony, Isabella would try her best to get clear of anyone who was accompanying her; my wife, myself or her nurse. And as soon as she had mastered the grey mare we bought her for her fifteenth birthday, there was no holding her back. Each day she was out riding, in all weathers, galloping across the downs in every direction. There was no longer anyone who could keep up with her. She grew defiant, wilful... You think we should have beaten her, no doubt. Locked her in her chamber. People told me to my face that I was too weak with her. That if she had been their daughter...' He shrugged. 'Oh, you can guess the sort of thing.'

I could, only too well. I had a daughter of my own and could foresee myself receiving just the same sort of advice when that strong-minded damsel reached maturity.

'But,' I prompted, when my companion threatened to lapse into silence once again, 'Isabella always did come home? She never did run away?'

'No,' he agreed sadly. 'She never did run away. I know that now.' He made a sudden, visible effort and roused himself from his reverie. 'Of course I do. But twenty years ago, my wife and I believed differently. We believed that Isabella had finally carried out her threat and run away

63

with one of her suitors.'

A log fell with a crash on to the hearth behind me, sending up a comet's tail of sparks. One of the old men at the next table hurried forward importantly, seized the tongs and put the crumbling log back on the fire, glancing around as he did so for applause. When none was forthcoming, he huffed his way back to his seat, offended. I felt sorry for him.

'You say suitors in the plural,' I said, turning back to face Jonathan Linkinhorne. 'There was more than one?'

'So we were told.'

'Did you never see them?'

His jowl quivered defiantly. 'No. Isabella always denied their existence when we questioned her concerning them.'

'In that case, how can you be sure these men ever really existed?'

He gave a faint, fleeting smile and confirmed what Sister Walburga had already told me.

'Neighbours, well-wishers, friends. People who knew people, who knew people, who knew people... Someone's mother-in-law's aunt had seen Isabella riding with a male companion near Westbury village, or on the Gloucester road, or as far away as the track that runs south to Bath. There were also reports of her visiting Bristol on her own, stabling the mare at the Full Moon, near Saint James's Priory. Sometimes, of course, she accompanied her mother and me to the city, when we went to visit the market or for another reason. And I recall there were several occasions when we lost her. She always turned up again, later, but would never say exactly where she'd been in the meantime.'

'Is there any chance she could have gone to visit your cousin at the Magdalen nunnery?'

Jonathan Linkinhorne shook his head glumly.

'Jeanette – Sister Walburga that is – didn't enter the nunnery as a postulant until just a few weeks before Isabella vanished.'

I thought over what he had told me for a moment or two while he once more lapsed into silence. Then I asked, 'Why are you so certain that, in all these sightings of your daughter in the company of a man, it was not the same man every time? Why are you so sure that there were three?'

With a visible effort, Jonathan Linkinhorne dragged his eyes back to my face.

'The descriptions didn't tally,' he said, at last raising his beaker and taking a few sips of ale. He licked his lips and wiped his mouth on his sleeve. 'One account was of a tall, fair man, very handsome. Another described a stocky, sandy-headed fellow, while a third fitted neither of those descriptions.'

'What was that?'

'Oh, brown-haired, blue-eyed, nothing re-markable or noteworthy. A man like a hundred others. Although...' My companion broke off, pressing a hand to his forehead, peering back into the dim recesses of the past and trying to conjure up a memory. 'Someone said – I think it was of him, and yet I wouldn't be sure – that he was a jolly fellow, always laughing. Or was that one of the others?'

I struggled against a growing sense of disbelief.

'But you and your wife never saw any of these men? You never thought to follow your daughter when she went out riding? You mentioned a nurse. Could she not have ridden with Isabella?'

Jonathan Linkinhorne grew testy, snapping at me, suddenly impatient.

'You can't have been listening, Master Chapman. I told you, my wife was over forty when our child was born. I was forty-five. So by the time we are now talking about, Amorette and I were both over sixty. Indeed, my wife had celebrated her sixtieth birthday shortly before Isabella disappeared. And Emilia – Emilia Virgoe, Isabella's nurse – as well as being in her forties, was no horsewoman. There was no possible way that either one of us could have kept up with my daughter when she was on horseback.' He was beginning to sweat and jerked his stool away from the fire's heat before continuing. 'You must understand that Isabella had an instinctive bond with horses from the moment she first clapped eyes on one. She was a superb horsewoman. There was no possible way anyone could have kept up with her, followed her, if she didn't wish it.'

I, too, was starting to sweat, the heat on my back making me feel slightly sick and lightheaded. I got up and walked round the table to sit beside my reluctant host. My mouth was parched, and I looked longingly at Jonathan Linkinhorne's still quarter-full beaker of ale. He pushed it towards me.

'Take it,' he muttered. 'Small beer's all you get here and I can't bear the stuff. Wine's the only fit drink for a civilized human being.'

'If you can afford it,' I retorted, swallowing the remains of the ale in a couple of gulps.

'Oh, I could always afford it,' he declared, suddenly boastful. 'The holding I worked for Lord Cobham was a flourishing one. Four or five hands I had under me at one time, and two girls to do the milking and feed the hens and work in the house. I provided near enough the whole manor with vegetables, and sufficient over to sell in Bristol market at least once, sometimes twice a week.'

He was silent again, staring into space. Then, after a while, he buried his face in his hands.

'Master Linkinhorne?' I murmured, gently squeezing his shoulder, aware, as he apparently was not, that his conduct was beginning to attract attention. Nudges, winks and nods were being exchanged among the other old people nearby, who, although probably at least partially deaf, had nevertheless been taking a close interest in our conversation. My brief acquaintance with my companion had convinced me that he would hate to make himself conspicuous in any way, or be the subject of whispered speculation among his fellow inmates, all of whom, I felt sure, he deeply despised. He was that most pitiable of creatures; a man with more than his fair share of pride, fallen on hard times. I lowered my mouth to within an inch of his ear. 'Master Linkinhorne, people are looking.'

He raised his head, sat up straight and gazed

belligerently around him. There was an uneasy shuffling of feet, an awkward avoidance of glances before the others turned back to what they had previously been doing; playing board games, reading or simply chatting and bickering amongst themselves.

Jonathan Linkinhorne shrugged off my hand and reached for his beaker, forgetting that he had allowed me to empty it. When he did remember, he slammed it back on the table in disgust.

'Let me fetch you some more,' I offered guilt-ily, half-rising from my seat.

He shook his head.

'You don't understand, Master Chapman,' he said fiercely. 'When you live on charity, you don't ask for more.'

'I'm sure that if I explain...'

'No!'

I sank back on to my stool. 'Very well.'

'In any case, I hate the stuff.'

'So you said. But if you're thirsty—'

'For God's sake, fellow, do as you're told.'

Yes, I thought to myself, this is more like the man you once were before disaster and indignity blighted your life. I waited a few seconds to let reality sink in again, then asked neutrally (although I already knew part of the answer), 'What happened after Isabella disappeared? Did you and your wife continue as you had before?'

Jonathan gave a snort of mirthless laughter.

'Use your imagination, man! If, that is, you have any! How could we? Our one and only chick had gone. Flown the coop. Everything we had done and thought and said for twenty years had been for Isabella. Now there was no one. Nothing! Of course, for a while, for weeks, months, we half-expected that she would return, bringing her husband – that is, whichever of the three men she had finally chosen – with her. But when a year had passed and we had heard nothing from her, we began to suspect that she was never coming home.'

'But surely,' I persisted, 'in the early days, you must have made some push to find her? You must have made enquiries?'

'Of course we did! The day she failed to come back from riding, we sent to Emilia at her cottage and I went myself to my cousin at the nunnery, to discover if either of them had seen Isabella. If, by chance, she was with one of them. The following morning, we took the hands from their work and sent them to scour the countryside in case our daughter had met with an accident. We sent both girls to Clifton village to find out if anyone there had seen her since she rode out the previous morning. Lord Cobham was away from home – he often was – but Amorette and I visited the house and made enquiries of the housekeeper.'

'Without result? No one had seen Isabella at all the day she vanished?'

'Oh, people had seen her. There had been several sightings of her in the morning near Westbury village, in the company of a man. But nobody could say which one. At least, there seemed to be disagreement about his identity. It was a wet March day, cold and windy, and with a hint of sleet in the air. It seems that both

Isabella and her companion, whoever he was, had the hoods of their cloaks pulled well forward, making it difficult to see their features distinctly.'

'In that case, how were your informants certain that it was your daughter that they'd seen?'

'They knew her by her cloak. It was dark blue, lined with scarlet wool.'

'Ah... And did you find out how late in the day it was when Isabella was last observed?'

Jonathan Linkinhorne shook his head. I could tell by the shuttered expression on his face that suddenly he had had enough. He did not want to think or talk about the subject any more.

'I've told you, Master!' He slammed his open palm against the tabletop, again attracting the attention of his neighbours, but now past caring. 'It's too long ago. I'd like you to go.'

I had often seen this happen with older people: for a while they were bright and energetic, then, without warning, they wilted like flowers in the summer heat, overcome by fatigue. I patted his gnarled and brown-spotted hand.

'I'm leaving,' I said. 'Just one more question. This nurse, this Emilia... Virgoe, did you say?' He nodded. 'Is she still alive?' He nodded again. 'Do you know where I can find her?'

'That's two questions,' Jonathan reminded me, but answered all the same. 'She has a cottage on Lord Cobham's estate. Ask for her in Clifton village. Anyone will tell you where she lives.' His gaze and voice sharpened, the milky blue eyes focusing on my face, almost as if he were seeing me properly for the first time since my arrival. 'What do you want with Emilia? She can't tell you any more than I have done. She's over sixty now. Old people don't want to be bothered cudgelling their brains to remember things long gone and best forgotten. It's upsetting. And the plain truth is, Master Chapman, that Isabella's been dead to me – and, I suspect, to Emilia – these many years. Finding her body hasn't made her death any more real, except in the sense that now I know for certain, for a fact, that I'll never set eyes on her again.'

He was lying. I could tell it by the tremor in his voice, which he strove valiantly to keep steady, and by the rogue tear that had escaped and was running down one cheek. But I could understand his reluctance to dwell, publicly at least, on the gruesome discovery of his daughter's corpse. He must blame himself, and also feel that others blamed him, for not making more effort to trace her whereabouts twenty years ago. Had he done so, her true fate might have become known, with a far better chance of bringing the murderer to justice.

I rose to take my leave of him, but the sight of Miles Huckbody and Henry Dando loitering near the door made me pause and risk asking yet another question.

'Master Linkinhorne,' I ventured, 'the jewellery your daughter was wearing – the rings, necklace and girdle by which your cousin was able to identify the body as Isabella's – was it familiar to you?'

He shook his head.

'No. Sergeant Manifold brought it to show me,

71

but I'd never seen any of it before. Obviously,' he added bitterly, 'Jeanette – Sister Walburga – recognized it.'

'Sister Walburga told me it was given to Isabella by one of her admirers, who was a goldsmith by trade.'

The old man gave vent to a sudden explosion of furious laughter.

'Then my cousin knows far more than I do. Far more! You'd better go and talk to her again.'

I could see that he was trembling, his left hand jerking uncontrollably against the tabletop. Guilt consumed me. I leaned forward, once more pressing his shoulder.

'I'll leave you in peace now, Master Linkinhorne. Thank you for your time and patience.'

He made no reply. I'm not sure that he even heard me. I pushed past Miles Huckbody and Henry Dando without looking at them, resolutely ignoring their whispered questions and muttered indignation when I didn't answer. Then I was out in the fresh air of the April afternoon, breathing pleasurably and deeply, but possessed by the uneasy reflection that one day I, too, would be old.

Five

I walked home through the April afternoon with
a growing sense of unease; but by the time I
approached the Frome Bridge I had managed to
pinpoint at least three causes of my discomfort.

Firstly, I had never before used my talent to
make money; never allowed my services to be
hired. I had solved mysteries for many people,
but always maintained my independence, sup-
porting myself, Adela and the children by my
efforts as a pedlar while sorting out those God-
sent problems; problems which usually – I'm too
modest to say always – resulted in some wrong-
doer being brought to justice. Once, the Duke of
Gloucester had sent money after me, but it had
only supplemented what I had managed to earn
for myself and, although undeniably welcome, it
had not been vital to my or my family's survival.
Now, however, I had broken my golden rule and
was living on John Foster's bounty while I did
my best to unravel the puzzle of who had killed
Isabella Linkinhorne. I had established a prece-
dent. And that worried me.

The second thing disturbing my peace of mind
was something I suppose I had always secretly
acknowledged, but considered it as yet too early
in life to face up to: the difficulties, the clash of

73

wills that inevitably arose between parents and children as they all grew older. Jonathan and Amorette Linkinhorne's relationship with their daughter had plainly been an extreme one, but it demonstrated the depths of misunderstanding – indeed of total alienation – that could develop through selfishness and pride on the one hand, and deep-seated resentment and rebellion on the other. I knew that both Adela and I were unusual in our concerns for our offspring; that many people, including Margaret Walker, regarded us as lax preceptors because we spared the rod and, in their eyes, spoiled the child. I even worried about it myself, sometimes. And although I often, loudly and forcefully, expressed contrary views and made threats that I, and everyone else, knew I had no intention of carrying out, I doubted if Adela and I would ever reach such a state of wilful ignorance concerning our children's doings as the Linkinhornes had with Isabella.

Finally, there was the thought of old age itself, provided either disease or disaster failed to carry me off before my allotted three score years and ten; the expectation of diminished eyesight, impaired hearing, creaking joints and incontinence. (And although the reality hasn't proved to be quite as bad as I had anticipated, there is still the shock of waking up each morning and realizing that my tomorrows are numbered.)

So I crossed the Frome Bridge to the gateway feeling thoroughly despondent, glancing up at the great keep of the castle where it brooded over the town, hanging in the sun-threaded air like some fairy palace. Only it wasn't a fairy

74

palace, but rather a place of darkness and misery, suffering and despair. In stark contrast, from the chapel of Saint John-on-the-Arch floated the voices of children singing, a little ragged at the edges but with a heart-rending purity of sound, bringing hope and comfort and joy to everyone who heard them. The thin spring sunlight sent grey and silver shadows rippling across the surface of the water; and the small stone customs house that stood near the river reminded me of a pebble washed up by the tide.

Edgar Capgrave was still on duty at the gate, and still arguing, this time with the stream of homeward-bound visitors who were objecting to the toll on goods being taken out of the city.

'I don't make the laws, mother!' he was bellowing at a deaf woman with a basket of goods weighing down her frail old arms. 'Them's Bristol goods for Bristol people you'm squirrelling away to your hidey-hole in the country. So course you've got to pay a toll! It's only right and proper.'

'I'm not your mother!' the crone screeched in reply. 'I just wish I were! You'd feel the weight of my fist! Such incivility to a poor, defenceless old woman!'

Once again, I left Edgar to it and went home for my supper – only to find myself faced with a domestic crisis.

'The night-soil man hasn't come today,' was Adela's greeting. 'The privy's full to overflowing. You'll have to do something about it, Roger. We can't have turds being trodden all over the yard.'

'Turds!' shouted Adam, beaming all over his bread-and-milk-spattered little face and waving his spoon at me.

Wonderful! Cleaning out the privy was just what I needed before tackling my rabbit stew. But it wasn't the first time I'd had to do the night-soil man's job for him. He seemed to be constantly going sick. Perhaps it was genuine. Either way, who could blame him?

When I'd finished – in the absence of the night-soil man's horse and cart, transferring the privy contents to the street's central drain – Adela shooed all three children upstairs while I sat naked in the old wooden tub in front of the kitchen fire and she poured pitchers of alternate cold and hot water into it until I was covered to my waist. Then she scrubbed my back, laughing and wrinkling her nose at the disgusting smell of the clothes I had dropped on the floor. One thing very nearly led to another, but the patter of feet up and down the stairs reminded us that it was far too early in the evening for any kind of dalliance. So Adela found me a clean shirt and my only other decent pair of hose and, when I had got out of the tub, set about soaking the offending garments in my bath water. While all this was going on, and I was rubbing myself dry on the piece of rough sheeting we kept for that purpose, I took the opportunity to tell her about my conversations with Sister Walburga and Jonathan Linkinhorne.

'What I don't understand,' Adela said, as she laid the kitchen table with plates and spoons for supper, 'is how Isabella's body came to be

76

buried in that plot of ground if, as everyone insists, it had never been used as a graveyard. Digging a grave, even a shallow one, can't be easy. And that spot is near enough to both the nunnery and Saint Michael's church that anyone doing so would surely have been bound to attract attention at some point in the proceedings. Even under cover of darkness, you'd think that someone would have seen or heard something at some time.'

She was right. I hadn't until that moment thought of it myself, although no doubt I would have done so eventually. But then, there was much about the case that I hadn't had occasion to consider as yet. All the same, I used it as an excuse to get my arm around her waist and tell her what a clever woman she was, while at the same time trying to insinuate one hand into the top of her skirt.

She gently pushed me away, a warning glint that I recognized in her fine dark eyes.

'Don't patronize me, Roger.'

I held up my hands in surrender. 'Pax! Pax!' I said, laughing. 'I'm sorry.'

She accepted my apology with her usual good grace, and called the children down to supper. Elizabeth and Nicholas, ever hungry, stormed in and climbed on their stools, waiting impatiently for their bowls of stew to be passed to them. Adam, who had already been fed, was free to roam about the kitchen at will, but most unexpectedly chose to clamber on to my knees and lay his head against my chest. It made eating difficult, but when Adela offered to relieve me of my burden, I smiled and shook my head.

'No. Let him be.'

She returned my smile, knowing, with that intuition wives develop, that I was thinking of those other parents whose understanding of their child and her needs had led eventually to total estrangement. And when, after ten minutes or so, Adam wriggled free of my embrace and trotted off about his own small affairs without any reproaches or efforts to detain him on my part, she smiled at me again, more lovingly than ever.

'What will you do next?' she asked.

I shrugged. 'I can do nothing tomorrow, it being Sunday. But on Monday, I think I must walk to Clifton and try to find this Emilia Virgoe, Isabella's nurse.'

But late that night, lying in my arms, content and drowsy after making love, Adela suddenly roused herself, raising her head from the pillow to ask, 'How could any mother and father be so ignorant of what their child was doing? Who she was seeing? And surely when she disappeared like that, they should have bestirred themselves to make more enquiries than they did?'

I could tell from her tone of voice that she was worried, foreseeing, as I had done, a future when these problems might be ours, and frightened for the outcome. I tightened my hold on her.

'We're not the Linkinhornes,' I reassured her. 'We shan't expect to command our children's love, or feel slighted if they withhold it. Or at least not so that it shows. And we'd never let our resentment of their behaviour get in the way of doing what was right. If Elizabeth or Nicholas or

Adam vanished without a word, we'd move heaven and earth to find out what had happened to him or her.'

'Is that what you think it was, resentment?'

'Oh, yes. I feel certain of it. Isabella had shut them out of her life, even flagrantly lying to them. And they must have known in their hearts that she was lying, even while pretending to themselves that they believed her. They'd given her everything, including more love and attention than one person could cope with. So when, as they thought, she left them without a word for the love of someone else, they only made a pretence of trying to find her. But I think the lack of effort must have preyed on Mistress Linkinhorne's mind. A year after Isabella's disappearance, she was dead. Drowned in the Avon.'

'Suicide?' Adela whispered.

'Not officially. An accident; and maybe it was. But I can't help wondering if remorse played any part in her death.'

'Poor woman.'

Adela spoke so softly that I barely heard her, as a sudden squall of rain rattled the bedchamber shutters and wind moaned down Small Street between the overhanging eaves of the houses. I kissed her gently on the forehead.

'Go to sleep,' I murmured, 'and stop worrying over matters you've no hope of mending. Our lives can never be that bad, not while we have each other.'

She settled her head contentedly once more against my shoulder, and I thought I caught a half-laughing, disjointed mutter about men and roving eyes and their general untrustworthiness, which I considered it best to ignore. I gave her another kiss, which was received with sufficient, if somewhat sleepy, passion to make me think of assaulting the citadel again, but tiredness won. Before the thought was even half-formed, I was (so Adela informed me the following day) snoring.

Sunday passed, as Sundays generally do, in a haze of churchgoing, reading of the Scriptures and boredom. There was no sign of John Foster at Saint Giles. It being the Sunday before his swearing-in as the city's new Mayor, he would have gone in procession with his fellow aldermen and the out-going Mayor to Saint Mark's chapel at the Gaunts' Hospital, and I was relieved to be spared his anxious queries as to how my investigation was proceeding. (People always thought that facts just fell into my lap without any work on my part.) It continued raining all day, which meant that the children were housebound and forbidden to play games for fear of disturbing the Sabbath calm and the religious scruples of the neighbours. So I gathered the family around the kitchen table and told them the story of Noah and the flood; although I wondered afterwards, noting the look of rapt attention on Adam's face, if it had been a wise choice. There was never any knowing what was going on in that devious little head of his.

But no Sunday, however dismal, can last for ever, and by Monday morning the weather had improved. Daybreak brought sun and gently steaming cobbles, and even the men who rattled into the city on their carts to clear the drains sounded cheerful as they called to one another or returned greetings with people already abroad in the streets. The night-soil man actually made an early appearance, apologizing for his absence on Saturday, which, he said, had been caused by a bad back. I grunted to Adela that I wished I had a groat for every time I'd listened to that excuse, but she hushed me quickly. As a woman, she knew that there were certain people who should never be antagonized.

I ate my breakfast of dried herring and oatmeal biscuit, then grabbed my cudgel and whistled up Hercules ready for the long uphill trudge to Clifton. The strangeness of leaving my pack behind still irked me and made me feel guilty, but as Adela sensibly remarked, the sooner I found the answer to this particular problem, the sooner I would be free to pursue my rightful calling. I kissed her soundly and told her she had more faith in my abilities than I had, at least in this particular case, but she only laughed and retorted that modesty didn't become me.

'On your way!' she ordered, before sitting down at the table and beginning the arduous task of binding new broom twigs on to the ash sapling handle that had served her as the mainstay of her besom for so long.

I had recently found in a pile of street rubbish an old, very long leather belt that must once have belonged to an extremely fat man. It proved ideal as a new lead for Hercules, with the buckle end lightly fastened around his neck and the

81

other coiled around my wrist. He was at first inclined to resent this tougher and wider restriction against his throat and strained angrily at the leash all the way across the Frome Bridge and along the Backs; but by the time we reached the open ground above the straggling streets and houses that had proliferated beyond the city walls, he was trotting along quietly and proudly and looking disdainfully at other dogs confined simply by a piece of rope.

We climbed past the summit of Saint Brendan's hill and then further up until finally, hot and breathless – well I know I was – we achieved the plateau of land to the east of the great gorge. After yesterday's rain, it bid fair to be a fine day with a promise of that warmth so characteristic of an English spring, when the weather has not quite made up its mind that winter is past, but can't help hinting at summer joys to come. Still slumbering trees brooded over sun-dappled grass, distances shifted in the soft morning haze and a ragged string of geese rose, gobbling, into a pale green sky. There were plenty of fellow travellers already on the road; pedlars like myself, a party of mummers probably moving on from the house which had given them shelter throughout the winter months, people with baskets and carts of vegetables or driving animals, all of them heading downhill to Bristol in its marshy bed, hoping to sell them at market. Two stalwart churchmen sailed like a couple of black swans through the early mist.

The manor of Clifton lives up to its name; the cliff town perched on the edge of Ghyston Cliff, the great rock face on the Bristol side of the gorge that rises sheer from the bed of the River Avon. It still being very early, and not wishing to disturb Emilia Virgoe's slumbers, should the old lady not feel the urge to rise at the crack of dawn, Hercules (long since let off his leash) and I made our way to the great tump, about a quarter of a mile from the edge of the cliff. Here we sat down and from my satchel I produced the hunk of rye bread and scraps of meat that Adela had given me. There was also a piece of cheese wrapped in dock leaves, but Hercules turned his nose up at that, so I had it all to myself. Then we both stretched out on one of the grassy mounds of the tump and let our tired limbs slowly recover from the rigours of the climb.

The tump is a strange place, full of ghostly echoes. Some say that our Celtic ancestors used it as a fort until the Romans drove them out and turned it into a look-out post from which they could survey the river and its approaches, so that raiding parties of Welshmen shouldn't take them by surprise. Then there are other wilder stories that the mound was built by either the Saracens or the Jews. Ridiculous, of course, but these odd notions take a hold in the minds of country people, often gaining ascendancy over the far more likely, rational explanations. And then there's the legend of how the gorge itself was hewn out of living rock by the two giants, Goram and Vincent, using one pick which they threw back and forth to one another until the latter accidentally killed the former, and spent the rest of his life in prayer and good works in order to atone.

The memory of this tale reminded me that if I walked down a narrow cliff path I would come to Saint Vincent's chapel and hermitage, perched high above the gorge like a nesting bird, where Hercules and I might be offered a drink of water and I could make enquiries as to the whereabouts of Mistress Virgoe's cottage. It turned out that the path was narrower and slightly more dangerous than I had supposed, viewing it in the past from the ground, and rather than risk Hercules plunging to his death over the edge, I carried him in my arms. This proved to be a mistake as he wriggled indignantly throughout most of the descent and I was forced to grab on to the pitifully inadequate rope railing, fastened to the cliff face, with all my might.

The hermit, whose abode was a cave alongside the tiny chapel, greeted us without much enthusiasm; a thin, ascetic-looking man with untidy strands of hair plastered to his otherwise bald pate, watery hazel eyes and rheumatic joints. Very much, I suppose, as you would expect a hermit to be, except that this one seemed to bear a grudge against the world in general and against me in particular for disturbing his morning rest. He took an immediate dislike to Hercules, whom he bade me leave outside, which I refused to do.

'He'll be over the cliff edge as soon as I take my eyes off him,' I protested, 'and I'm fond of him.' I was suddenly conscious of the fact that this was true. 'Besides, I won't trouble you long. I just want to know where I can find Emilia

Virgoe.'

'Why do you want to know?'

The man smelled offensively, a sour mixture of dried sweat, vomit and old food. The cave was a shallow one, going back only six or seven feet into the rock face and containing nothing but a straw mattress covered by a moth-eaten grey blanket, a couple of pots for cooking, a tinder-box and a knife on a shelf near the entrance. The man's brown robe was stained with food and various other marks on whose origin I preferred not to speculate. Living in such circumstances, perhaps anyone would be short-tempered and suspicious. On the other hand, living close to God and contemplating the work of His creation was surely intended to make one humble and happy.

'I wish to ask Mistress Virgoe some questions,' I said.

The hermit sneered. 'About that strumpet, Isabella Linkinhorne, I suppose. Oh, don't think we haven't heard about the discovery of her body up here! News travels fast where death and scandal are concerned.'

'Scandal?' I queried innocently.

'That girl was a disgrace,' he declared viciously.

'You were acquainted with her?'

'I knew her. I was about her own age and lived on the manor. She was brought up to be a decent, God-fearing girl, and could have had a decent, God-fearing husband had she so chosen. Instead of which, she preferred the ways of Satan.'

Oho, I thought, so you were after her, too, my

lad, were you? Except, of course, he was no longer a lad, but a sad, middle-aged man who had embarked on the life of a solitary as a shield against his bitterness and frustration.

'So,' I said, 'these men I've been hearing about really did exist, did they? They weren't just figments of other people's imaginations? Jonathan Linkinhorne told me that Isabella always denied them.'

'The man is a fool!' the hermit rapped back violently. 'He and his wife believed what they wanted to be true – until it was too late and Isabella had gone. They ignored what everyone told them because they were too old to face up to unpalatable facts.'

'Did you ever see Mistress Isabella with one of these men?'

'With all three at one time or another.' My companion's voice was full of loathing and resentment, yet tinged with a longing that indicated more clearly than his previous contempt just what his true feelings had been.

'Where did you see them?'

'I had an aunt who lived near Westbury College. She's long dead, but in those days I often used to walk over to see her.' More often than was necessary, I surmised. 'Westbury was a convenient rendezvous for all three men to meet Isabella. I'm sure one of them came from Bristol, but not having been there for many, many years I wouldn't know if he were still living there or not.'

'And the other two?'

The man shrugged. 'From round and about. No

one I ever spoke to seemed certain of their origins. There was talk of Gloucester and Bath, but whether that was true or not, or just guesswork on the part of others, I had no means of knowing.' The skinny chest swelled. 'I did once try reasoning with Isabella, when I met her in Westbury village, but she laughed at me and her companion threatened me with his riding crop and told me to mind my own business or he'd lay it about my sides. I was so incensed that when I returned to Clifton, I went straight to Master and Mistress Linkinhorne and laid the facts before them.'

'And?'

The hermit's face darkened with anger. 'They refused to listen. Accused me of being like everyone else who attempted to make them see reason. Accused me of trying to destroy Isabella's reputation because she had refused my suit. *My* suit! I had never offered for the trollop!' Only because he had had a good idea of what, and how scathing, the answer would be, I was sure. 'Besides, I was already experiencing a calling for the religious life.'

Hercules, whom I was still holding, nudged my face with his cold, wet nose to remind me that we had been stationary for long enough and that it was high time we were moving. I scratched his ears with my free hand and gave him a little squeeze.

'Had you taken up your office of manor hermit before Isabella disappeared?' I asked.

He shook his head. 'The job didn't fall vacant until three or four years after that. When the old

87

hermit died, Lord Cobham offered it to me, knowing from his chaplain that I had a religious bent and had no intention of marrying.'

I moved the few steps towards the cave mouth, as if about to leave, but turned back at the last moment as though struck by a sudden thought.

'Did you, by any chance, happen to see Isabella at any time on the day she vanished? On the day, I suppose, we now know that she died.'

There were a few seconds of complete silence, while the hermit made up his mind whether or not to answer my question. The narrow face was a battleground of conflicting emotions before he finally replied hoarsely, 'Yes, I saw her.'

'What time of day?'

'Around mid-afternoon, perhaps. It was a cold, wet day. Grey skies, overcast, so difficult to tell. And twenty years is a long time ago.'

I agreed, but persisted. 'Do you happen to remember exactly where you saw her?'

'She was on horseback, riding down the village street. I tried to catch her eye, but although I'm fairly certain she'd seen me, she pretended she hadn't and continued on her way. Off on one of her gallops, I thought to myself, to meet one of her men. I used to think that if only I could get her to listen to me, I could show her the error of her ways. But she'd never give me the chance.'

I wasn't surprised. I could imagine this man twenty years ago; self-righteous, priggish, intolerant, always trying to convert others to his own narrow point of view. I'd met people like him many times in my life and never warmed to any of them.

'Can you recollect what Isabella was wearing?' I asked him.

The hermit shrugged again; a favourite gesture it seemed.

'A cloak probably. I've told you, it was cold and wet. A typical March day. At least, I think it was March.' He considered this statement for a moment or two, then nodded, as though satisfied. 'She was wearing a cloak,' he added, just as I thought he was going to jib at telling me anything further. 'I remember she had the hood pulled well forward, but I knew it was Isabella because I recognized her horse.'

'You didn't recognize the cloak she was wearing?'

'Her cloak?' He looked affronted. 'I've never taken much notice of women's clothes.' He immediately belied this statement by continuing, 'It was that dark blue cloak of hers with the scarlet lining. It was billowing all around her, like a great sail. Why she hadn't fastened it properly I don't know. It would have stopped the wind blowing her skirt up and showing her legs in those red silk stockings and green leather garters she was wearing.' For one who took no interest in women's clothing, it occurred to me that he had noticed a very great deal. He confirmed this by repeating, 'Red stockings, I ask you!' His tone was scathing. 'With that gown!'

It was at this point that Hercules finally managed to squirm free of my arms and perform the trick he always tried whenever he was annoyed at being kept waiting: he cocked his leg against mine and peed all down my boot. The hermit suddenly proved that he had a sense of humour – of a sort – and burst out laughing. In fact he was doubled up with mirth and appeared in imminent danger of having a seizure.

I grabbed the miscreant and left.

Six

It was not until I reached the top of the path that I realized my original question had remained unanswered. The hermit had failed to tell me where I might find Emilia Virgoe. This, however, proved to be no problem as the first person I encountered, a smiling countrywoman in a brown homespun gown and a snowy-white hood and apron, immediately directed me to the nurse's cottage.

This stood a little apart from the village, set back from the track known generally as Stonelea; a track that led eastwards and downwards to Bristol in the vicinity of Steep Street. Somewhere near the beginning of the descent the road divided, the left-hand fork being the approach to the village of Westbury which, in all probability, I would be taking later. But not before I had had a word with Mistress Virgoe.

Judging by the height of the sun, the morning was by now well advanced, and I was afraid she might be out and about, gathering wood for her fire or looking for mushrooms that had sprung up in the fields overnight after the previous day's wet weather. But I need not have worried: Emilia Virgoe was at home, clearing away the remnants of her seemingly frugal dinner. There was no smell of cooking, no pot over the fire and only a crust of bread and a rind of cheese on the plate remaining on the table.

She was a small woman, neat, compact, with a pair of intelligent brown eyes in a wrinkled, weathered face, a short, straight nose and thin lips that curled upwards at the corners as though their owner was ready at any moment to break into a smile. Jonathan Linkinhorne had told me that she was well over sixty, and there was nothing to contradict this statement in the badly gnarled hands that were clasped composedly in front of her once she had opened the cottage door to my knock. But in spite of the wrinkles and knotted joints there was an indefinable air of youthfulness about her that I have noticed in some old people. Spry is the word that I think best described her.

'Yes?' she queried. 'And what do you want, young man?'

I explained as clearly and succinctly as I could, but I need not have feared for her powers of understanding. She listened quietly, her head cocked slightly to one side, and at no time did she ask me to repeat myself. When I had finished, she invited me to enter, holding the door wide and stooping to pat Hercules's head. He licked her hand and at once made himself at home, stretching out in front of the fire on its central hearth and promptly settling down to sleep.

'He likes you,' I grinned. 'He doesn't take to everybody.'

Her lips twitched. 'And I don't take to every dog I meet. But he's a nice little fellow. I knew it the second I set eyes on him.' She saw me looking at the bread and cheese and quietly removed the plate to a broad shelf near the water barrel, then told me to sit down on one of the two stools drawn up to the table. She took the other, facing me, and asked with the same composure she had shown throughout, 'Now, what is it you want from me? You say you've spoken to Master Linkinhorne, so what more can I tell you?'

I countered with a question of my own.

'Were you shocked to hear the recent news of the discovery of Isabella's body?' A sudden thought struck me. 'You have heard, I assume?' I did a quick calculation in my head. 'Now I come to think of it, it's only four days since she was found.'

The brown eyes lit with amusement.

'My dear – Roger, did you say your name is?' I nodded. 'My dear Roger,' she went on, 'how long do you think it needs for such tidings to reach as far as Clifton? We are not living on the moon. The news was all over the manor by Friday morning, and as Sister Walburga had by then identified the remains as those of Isabella, I was naturally one of the very first to be informed.'

'So...were you shocked?'

Emilia Virgoe hesitated before saying primly,

92

'Of course.'

I regarded her severely. 'Shocked, yes. Naturally. But surprised?'

There was a longer pause, and I sensed my hostess's sudden discomfort.

'What do you want me to say?' she asked at last.

'The truth would be helpful.' Then, feeling that this was a little blunt, if not downright rude, I added meekly, 'Please.'

She gave me a swift smile that puckered the corners of her eyes, but faded to leave her looking sad and somewhat apprehensive.

'No,' she admitted at last. 'Not surprised.'

I leaned my elbows on the table. 'Mistress Virgoe, did you suspect that Isabella could have been the victim of foul play at the time of her disappearance?'

She delayed her answer by getting up and taking two beakers and an earthenware jar from a wall cupboard and bringing them back to the table. When she unstoppered the jar, the pungent scent of elderflower wine teased my nostrils and I knew that unless I managed to restrain my natural appetite, I should be in trouble. There are fewer drinks more potent, at least in my experience, than elderflower wine brewed by enthusiastic old ladies. The dames themselves usually regard it as harmless, even after it has been stored and allowed to ferment throughout the winter; just a refreshing draft to revive you, they say. Never believe them! It can lay you out flat, to be followed by a splitting headache.

I accepted my beaker but, after a sip or two to

show willing, pushed it to one side.

'You haven't answered my question,' I reminded Emilia gently.

'Which was?'

'Did you suspect that anything sinister had happened to Isabella when she vanished?'

The nurse took a deep breath. 'No, not really.' When I would have spoken again, she held up her hand to stop me. 'I know! What do I mean by "not really"?' She drank some wine before continuing. 'It was nothing but a fleeting suspicion. A faint feeling of unease, if you like, but no more than that.'

'Did you voice your unease to Master and Mistress Linkinhorne?'

'Once. But not with any conviction.'

'They thought it unlikely?'

'They both dismissed the notion out of hand. Although...'

'Yes? Although?'

Emilia Virgoe shrugged her thin shoulders. 'I remember thinking that Mistress Linkinhorne was less sceptical than her husband. But Amorette was always greatly influenced by him, and Jonathan soon persuaded her that the idea was nonsense. She agreed at once. And I didn't press it. I didn't truly consider it likely, myself.'

'Why not?'

Suddenly she was angry.

'What is this? An inquisition?'

I had the grace to blush. 'I'm sorry. It's just that for Mayor Foster's sake, I'd like to get at the truth. As I explained, he wants to build his chapel, dedicated to the Three Kings of Cologne,

94

alongside his almshouses. But he feels that unless Isabella's killer can be brought to justice, he can't ask for the ground to be re-hallowed.'

My companion nodded. 'I can understand that. I know of Master Foster by reputation. A good man and a devout Christian. Very well! I'll answer your questions, although if you've spoken to Jonathan Linkinhorne, I doubt if there's much else I can tell you.'

'You were Isabella's nurse. Did she never confide in you? These three men she was reported as meeting – did she never tell you their names?'

Emilia Virgoe shook her head. 'No, for the simple reason that she knew whatever she told me I should feel in duty bound to report to her parents. They were the people who paid my wages and I considered my loyalty was to them. In any case –' she took another sip of wine – 'I was never sufficiently attached to Isabella to stand as her friend. Perhaps that sounds strange to you. I was her nurse from her earliest years, and nurses are generally regarded as the confidantes of their charges, very often taking the place of parents, who have other and more pressing concerns. But Master and Mistress Linkinhorne were doting parents and involved themselves in everything Isabella thought and said and did. I had little to do other than the washing and dressing of her, taking her for walks, singing her to sleep. So, in fairness to myself, I suppose I was never allowed to grow too close to the child.'

'But after Isabella grew up, after she began to rebel against her parents' smothering affection,

95

didn't she turn to you then?' I urged.

Emilia shook her head. 'My sympathies were with the mother and father. Isabella sensed that, and although we never discussed the subject, I can see now that she probably resented the fact. With hindsight, I can also see that it was a mistake. If my attitude had been less condemnatory, she might have taken me into her confidence more. You talk of Jonathan and Amorette Linkinhorne's smothering affection, a phrase I have often heard repeated in the years since Isabella's disappearance and which, I must admit, I have come to accept might have some justification. But at the time, all I could see was two people who desperately wanted the love of their only child, and who had no reason to be rejected so harshly.' She smiled faintly. 'I can tell by your expression that you don't agree with me.'

I made no reply to that.

'These three men,' I said, 'in whose company Isabella was reported as having been seen, did she never let drop a hint as to their identity?'

'None. Oh, unlike Master and Mistress Linkinhorne, I never believed her protestations that the stories were all lies, made up by spiteful neighbours. That was ridiculous. There were too many of them. One neighbour might bear her a grudge, but not everybody. Besides, the various descriptions of the three men tallied with one another.'

'So why do you think Master and Mistress Linkinhorne were so gullible? Why did two intelligent people allow themselves to be deceived?'

The nurse took another long draft from her

beaker, while I watched, fascinated. The elder-flower wine seemed to have no effect on her whatsoever, while my head was already whirling from the half dozen sips I had ventured to drink.

'Because they couldn't bear to think that Isabella was lying to them,' she replied, replacing her now nearly empty beaker on the table and refilling it. 'It's a simple answer, but the truth often is simple, haven't you found?'

It was my turn to nod, while moving my beaker out of range of the jar, as Emilia tried to replenish its contents.

'What can you tell me about the day Isabella disappeared?'

'Now there, I'm afraid, you're unlucky,' she said regretfully. 'I was away visiting my sister in Bristol. Marian had been taken ill some days before – indeed, she died a fortnight later – and Master Linkinhorne had given me leave to visit her and to stay as long as I was needed. He and Mistress Linkinhorne only kept me on out of the goodness of their hearts. Isabella had far outgrown the necessity for a nurse. Dear heaven! She was twenty and past marriageable age, but averse to all suggestions by her parents that she should look about her for a suitable husband and settle down. I remember her saying once, "What do I want with a husband? Just another man who'd try to cage me!" So, by the time I returned home, Isabella had been missing for over six weeks.'

'What were you told?'

Again, Emilia Virgoe gave that slight shrug of her shoulders.

'Master Linkinhorne said that Isabella had run away. That she had been seen on the day she vanished with a man near Westbury village; that she had obviously eloped with him and that no doubt they would hear from her in due course when she needed their assistance. I asked what they had done to try to trace her, and I have to confess that it struck me as very little. But I could tell how bitter they were and how angry. I did suggest, as I told you, that some harm might have come to the girl, but the idea was dismissed, and indeed, knowing her reputation, I did not believe in it myself.'

I frowned. 'She seems to have been remarkably successful in keeping the identities of three men a secret from almost everyone. Most young women like to boast of their conquests.'

'Isabella was not like most girls. She was extremely secretive. One might say excessively so. I suppose I could agree with you that her parents had made her like that.'

'Did you ever have the impression that she was afraid of them? Of her father, anyway?'

Emilia Virgoe laughed. 'Never!' She was emphatic. 'Where the love and the need to be loved is all on one side and not on the other, it is the person without affection, or even the desire for it, who holds the whip-hand. Surely you can see that. I have always believed that love can inflict more damage than hatred ever can.'

I shifted uncomfortably. 'You're a cynical woman, Mistress.'

'A philosophy too close to your own, perhaps?' When I didn't answer, she smiled wisely and nodded towards my beaker. 'You haven't finished your wine.'

I gave her a shamefaced grin. 'To tell the truth, it's too strong for me.' I pushed my stool back from the table. 'Well, thank you for your time. I won't disturb you any further.'

She looked apologetic. 'I'm afraid I haven't been of much use to you, young man, in your quest for the truth. It's obvious, of course, that one of those three men – the one she was seen with that day – murdered Isabella. But until you can discover who they were, I don't give much for your chances of ever finding the poor girl's killer. And after twenty years...' Emilia broke off, shrugging.

'I have been told that one of them was a goldsmith and gave her the jewellery she was still wearing when her body was uncovered.'

The nurse raised her eyebrows.

'Then you have already found out more than I know,' she acknowledged, not, I thought, altogether pleased.

I called to Hercules, who opened one bleary eye a slit before closing it again. While I was busy rousing him and fastening the leather belt around his neck, Emilia Virgoe seemed to be lost in thoughts of her own. As I straightened up, she said, 'What you were saying, about girls liking to boast of their conquests, has made me remember Isabella's maid, Jane...Jane...' She wrinkled her nose in an effort of memory. 'Jane Honeychurch! That was it! An ugly, mousy little thing about Isabella's own age. Very quiet. Frightened of her own shadow. I don't know where she came from. Bristol, I think. Yes...Master Linkin-horne brought her home with him about a year before Isabella disappeared, and I believe I'm right in saying that it was after one of his trips to the city. What happened to her in later years, I really don't know. In fact, I'd completely for-gotten her until this minute. But I suppose it's possible that Isabella could have confided in her. Mistress and maid, what could be more natural?'

I nodded. 'Highly probable! Indeed, almost certain, I should say. And you have no idea at all where this young woman might be now?'

Emilia shook her head. 'But there's one thing I can tell you. Jane Honeychurch won't be a young woman any more. If she's still alive, she'll be forty or a little over. The same age that Isabella would have been had she lived. Indeed, the age I have always assumed she was until a day or so ago.'

'And of course she – Jane – might have married,' I added gloomily.

'There is that,' my hostess concurred, 'but I wouldn't stake my life on it. She was not a prepossessing girl. On the other hand,' Emilia added with a certain amount of bitterness, 'good looks aren't necessarily everything. I've known some very odd-featured women who have not only captured husbands, but who have been the object of those husbands' adoration.'

I guessed from this that Emilia Virgoe had never married. As a young woman she must have been very pretty, but for one reason or another had failed to ensnare a man. It had plainly galled her to see other, far less attractive females experiencing no difficulty in finding mates. Perhaps her attitude to love explained matters.

I thanked her again for her patience and time, adding, 'You see, you have been of great help to me, after all. If I can only find this Jane Honey-church, I might discover the names of Isabella's beaux.'

'I wouldn't pin your hopes on it,' the nurse advised me. 'Even if you do find the woman, there's nothing to say that Isabella ever told her anything more than she told anyone else. Where will you go now?'

'To Westbury village, in case there is anyone still living there who can recall seeing Isabella on the day she disappeared and can add anything to what I already know.'

'And that is?'

'That it was a cold, wet and windy March day and both Isabella and her companion had the hoods of their cloaks pulled well forward to conceal their faces.'

The nurse smiled and said, 'I wish you luck.' She nobly refrained from repeating a warning about the length of time involved or from adding a rider concerning the general unreliability of people's memories over a span of twenty days, let alone the same number of years. But she did wonder aloud, as I had wondered to myself, about the advisability of searching out the truth. 'After so lengthy a period, does it really matter now?'

I spoke sternly, partly to appease my own conscience.

'Where murder is involved, isn't it everyone's duty to bring the murderer to book if he can?' I asked. 'The taking of human life is surely the most heinous of all crimes.'

Emilia Virgoe laughed shortly. 'It depends, doesn't it, whether you are taking life for your own reasons or for those of your overlord, who commands you to do so on his behalf.'

I decided it was definitely time to go. We were getting into deep water; on the borderline of treason. I thanked my hostess yet again and left.

I had been to Westbury once before and knew it to be little more than a scatter of cottages along the River Trym and grouped around the college, which dominated the area. There had been a monastery there in Saxon times, under the control of the then Bishop of Worcester, who had brought over twelve Benedictine monks from Fleury in France. By the time of the Conquest, however, it had fallen into decay and the monks had long gone, leaving one solitary priest to carry on God's work. Thirty years later, another Bishop of Worcester, Wulfstan, had restored the building and reinstated the brotherhood, but further on in its history it had become a college, with secular priests who went out among the people, the control of the establishment passing into the hands of a dean and canons instead of an abbot. Its most famous – or infamous – son had been the heretic, John Wycliffe, who had held a prebendary stall there sometime in the preceding century. In recent years the building had been greatly enlarged under the auspices of Bishop

Carpenter and due to the patronage of Bristol's own William Canynges, who, before his death twelve years ago, had become first a canon and then dean of the college.

But my present visit had nothing to do with this august edifice, and instead I went knocking on the doors of cottages, asking if there was anyone who remembered a March morning, twenty years previously, when a girl by the name of Isabella Linkinhorne had been seen with a male companion somewhere in the vicinity of the village.

As was only to be expected, I was treated to blank stares, often accompanied by loud guffaws and suggestions as to what I could do with myself (and my dog), or to downright rudeness and the deepest suspicion as to my motives. I began to realize that leaving my pack at home had perhaps not been such a good idea. As a pedlar, people regarded me either as a welcome visitor or a nuisance, but not as a potential thief, poking my long nose into their homes to spy out the land with a view to robbing them later. Even Hercules failed to win friends, especially after he leaped over a fence to chase an old couple's geese into the lane through a gate that someone had carelessly left open. Needless to say I was blamed for this catastrophe, although it was none of my doing, someone else having failed to close the gate. But in the event it proved to have a satisfactory ending, for me, at least. The old couple, angry and abusive at first, were won over by my abject apologies and willingness to help capture the errant birds, who were making a determined dash for freedom. By the time the final one was penned inside the fence again, we were all three exhausted, and the dame, taking pity on me, invited me into the cottage for a drink of ale.

'Anything, mother,' I gasped, 'as long as it's not elderflower wine.'

'Elderflower wine?' she screeched. 'Got enough to do what with looking after the geese, the pig, the donkey and him –' she jerked her head towards the old man – 'without wasting my time making elderflower wine. Sit down, lad, sit down! And make sure that pesky dog don't get off his leash again.'

I promised humbly to keep the pest under control and ordered Hercules to sit at my feet and keep quiet. To my surprise, he obeyed instantly, which made me suspect that the geese had frightened him a great deal more than he had scared them. The old man turned out to be the dame's brother, not her husband as I had presumed, and they introduced themselves as Judith and Alfred Humble. An enquiry by the latter as to what I was doing in Westbury and why I was knocking on doors produced the whole story; a tale of murder which not only thrilled them to the marrow of their ancient bones, but also led to Judith Humble banging excitedly on the cottage table with her fist, crying in her piercingly shrill tones, 'I can remember that girl! Never knew her name, but she was always around here at one time, meeting some man or another. You recollect her, Alfred. You must do! She'd hang around here, talking to you over the fence. You weren't a bad-looking man in them days, before your hair went white and your teeth fell out.'

'Ar,' her brother agreed, when he'd thought the matter over. 'It were a long time gone, though. Must be. I ain't had all me teeth for ten year or more. But I do recall her now you bring her to mind. Young, she were. Lovely. Sit on that horse of hers, she would, and chat to me like I were a proper gentleman, not just a cottager. I often wondered what had become of her. Stopped coming all of a sudden like, and I never set eyes on her again. And now you tell me she's dead. Murdered.' His faded eyes slowly filled with tears.

His sister sniffed disparagingly. 'Well, I can't say I'm that surprised. All those different men she used to meet! I clearly remember thinking to myself, "You're asking for trouble, my lady! Just begging for it, with your fine clothes and your airs and graces. You'll come to a bad end, my girl!" And you see, I was right!'

'When you say "all those different men",' I asked, 'how many exactly were there?'

'Three,' was the prompt reply. 'I remember as though it were yesterday. But she never met them all together, that goes without saying. They each had their appointed days, and I doubt if any one of them knew the other two existed. But she was bound to make a botch of it one day. One day, one of 'em was bound to find out he was being made a fool of, and then, I thought, you're for it, my young mistress.'

'Can you recall at all what the three men

105

looked like?' I leaned forward eagerly on my stool.

Judith Humble frowned. After a minute or two's deep cogitation, she finally answered, 'If memory don't play me false, one – the one I recollect best – was tall and fair and very handsome. Too good for her, although it was obvious she didn't think so. She thought herself better than him; but then, I could tell, she thought herself better than anybody. Mind you, to be fair, the other two weren't nothing remarkable. I can't really remember either of them.'

'I've been informed that one might have had red hair.'

The dame sipped her ale and wiped her mouth on her apron. 'You could be right, at that,' she agreed.

'And Mistress Linkinhorne always met them here? In Westbury?'

'I can't say that for certain, but this did seem to be her trysting place. What do you tell me her name was?'

'Isabella Linkinhorne.'

Judith Humble nodded her head. 'That explains it, then. For years there was the letters I and L and R and M carved into the trunk of one of the trees hereabouts, enclosed in a heart. Could have shown it to you, but the tree came down in a storm three or four years ago.'

I too drank some of my ale while I pondered on this newly acquired information.

'So, one of the men had the initials R.M.,' I mused.

The dame nodded. 'It would seem so.'

Alfred Humble suddenly spoke up. He had been so quiet for the last few minutes that I had almost forgotten his existence, especially as he had left the table and gone to sit by the fire, lost, I suspected, in memories of a young and beautiful girl who had carelessly made a friend of him; memories half-forgotten, but now recalled to mind.

'One of them three men she met lived in Bath. She told me so,' he said.

I turned my head sharply to look at him. 'Which one? Do you know?'

The old man shrugged. 'She never said and I didn't ask. Weren't my business.' He added softly, more to himself than to me or his sister, 'The last time I ever recollect seeing her was on a blustery March morning, when it weren't fit for a dog to be out. Wrapped up in that blue cloak of hers, she were. She waved at me and smiled.'

Seven

'Did you see anyone with her?' I asked. 'Or was she alone?'

The old man furrowed his brow. 'Can't rightly recollect,' he said after a moment. 'It's a long time ago.'

'Try to remember,' I urged him. 'It could be very important.'

Judith Humble sniffed. 'Well, I can tell you that,' she announced surprisingly. 'I saw her that morning, too, when I looked out the door to yell at you –' she nodded at her brother – 'to come inside and not catch your death of cold, standing there gawking, like some mazed youngling instead of a grown man in possession of his senses. And the wind and rain blowing that hard across the downs it was enough to give you an inflammation of the lungs.' She turned to me. 'Alfred's always had a weak chest, ever since he were a child. Many's the time my poor mother—'

I stemmed these reminiscences without compunction.

'And was there anyone with Mistress Linkinhorne?'

'Mistress Link—? Oh, yes! Her! I'd forgotten what you said her name was. Of course there was someone with her. A man. There always was.'

'Not always,' Alfred Humble protested. 'Sometimes she was on her own.'

'Not often,' his sister snorted. 'She played those three fools one against the other...'

Once again, I interrupted. 'Did you get a glimpse of his face? Do you know which of the three men it was?'

Judith Humble thought a minute, but then shook her head. 'He had his hood pulled well forward over his face against the weather.'

I sighed. This information agreed with that given me by Jonathan Linkinhorne. I asked, 'Did anyone, to your knowledge, come here making enquiries about Isabella in the next few days?'

The old lady nodded briskly. 'They did that. Which is why the sighting stuck in my mind, I suppose. It were a couple o' young men, as I recall. Said they worked for her father, though no names were mentioned.'

'Did they say why they were enquiring?'

'Said their young lady hadn't been home all night. Ho, ho! I thought to myself. There's a surprise!' The sarcasm was heavy. 'I'd have wagered my last groat that that girl was going to cause trouble one fine day. Gone off with the man I saw, was my reckoning. And now you've brought it all back to mind, I guess that was the last time *I* ever clapped eyes on her. Not that I'd have sworn to it until this minute, but, yes, that was the last time. And now you tell us that the poor creature didn't run away at all: she was murdered.'

'Probably by the man she was with that day,' I

answered sombrely. 'A thousand pities you didn't see his face.'

'Well, I didn't,' she replied with some asperity, as though she suspected I didn't quite believe her. 'It wasn't a day for lingering at the door, and I was more concerned with getting Alfred to come indoors than in discovering which gudgeon she had persuaded to keep a tryst with her in such bad weather.'

'I believe you,' I said placatingly. 'And I can only thank you for all you've told me. You have a remarkable memory, Mistress.'

'Always have had,' she answered proudly. 'My dear mother used to say to me, "Judith, if we had a silver shilling for every time you remember something aright, we'd be richer than a bishop." Ain't that so, Alfred?'

'That be so, my dear,' her brother concurred, but I could tell that he wasn't really listening. He was lost in a dream of his own; a dream of youth and a beautiful girl who had once, long ago, smiled at him and brightened his humdrum life, if only for a moment.

I rose to my feet, picking up Hercules and apologizing once more for the incident with the geese.

'No harm done. As it happens.' Judith Humble could not resist the rider, nor wagging an admonitory finger at me as she spoke. She, too, got to her feet.

I recollected something.

'This girl we've been talking about, this Isabella Linkinhorne, she had a cousin who lived in, or near, Westbury. A Jeanette Linkinhorne.

She entered the sisterhood of the Magdalen nuns in Bristol a few weeks before Isabella disappeared. Did you by any chance know her? Or of her?'

My hostess clapped a hand to her forehead. 'I knew the name Linkinhorne seemed familiar to me when you first mentioned it, but I couldn't for the life of me think why. Yes, I do recall the woman, vaguely, although I never knew her well. She lived a little way out of the village, in a cottage that stands by itself at the top of the hill as you come down from the Clifton track. But I'd no idea she was kin to this Isabella. No good reason why I should. Any visit to her cottage would have been paid before the girl reached as far as here. Became a nun, did she? Well, there again, I knew her so little that, according to what you say, she's been gone these twenty years and I haven't even missed her. Just an echo of the name must've stuck in my mind.'

I thanked her yet again, took my leave of Alfred Humble, still wandering somewhere among the stars, and started the long walk home.

It was almost suppertime when, tired out and weary, I finally reached Small Street. Adela was where she was usually to be found, in the kitchen, squeezing the last of the whey from a muslin bag of curds that, with further hanging, would make a palatable cream cheese. The children were nowhere to be seen, although I could hear them upstairs, rattling around like so many peas in a pod. Hercules went straight to his water bowl, while I kissed my wife and sank

111

thankfully on to a stool and pulled off my boots.

'It looks like it might be a dry summer,' I said, tossing them into a corner and stooping to rub my aching feet. 'I noticed on the way home that the oaks are coming into bud before the ash trees.'

Adela smiled and quoted, 'Oak before ash, we'll only have a splash; Ash before oak, we're in for a soak. That's good news. You look exhausted. Supper's nearly ready.' She went to the pot over the fire and stirred the contents. A delicious smell of herbs scented the air. 'Mutton,' she added. 'They've been slaughtering sheep in the Shambles today, so Margaret and I shared the price of three collops between us. Fresh meat on a Monday, my lad! You're being spoiled, but there was more money in Mayor Foster's purse than I at first thought.'

I frowned. 'We mustn't get used to good living, sweetheart. What we don't use, I must give back to him.'

She grimaced. 'I know. You like your independence. You don't want to work for other people. But just now and then,' she went on wistfully, 'it's nice not to have to worry about the price of things.' She changed the subject quickly. 'Have you found out anything of importance today?'

'A little. I must go and see Margaret again. Her and the other two wise women of Redcliffe.' Adela giggled. 'I need to find out if they know, or knew, of anyone living in the city called Jane Honeychurch. She was Isabella's maid,' I explained, answering my wife's look of enquiry.

I gave her a brief history of my day's doings, and of the various scraps of knowledge I had garnered from the hermit, from Emilia Virgoe and from Judith and Alfred Humble, by which time the children had made their appearance, all clamouring to know if I had brought them anything. Fortunately for household peace, I had remembered my obligations before making my way to Small Street, and purchased some sugared violets from an itinerant sweetmeat seller. These I now proceeded to distribute equally between the three of them (with dire warnings not to eat them until after supper), which reminded Adela that it was the season for candying both flower heads and some of the early fruits.

'I must ask Margaret if she can spare me a few scrapings of her sugar loaf,' she remarked, starting to ladle the mutton broth on to our plates. 'I know some of the Redcliffe dames share half a one amongst themselves.'

'I'll ask her tomorrow,' I volunteered. 'It will give me an excuse for calling on her again so soon. She might otherwise get the impression that I'm hankering after her company.'

My wife smiled, but shook her head reprovingly.

'Margaret's a good woman, Roger, and she's been an excellent friend to us. To me, especially, when you're away from home.'

'Away!' shouted Adam, exploring one nostril with a grubby forefinger whilst spooning broth into his mouth with his other hand. The combination of all three activities resulted in the gravy running down over his chin and staining his little smock. Adela gave an exasperated groan, while the two older children tried to suppress their sniggers. It was, I reflected, a fairly normal mealtime and I attempted to maintain my good humour.

I was in Redcliffe bright and early the following morning, only to find my former mother-in-law already spinning busily, the basket of unbleached wool having been delivered to her from the weaving sheds probably just after dawn.

'You've started betimes. I thought the guild regulated spinners' hours,' I said, frowning.

Margaret snorted in derision. 'So they might have, my lad! But I'm a poor woman and I can earn a deal more money by adhering to Master Adelard's hours than going along with all this new-fangled nonsense.'

'The guild's rules are made for your own good,' I protested.

'You mind your own business,' she answered tartly, 'and I'll mind mine. What can I do for you? Two visits in four days! I am honoured.'

I asked first about the sugar loaf, and she nodded. 'I'll divide my share with Adela most willingly.' Then when I showed no sign of immediately taking my leave, she stopped the loom and regarded me shrewdly. 'Well? What else?' she demanded. 'Out with it! I'm very busy today, as you can see.'

I pulled up a stool and sat down beside her. 'It's to do with this present enquiry of mine for Mayor Foster.' And I launched into as brief an explanation as I could of what I had so far discovered. 'So,' I asked, when I had finished, 'does the name of this Jane Honeychurch mean anything at all to you? Married or not, the woman would be forty or so years of age by now.'

Margaret sat, chewing her bottom lip for a moment or two before giving a decisive shake of her head.

'I'll have to go and consult with Maria and Bess,' she announced, getting up from her loom and putting on her cloak. Obviously, helping me took precedence over her own work, however urgent that might be. 'Stay here,' she added. 'I'll be back shortly.'

She was optimistic. I reckoned that a good hour had passed before I saw her again, looking refreshed after a long gossip and exchange of information with her two bosom friends. During her absence I took in another basket of wool from the weaving sheds, a loaf of oaten bread which she had sent to be baked in the ovens in Water Lane and lied about her whereabouts to another caller, who urgently needed her advice on how to use alkanet as a colouring for cheese.

'You've been in demand,' I said as she closed the cottage door and divested herself of her cloak.

'Never mind that,' she retorted. 'That nurse – Mistress Virgoe, or whatever she's called – was in the right of it. Jane Honeychurch was a Bristol maid. Furthermore, you're in luck. She still lives here. She's married to one of the scullions who works in the castle kitchens. Jane Purefoy, her name is now. Her husband's known to Maria's nephew, although, apparently, Nick doesn't care much for the man. Still, your business won't be with him.'

'True,' I agreed. 'Where does Goody Purefoy live?'

But here Margaret's information was deficient. 'Maria didn't know for certain, but it'll either be in one of those hovels just outside the castle walls or in the domestic quarters of the castle itself. Knock on a few doors. Someone will know where to find her. But watch your purse, if you've one on you. There are some rogues and villains living in that part of the town.'

'There are rogues and villains everywhere,' I said, bringing a hot defence of Redcliffe springing to her lips. I forestalled this diatribe by pointing out the new basket of wool, the loaves of baked bread and telling her about her neighbour's enquiry concerning alkanet for colouring cheese. Then I took a hurried leave of her, before being forced to admit that I had failed to ask the neighbour's name, and made my way back across Bristol Bridge, through a network of narrow side streets and alleys that eventually brought me to the towering bulk of the castle walls and the huddle of little cottages which surrounded them.

It needed no more than a couple of enquiries to elicit the information that Goody Purefoy lived in a cottage close to the great barbican gate, and a toothless crone with only one eye (a gaping, raw socket suggested that the accident had been of recent date) led me to a mean little hovel so closely crammed against the wall that it seemed part of the very stones themselves.

The woman who answered my knock looked far older than I had expected – more like someone of sixty than forty – but otherwise corresponding to Emilia Virgoe's description of an 'ugly, mousy little thing'. I imagined that the intervening years had not dealt kindly with her. Her hair, straggling from beneath a dirty linen coif, was now grey and very thin, her pale eyes almost colourless beneath non-existent brows, her complexion muddy and her skin wrinkled. She reminded me of a plant that had withered through want of light and air.

'Goody Purefoy?' I asked. 'Jane Honeychurch that used to be?'

Reluctantly, she edged the door a little wider.

'You're the law,' she said resignedly. 'Ranald warned me to expect 'ee soon as we heard that that there body they've found is the mistress's. Mistress Isabella's. My man said you'd be round sometime or other, asking questions.'

'I am enquiring about Mistress Linkinhorne,' I replied with what I trusted was a reassuring smile. 'But I'm not the law.'

'Oo are you then?' The door inched shut again and I quickly put a foot in the narrowing gap.

I explained as best I could to the small, suspicious face staring at me through the aperture, at the same time trying to ignore the chorus of sniggers, shuffling and insulting remarks from a gaggle of urchins who had left their play to come and harass this stranger who had been foolhardy enough to stray into their midst. A pebble from a

117

homemade catapult struck me painfully between the shoulderblades. I swung round menacingly and the little army retreated a step or two, but as soon as my back was turned once more, I was hit again. I knew that I probably could, by sheer strength and size, send them packing, but guessed that I should then be confronted by the urchins' mothers – a far more terrifying prospect.

'I promise you, Goody Purefoy, I'm not the law,' I repeated. And just at that moment, with a grating of wood against stone that set every tooth in my head on edge, the hovel door was opened wide enough to admit me. I slipped inside, enduring a repetition of the screech as the door was closed. 'Thank you,' I uttered gratefully.

'Little varmints!' my saviour muttered, jerking her head in the direction of the street, where, to howls and yells of disappointment, my small persecutors were trying to hammer their way in.

'They'll get tired of it in a minute,' I said, 'and go away.'

Jane Purefoy gave me a scathing look. 'I know that, don' I? I lives here.'

Reproved, I humbly bowed my head. A brief glance around the single room had told me there was very little to see. The floor was simply beaten mud with no covering of any sort, while the basics of table, two stools and a shelf holding a couple of pots and pans took up what space there was. A rolled-up mattress in one corner suggested that sleeping arrangements were equally primitive, and a meagre fire on a raised hearthstone belched more smoke than flame. Over all hung a pervasive smell of urine, and such light as there was came from an unshuttered window at one side of the room, opening on to the wall of the next hovel, only a foot or so away. The knowledge that this was the lot of so many of my fellow citizens suddenly made me ashamed of the comparative comfort I and my family enjoyed, and engendered in me a (short-lived) resolve never to complain about anything again.

'Well?' my hostess demanded. 'What is it you want? You're working on behalf of Mayor Foster you say.'

I started to repeat what I had already told her, but Jane Purefoy stopped me with an impatient wave of her hand.

'I'm not daft, young man, nor am I deaf. I don't need telling everything twice. I know I looks stupid, but I ain't.'

'No, no!' I agreed eagerly. 'Of course you're not. I never thought so for a minute. It's just that... What I mean is, I'd be grateful for anything you can tell me about Isabella Linkinhorne. You were her maid, Mistress Virgoe informs me.'

Jane Purefoy sniffed. 'You been to see her, have you, as well as the old master? She was never a friend to the young mistress. Hand in glove with the old folks, she was.'

I nodded. 'Mistress Virgoe did admit that her sympathies lay with the parents rather than the daughter.'

A faint smile lifted the corners of her thin lips.

'My, my! You do talk fancy! A funny sort of chapman you be, if that's your real calling, like what you say it is.' She paused, waiting for my affirmation, but I merely nodded again, saying nothing. I had no intention to delve into my life history: I had done it too many times in the past and the constant repetition had long since begun to pall. When she realized that she was not about to get an answer, Goody Purefoy shrugged and waved me to one of the stools, perching herself on the other. 'Well, what do 'ee want to ask, then?'

'These three swains of hers – at least everyone seems to think that there were three – did she ever talk to you about them? Or was she as secretive with you as she was with everyone else?'

My companion grimaced. 'Oh, she were secretive all right. Didn't trust no one. Not even me. And I dessay I was as near to a friend as she ever had. She didn't like women as a general rule. But then, she didn't like no one, really. Hated her parents. I told her once she was lucky to have a mother and father who were so fond of her and gave her everything she asked for.' Jane scratched her head through her hood. 'I've never forgotten her answer, nor the look on her face when she made it. "Having everything you want's no good," she said, "if you've got to give your soul in return." I told her I didn't know what she was talking about, and that I'd never known my ma and pa. I was an orphan, brought up on charity and sold on to anyone 'oo'd have me. That's how I went to live with the Linkin-

120

hornes.'

'And what did she reply to that?'

'Said I was a fool. Ignorant, Stupid.' The woman broke off, staring into space, musing resentfully.

'Did she ever tell you the names of these three men?' I asked eventually. 'Or even of one of them?'

'No, not that. But she told me some things.'

'Such as?'

'That there were three of 'em, like you say. She used to laugh about the way she had to be so careful not to arrange a meeting with two on the same day. "They all think they're the only one," she'd say. And when I'd ask her if she didn't think it was unfair on them, she'd answer she hated men, and deceiving them was all they were good for.'

'Did she tell you where she met them?'

'Over in Westbury village. She used to ride that way 'cause Master had a cousin who lived in that direction. She used to tell her parents that she was visiting Mistress Jeanette.'

'Master Linkinhorne vows that he and his wife knew nothing of these three men. No, that's not quite right. They got to know of them through other people, but Isabella always denied their existence to him and Mistress Linkinhorne. Assured them the talk was nothing but vicious rumours and lies.'

Jane Purefoy nodded. 'True enough.'

'But why did she not wish them to know? Did you ever ask her?'

'I did. She said lying to them was part of her

121

revenge. When she did, at last, admit the truth, or when she finally went off with one of those men, it would be so much more terrible for them to realize they'd been hoodwinked.'

There was silence for a moment or two while we both contemplated the depth of Isabella Linkinhorne's loathing for her parents. I thought of my own children and the pitfalls, the great yawning chasms that can open up between the generations. I felt the sweat start to prickle across my skin. Eventually, finding my voice, I said, 'She may not have told you their names, but did Isabella confide in you anything else about these three men?'

'She told me one o' them were a goldsmith, and she showed me some of the jewellery he'd given her. Said he lived in Gloucester and came down this way now and then to visit one of the manor houses north o' Westbury, where he had a customer. As far as the other two go, one lived in Bath and t'other in Bristol. And it's no good you asking me more about them; that's all I know. Who they were or what they did for a living, she never mentioned. Nor how she came to meet them. Nor why Westbury was their trysting place. Well, I can see why it might have been for the goldsmith, but as for the others –' she shrugged '– your guess will do as well as mine, I dessay.'

I was a little further on with my enquiries. Jane Purefoy had confirmed what Alfred Humble had told me; that one of the men had lived in Bath. And I also knew now that it was the goldsmith who had lived in Gloucester. Concerning the one

122

reported to have lived in Bristol, I was little the wiser.

'Did Isabella ever describe the men to you?' I asked. I was feeling desperately thirsty, but suspected that I was unlikely to be offered any refreshment. Money was tight and did not run to free ale. And I was wary of drinking the water, even though there was a small water barrel beneath the shelf. It might not come from the local well, but be taken straight from either of the rivers. I swallowed hard and repeated my question.

'I told you before, I'm not deaf,' was the tart response. When I apologized, my companion continued, somewhat appeased, 'Young mistress did say as how one of 'em was very good-looking. But no, she never said which one. Did remark once that looks ain't everything. You can make o' that what you like.'

There was nothing to be made of it: it told me nothing that I did not already know. 'What do you remember of the day Mistress Isabella disappeared?' I demanded.

Jane Purefoy arched her back and rubbed her thighs, a hint that she was growing tired of this interrogation.

'I recollect it were an awful day, wind and rain. Proper March weather. But young mistress would go out, even though Mistress Linkinhorne begged her not to. She went riding every day, across the downs, and nothing would stop her. I didn't see her leave, but I remember her shouting for her horse to be saddled – one of the hands who worked for the master always did that – and she came upstairs to her chamber to put on her cloak. It was a dark blue one with a scarlet lining. Oh, yes, and I remember she'd snagged her stockings on a chair in the dining parlour. Real angry she was, because the only other pair she had were the red ones with the darn in the heel. Later in the day, Master let me go into Bristol to visit my foster mother. Mistress was going in to see a friend and she took me with her in the covered waggon.'

'Did she also take you home again?'

Jane Purefoy grunted assent. 'When we returned it were after dark and Master was in a right taking because Isabella hadn't returned.' There was a pregnant pause, before she added with a strange lack of emotion, 'She never did.'

'Why do you think Master and Mistress Linkinhorne didn't suspect that some harm might have come to Isabella? Why did they believe that she'd simply run away with one of her swains? Men you say they refused to believe in?'

The colourless eyes regarded me with faint contempt.

'There's a difference between saying you don't believe in something and really not believing it.' Someone else had said something similar to me in the past few days. 'They asked around for her, o' course they did. But when it was made plain to them that young mistress had been seen with a man near Westbury village, I think they couldn't pretend to themselves any longer that all the things people had been saying about Isabella were rumours and lies. Hit them all of a heap, it did. Master was quite ill for several weeks after, and I don't think Mistress ever recovered. Drowned she was, a year later, and although it's always been claimed it was an accident, I'm not so certain. I reckon she made away with herself.'

Eight

It was at this moment that the door of the cottage was flung open and one of the largest men I had ever seen thrust his bulk, not without some difficulty, through the doorway. He was as broad as he was tall and his massive presence filled the cramped space to the exclusion of all else. Even I, who was then over six feet in height (like all old people, I've grown shorter as I've grown older) and well fleshed out, felt overpowered, squashing myself up against the hovel's further wall. He wore a greasy, blood-stained apron and smelled strongly of fish, raw meat and garlic.

'Who's this?' growled the giant.

'No need to get in a taking, Ranald,' my hostess remonstrated. This, then, was the master of the house. Beside him Jane Purefoy looked like a midget, a wooden doll that he might snap in half with a mere flick of his fingers, but she seemed unafraid of him. Indeed, if anything, she appeared mistress of the situation. 'Calm down, do. He ain't after me.'

125

After her? *After her!* My self-esteem took a tumble into my boots. It took a further nosedive through the floor when Ranald Purefoy's belligerent attitude softened a little and he grunted, 'That's all right, then. So long as he isn't bothering you.'

'He ain't bothering me. He ain't the law, neither. But he is asking questions about Mistress Linkinhorne on behalf of Mayor Foster. At least, so he says.'

'It's true,' I confirmed hastily as the scullion rolled a suspicious eye in my direction. And once again I was forced to give an explanation of my interest, adding, 'As a matter of fact, I was just going. I...I think your wife has told me all she knows.' I began nervously to edge my way around this man-mountain, making for the door, when a sudden thought gave me pause. 'Goody Purefoy,' I added, 'I know you said that your mistress never disclosed the names of her admirers, but, by any possible chance, do the initials R. M. mean anything to you?'

My hostess gave the question some thought before reluctantly admitting, 'Can't say as they does. Why d'you ask?'

I explained about the intertwined initials carved on the tree near Westbury village, but Jane Purefoy shook her head.

'You're certain?' I ventured.

'She's said so, ain't she?' Ranald growled. He was obviously growing restive. 'I didn't sneak home to talk to a blessed stranger, did I?' He turned to his wife. 'Get the mattress out, woman, and let's get on with it.' He removed his apron

126

and began to unbuckle his belt.

Jane gave him a seductive, if somewhat toothless grin. My mind boggled. I fled.

But I had only gone a few paces down the narrow, twisting street, when I heard the Purefoys' door scrape open behind me and Jane's voice call, 'Wait a minute, Chapman!' I swung round to find her behind me, while her husband bellowed from inside the cottage, 'Will you hurry up, you stupid old mare!'

'What is it?' I asked.

'I jus' remembered. I'd forgotten, but what you said jus' now jogged my memory. One day she – Isabella, that is – was writing summat on a piece of paper. Later on, she threw it away and I picked it up. I ain't much good at reading, but this was jus' letters. "R.M." she'd written three times, on three different lines, and put a query mark against each set o' letters. Tha's all,' she added abruptly. 'I gotta get back.'

I should have liked to question her further, but the maddened cries from within the hovel had by now reached fever pitch: Ranald Purefoy would be balked of his mid-morning love-making no longer. Thoughtfully, I went home to Small Street and my dinner.

'So what now?' Adela asked when I had finished telling her the story of my morning's doings and the two older children had vanished about their own nefarious business (which had involved much whispering and giggling throughout dinner). Adam for once was quiet, curled up on Adela's lap, sound asleep, thumb in mouth,

127

replete with bread and milk and a spoonful of honey to follow. (When I say 'spoonful' what I mean is that he was allowed to dip his little fingers in the honey jar, then smear them all over his face in the hope that some of the honey would find its way into his mouth. Some of it actually did.)

'I'll have to go to Gloucester,' I said. 'At least I know that I'm looking for a goldsmith there, and if I can discover one whose names begin with the letters R and M...'

'You may have found Isabella's murderer?' my wife enquired caustically. 'I doubt it, Roger. I doubt it very much. Even if you manage to find him after all these years, even if he admits to having known Isabella, there's no proof that he was the man she was seen with on that last morning of her life.'

'I know that. But I have to try, now that I've taken Mayor Foster's money. And when I return, I'll have to go to Bath. Thank goodness Balthazar is reported as living in Bristol.'

'*Who?*' demanded Adela with such force that Adam stirred and grizzled in his sleep.

'Who?' she repeated more quietly.

'Well, it's difficult not knowing the names of these three men,' I explained, a little sheepishly, 'so I've decided to call them after the Magi. I think I told you that when Master Foster's chapel and almshouses are eventually built, he intends to dedicate the former to the Three Kings of Cologne. The Three Wise Men. So the goldsmith has to be Melchior, who brought the Christ child gold. There's no obvious choice for the other two, but I've decided that the man from Bath will be Caspar, who brought frankincense, and the man from Bristol is Balthazar, who brought myrrh.'

Adela smiled at me in the way that told me she sometimes regarded me as even younger than Adam; a look that comprised humour, approval, but, most of all, indulgence, as though I were a precocious child.

'That should simplify matters,' was her only comment. I wasn't sure that she really meant it, but I chose to take it as a compliment and grinned inanely. 'Do you intend to walk?' she asked.

'If I have to. But I thought I'd call on Jack Nym and see if by any lucky chance he's going northwards in the next day or two.'

Jack Nym was a neighbour of Margaret Walker, a carter, who, from time to time, travelled to Hereford and the Cotswolds, as well as to London and in more southerly directions.

'A good idea.' Adela shifted Adam slightly to ease her aching arms. (Our nearly three-year-old son was, I knew from experience, no light weight.) 'But what still puzzles me about this business, Roger, is how Isabella came to be buried on that land.'

I sighed. 'I know. It puzzles me, too. As you said the other day, digging a grave is no easy job. Not something that can be accomplished in a few minutes, nor without making some stir. Ah well! I can't waste time on that particular mystery just at present. Finding my three kings is the first task.'

'And if you can't? Find them, I mean. Or if

you find them but can't prove one of them's the murderer? What then?'

'Then, sweetheart, I have to admit defeat and repay Mayor Foster what's left of his money.'

Adela smiled understandingly at me. 'You won't like that. It will hurt your pride.'

I grimaced. 'It will, indeed. But it might be good for me. I've begun to think myself invincible in these matters, and pride is a sin.'

'Not if you feel you're doing God's work. You do still feel that, don't you?'

I hesitated. Finally I said, 'Let's just say that I have to remind myself of the fact more often than I used to. I find myself taking too much credit and not according it where it's due.'

My wife looked worried. 'Perhaps you should guard your thoughts more strictly, Roger. I haven't known you and loved you for over four years without realizing that you hold some...' She lowered her voice almost to a whisper, as though afraid to speak the words aloud. 'Well, that you hold some heretical views.'

I couldn't deny it. There were moments when I even doubted the existence of God; moments when the sheer brutality of what was perpetrated in His name appalled me, or when His seeming indifference to the sufferings of His children denied the claim that He was a God of love. But I would never be irresponsible enough to voice these doubts out loud, not now that I had a wife and family who depended on me. Besides which, if the truth were told, I was far too much of a coward to put my skin in danger. So I smiled reassuringly. 'That's all in the past, my love.

130

Being married to you has shown me the error of my ways.'

Adela knew when I was lying: wives always do. But she also knew it meant that I wasn't going to do anything foolhardy to put her and the children at risk; that I wasn't even a secret Lollard, like Margaret Walker and so many of Redcliffe's weaving community. She leaned over and kissed me.

This woke our son, whose roars of disapproval at being squashed between us were accompanied by flailing arms and a face the colour of a crimson rose. For a few seconds outrage threatened to choke him as his breath became suspended and he frothed milkily at the mouth. But nothing could keep Adam quiet for long and he regained his breath to scream even more lustily than before. Adela and I were forced to abandon our fond embrace. She handed him to me – as a punishment for something, although I wasn't quite sure what – while she began collecting together the dirty dinner dishes for washing.

I was as good as my word, and went to see Jack Nym that very afternoon.

I wasn't even sure of finding him. The chances were that he was already away from home, carting goods somewhere or other, but it was worth a try. My fears proved to be well grounded, but then his slatternly wife, blowing her nose on her skirt, informed me that he had only gone as far as Clifton, where he was delivering a consignment of soap and sea coal to the manor, and added that, if I fancied a walk, I might either meet him there or on his return journey. Or else, if the matter were urgent, I was welcome to wait until he came home. I declined this latter offer. A glimpse into the cottage's interior and a strong smell of burning meat reminded me of the Purefoys' hovel, and I felt that two such experiences in one day was more than any man should subject himself to. Besides which, with the approach of noon, a certain warmth had displaced the chill of early morning, and an excuse for stretching my long legs and shaking off the noise and dust of the city seemed too good an opportunity to miss.

So I went home, told Adela where I was going and why, buckled the old leather belt around Hercules's neck and, with the excited animal capering around my legs and threatening to trip me up, set off for the heights of Clifton. With the houses left behind as I started on the second of the hills rising to the north of Bristol, the old sense of freedom returned. The grass beneath my feet was dotted with periwinkles, like a galaxy of pale blue stars, and the misty distances shimmered faint and pale like water under the morning sun. Trees and bushes dotted the landscape, spurting like fountains from the softening April ground and I whistled happily to myself until Hercules, maddened by my inability to carry a tune, turned and barked protestingly at me.

'Sorry,' I apologized, stooping to pat his head, but he couldn't wait for such nonsense and was away again, freed from his collar, chasing imaginary rabbits.

There were plenty of people about and plenty

of traffic to be met with on the various tracks, but no sign as yet of Jack Nym, not even on the approaches to Clifton. No doubt I had missed him somewhere in all that broad sweep of the downs, but it was no matter. I knew that he was returning home some time later in the day, and could call on him again after supper. I had achieved my real purpose: freedom of mind and body from the immediate problems and clutter of daily life. I wasn't even thinking about Isabella Linkinhorne or her possible murderer; I wasn't even really aware of where I was going, only of the general direction, when the ruined house suddenly appeared before me, like a wraith springing from the ground.

I stopped abruptly, looking about me like someone waking from a dream. I realized that I was within, perhaps, half a mile of Clifton village – I could see the first straggling cottages and outhouses in the distance – and also that I was close to that thick belt of trees, known locally as Nightingale Wood, which crowds along the lip of the gorge. I whistled loudly and imperatively for Hercules's immediate return and approached the ruin.

I could see at once from the blackened walls that the place had been destroyed by fire, and knew that this must be the remains of the Link-inhornes' dwelling, burned down some years previously, the result of an ageing man's care-lessness. The land that had once surrounded it, the thriving smallholding that had supported the family, had now returned to wilderness, and the house itself was little better. The roof, or what remained of it, had collapsed, allowing oak and alder to burst their way through, reaching slender boughs, green with budding leaf, to the sky. Brakes of hawthorn already stood within the crumbling palings and bindweed and ivy rioted everywhere unchecked. Another few years would see the ruin lost, swallowed up by the encroaching woodland.

But for now, I could still get in. I could see the smoke-blackened door hanging drunkenly on one hinge and, when I had cautiously pushed it open, I saw a flight of stone steps, its balustrade long since gone, rising to the upper floor. A stone-flagged passage, running the length of the house, led to an open doorway at the farther end, crowded now with foliage that flooded the corridor with an aqueous light, like an underwater cave. Other doorways flanked it on either side, but the rooms beyond were all empty, unless one could count the weeds, grass and saplings that thrust themselves between the flagstones, thin and attenuated as they reached for the light filtering through the greening canopy overhead.

I turned back and slowly and carefully started to mount the stairs, keeping one hand on the moss-covered wall to my left, damp and slippery with oozing slime. Hercules bounded ahead of me, unfazed by the lack of a banister to prevent our falling. I proceeded with equal circumspection along a narrow upper landing, but there was no entering any of the three bedchambers, whose floors had been made of planks and beams and had therefore been destroyed in the fire. Between the blackened rafters, I could see the foliage shooting up from the ground below. There was an air of desolation about the place and it was beginning to make my flesh crawl. I edged my way back to the top of the stairs.

I descended them with even greater care than I had taken going up – Hercules, of course, demonstrated his superior fleetness of foot by leaping the last four treads in a single bound – but having reached the bottom in safety I decided to take a final look around. I have no idea what prompted me to make this decision; perhaps because I felt a little ashamed of the sense of unease that was gripping me. But for whatever reason, I inspected again all the rooms on the lower floor, this time going into each of them in turn.

It was actually Hercules, with his quivering nose and inquisitive eye, who came across the chest, alerting me to its existence by his excited barking. Made of solid iron and banded with copper, it was half-hidden behind a clump of purple loosestrife, not yet in flower, but whose erect stems and hairy leaves had already reached almost their full three feet in height as they pushed their way in profusion through the broken flagstones. And it was the fact that the surrounding flagstones were so fragmented, and that the chest itself lay on its side, that suggested to me the thing had fallen from the chamber above, crashing through the burning floorboards as the fire had taken hold.

Hushing Hercules and kneeling down beside it, I inspected the chest, with its patches of flaking rust, and saw that the lock had burst asunder, confirming my theory that it had indeed fallen from the chamber above. I tried to open it, but it seemed to have rusted fast shut, and all that my attempts got me were raw and blackened fingers. The dog did his best to help, but only succeeded in getting in the way, incurring my wrath. Finally, I did what I should have done in the first place: I fetched my cudgel, which, on entering, I had propped against the outside wall of the house, and gave the lid several hearty blows with its lead-weighted end. Hercules thought this great sport and began barking like a fiend. Between us, we must have made enough noise to have awakened the countryside for some miles around, and to this day I cannot understand why nobody came to see what was going on. But no one did, and eventually the lid of the coffer buckled sufficiently for me to be able to force it open.

I don't really know what I had expected to find, but two undershifts, a pair of brown leather shoes and a gown of moth-eaten purple wool, embellished with fur around the neck, were a terrible disappointment. Further investigation revealed other female garments, and I came to the inevitable conclusion that the chest had been the property of either Isabella or Amorette Linkinhorne, locked up after either the one had disappeared or the other been found drowned, and probably never opened again.

I stood up slowly, brushing my knees and noticing that there were green stains, both on my jerkin and my hose. Adela would not be pleased.

Hercules, as though he understood and sympathized, licked my hand and tentatively wagged his tail. He was looking none too dapper himself (well, he never does, but even less so than usual), his rough coat dirty and the fur seemingly standing on end.

I sighed.

'You're right,' I told him. 'We're a scruffy pair and we shall no doubt be in serious trouble when we get home.' He licked my hand again. 'I know. Come on, lad, we'd better get on to the village and see if we can find Jack Nym.'

There was no sign of our quarry, but my enquiries elicited the fact that he had already delivered his consignment of soap and sea coal at the manor house and had left.

'Not these many minutes since,' the housekeeper informed me. 'A little bit earlier and you'd have caught him.'

It served me right, I thought, for wasting my time investigating old ruins instead of keeping to the job in hand. I could at least have begged a ride home for Hercules and myself in Jack's cart, for after the long and arduous climb up from the city we were both flagging somewhat, and the freedom of the open road began to appear a trifle overrated. However, it's no good being a chapman and balking at a little additional exercise, so I took a resolute grasp on my cudgel and, encouraging Hercules in his pursuit of rabbits, set off back the way we had come.

It was a little way past the great tump that I saw a cart that I knew to be Jack's pulled into the side of the track, and the man himself emerging from a clump of nearby bushes, adjusting his codpiece as he came. This unwonted coyness was explained by the presence of two young and decidedly pretty girls in the vicinity playing a decorous game of handball, watched with an indulgent eye by their nurse.

Jack saw me almost as soon as I saw him.

'Roger! What you doing up here, lad?' Then, lowering his voice, he added confidentially, 'Call o' nature.'

I grinned. 'So I'd surmised. And the reason I'm here is because I've come looking for you. Your goody said you were delivering soap and sea coal to the manor, so I came to find you.'

He sent me a shrewd, sly grin. 'You mean you wanted to get away for a while on your own.' He waved aside my half-hearted protest. 'D'you think I don't know all the tricks and excuses? Anyway, why d'you want to see me? What's so urgent that it couldn't have waited until I got home, eh? Tell me that.'

At his invitation, I climbed on to the cart's box seat, beside him, while Hercules leaped thankfully into the back and settled down. The two girls and their attendant waved happily to us before continuing with their game, and as we trundled downhill, I informed Jack of my need to get to Gloucester and my hope that he might be going in that direction some time soon.

'Or Bath,' I added. 'That would be just as helpful.'

'Well, make up your mind,' he grunted. 'Gloucester and Bath, they ain't exactly close together.

138

Opposite directions altogether, if it comes to that.'

'Of course they are!' I responded irritably. 'I'm not a fool, Jack! It just so happens I need to visit both places. It's to do with this business I'm engaged in for Mayor Foster.'

Jack nodded. 'Now, I've been hearing something about that.' Well, naturally he had. He lived in Redcliffe, not far from my former mother-in-law, and his wife was certainly on speaking terms with Bess Simnel and Maria Watkins. 'It's about this body they've dug up at the top of Steep Street. It's that Issybelly what's-'er-name, ain't it? His Worship the Mayor wants you to find out who done it. Who killed 'er. Before 'e builds 'is almshouses up there. But why? That's what I don' understand.'

'He also intends erecting a chapel for the inhabitants of the almshouses,' I explained. 'So Master Foster understandably wishes the ground to be re-consecrated before he builds anything to the glory of God. A sacred building must stand upon holy ground.'

Jack sniffed. 'And 'ow will it help, knowing who killed her and sending the poor sod to the gallows after all these years?'

'Justice will have been done.'

I was half-inclined to agree with my companion. Twenty years is a long time. People change. The guilty man was probably married. He might have a loving family, be a pillar of his community, looked up to, revered. Could any good be served by destroying the life of such a person? I had to remind myself sharply that this was

139

murder we were talking about; the destruction of a fellow human being; the most heinous of all sins.

It was getting on towards late afternoon. The light was beginning to drain from the day and the sky on the horizon was a whitish opalescent glow. Silken shadows inched across the grass and a sharp, salty tang freshened the air, as though to remind us that we had not yet done with winter.

'I don' know about justice,' Jack retorted. 'P'raps she were askin' for it.'

'Who?' I had momentarily lost the thread of our conversation.

''Er! That Issybelly what's-'er-name. Can't remember it. Never could. But I remembers 'er all right. A bold piece with a roving eye. The sort who played fast and loose with a man's affections.'

'You remember her?'

'That's what I said. Why shouldn't I? I weren't much more'n a lad at the time, 'tis true, but old enough. She and I were much of an age, I guess. I was a bit the younger in years maybe, but in all other ways, she could o' been my grandmother. There weren't no trick known to womankind she didn't employ, not from the time she were old enough to understand that men and women was different from one another.'

'When and where did you meet her?'

'I didn't meet her, exactly, but I saw her often enough when 'er father and mother brought her to market from Clifton. She were a pretty little thing, even when she were young, and she grew

140

into a beauty. But with a temper and a will of iron. If she'd been mine, I'd've whipped some respect and obedience into 'er, but as far as I can remember, neither parent lifted a finger against 'er.'

'No,' I agreed. 'At least that's the story everybody tells.'

'Probably true, then. Mostly, folks' memories don't agree on nothing.'

'There's a rumour,' I said, 'that Isabella had an admirer in Bristol. Do you know anything about that?'

Jack shrugged and narrowly avoided another cart, loaded with turnips, making its way up the track from the city.

'Never saw 'er with anyone particular that I can recall. She turned heads, mind, wherever she went. Strange,' he mused, pulling on the reins to slow his horse for a sudden steep descent, 'I'd forgotten all about 'er. It was like she'd never been. But now people are talking about 'er again, I can picture 'er as plain as though I'd just seen 'er yesterday.' He drew his breath in sharply. 'And now I comes to think on it... Get out the way, you blithering fools!' he shouted furiously at a band of travelling musicians, who were progressing jauntily along the middle of the track, playing their latest catchy little tune.

Without even faltering, and without any break in the melody, the five of them formed a single file, but as the cart passed, the man playing the nakers paused long enough to bite his thumb at us in a highly offensive manner.

'Ignore it,' I said to Jack, who showed every

sign of wanting to alight and have it out with the man. 'It's five against two – well, three if you count Hercules – and just at present I don't fancy the odds. Besides, brawling on the King's highway could land us in the bridewell. Go on with what you were saying.'

'And what was that?' Jack glanced longingly over his shoulder, still hankering for a fight.

'I asked you if you'd ever seen Isabella Linkinhorne with a particular man. You said no, but then you seemed to recollect something.'

Jack turned back and settled down, keeping his eyes on the track ahead (for which I was truly thankful). 'Well, you saying that reminded me all of a sudden about an incident I'd dang near forgotten about. I did see 'er once, kissin' a fellow. In the porch of All Saints Church, it were. And not just kissin' neither,' he added darkly. 'As I recall, there were a fair bit o' groping going on.'

'Did you see the man's face?' I asked excitedly, but after a moment's agonized reflection, Jack reluctantly shook his head.

'Nah! He were in the shadows. Recognized her, but not him. Pity, but there you are! 'Fraid I can't help you, Chapman. But as luck would have it, I am going to Stowe the day after tomorrow, so you can travel as far as Gloucester with me.'

Nine

This gave me a free day.

I rejected out of hand Adela's suggestion – delivered at breakfast as we all came to terms with another sunrise and the prospect of the morning ahead – that I should revert to my usual calling and try selling a few items in the neighbouring streets.

'I can't be about my own business while we're living on Mayor Foster's bounty,' I objected. 'If it came to his ears, he might feel that I was cheating him. But it makes me all the more determined that in the future I shall remain my own man and take money from no one except what I earn by my efforts as a chapman.'

'We're like to remain poor folks then,' my wife retorted, but cheerfully. Passing behind my stool, she stooped and kissed my cheek. 'But I prefer it that way. I don't care to be beholden to people either.'

I ignored this lack of faith in my ability as a chapman and, catching her round the waist, pulled her down to return her kiss with interest.

'Enough of that,' she reproved me, but giggled like a young girl all the same. 'What will you do today, then?' She added in a very wifely spirit, 'I hope you're not planning to remain indoors, getting under my feet. I've a lot to do.'

After a moment's reflection, I decided to visit the Magdalen nunnery again. 'I've a fancy to have another word with Sister Walburga. I suppose I could take Hercules with me.' I glanced enquiringly around the kitchen. 'Where is he?'

Adela said crisply, 'There's a bitch on heat in Bell Lane,' and seemed to think it sufficient explanation.

Which, of course, it was. Half the dogs in Bristol would be beating a path to the unfortunate creature's door. I doubted we should see Hercules, except when he was ravenous, for the next few days.

'Ah, well,' I said.

'You can take Adam with you instead,' my wife decided, 'in his little cart. It'll do him good, and Nick, Bess and I can concentrate on their lessons without any distraction. Neither's reading and sums are as good as they should be.'

The two elder children grimaced ruefully at one another, while I eyed up my son and he gazed limpidly back with the great liquid brown eyes that were so like his mother's. He was, as usual at breakfast time, smothered liberally with honey, and even as I watched, he put a small, plump arm protectively around the pot, as if in fear of having it wrested away from him.

'Mine,' he announced, clearly and defiantly.

'I can't take him to a nunnery,' I protested, but in vain.

'Nonsense!' declared Adela. 'Nuns love little children. And if they don't, then they should do. He'll be as good as gold, won't you, my lambkin?'

The lambkin dipped his fingers once more into the honey pot, managing to smear some of his plunder into his hair before finally locating his mouth.

'He'll have to be cleaned up a bit,' I demurred.

'Naturally!' Adela was indignant. 'You don't think I'd let him go out of doors like that, do you?'

So it was that, some appreciable time later, a clean and angelic little lad was put into his box on wheels, leaning against an old cushion that Adela had recently pronounced as too rubbed and faded for the parlour, lord of all he surveyed. (This box on wheels, with a long handle for either pulling or pushing the contraption, had been my own invention when Adam was very small, and had proved so useful that I had recently made a second, bigger one for when we were in a hurry and my son's erratic peregrinations were apt to prove too much of a delay.)

'Go!' he shouted, brandishing a little whip that Nicholas had made for him out of a stick and a piece of rope.

'He's going to be another Nero,' I remarked bitterly to no one in particular, but causing Nick and Elizabeth to snigger unsympathetically.

'He's a sweetheart,' my wife chided me. She could afford to be generous with the prospect of an hour or so free of Adam's disruptive company before her.

I kissed her reproachfully and set out across the Frome Bridge and through the Frome Gate, trundling my son behind me. Edgar Capgrave

145

was not on duty, for which I was truly thankful. I could do without his caustic comments on the subject of legshackled husbands. The smiles of approval I earned from the women we met were bad enough. I felt my reputation was at stake.

We reached the top of Steep Street, however, without incident – apart from Adam once trying to climb out of the cart to chase a stray cat and having to be forcibly restrained. Hob Jarrett and his team were leaning on their spades deep in discussion about something or another, so I didn't disturb them by attracting their attention. I noticed that very little progress in clearing the site had been made in the four days since I had last visited it, and reflected yet again that foreigners' strictures on the indolence of the English were not without some basis in fact.

At the nunnery I was informed by the Sister who answered my knock that Sister Walburga had gone to visit a sick woman who lived in Saint Michael's Hill, but was expected to return shortly. If I cared to wait...

I said I did, but in fairness indicated Adam in his cart. The nun stood on tiptoe, peering through the grille, out and down towards my feet. My son immediately stood up, somewhat precariously, and I held my breath, wondering what was coming next. But he only gave her a beatific smile. The door was opened at once and we were shown into the same little bare, whitewashed room where I had spoken to Sister Walburga. There was nothing there that Adam, even if he climbed out of his cart, could wreck. I heaved a silent sigh of relief.

The nun who had admitted us was a small, middle-aged woman with a gentle face and a retiring manner. Her voice was low and hesitant, and I guessed her to be the Sister referred to by Adela as shy and timid. She smiled tentatively at Adam, but then started to edge in the direction of the door with a muttered, 'I'll send Sister Walburga to you as soon as she returns.'

'I see work goes on apace in the graveyard opposite,' I said, but the heavy sarcasm was lost on my listener.

'They're good workers, all three of them,' she answered, failing to notice my look of incredulity. 'And now I must...'

'Tell me your name, Sister,' I requested, adding mendaciously, 'My wife thinks she might know you.'

'Sister Apollonia,' was the response. 'In the world, I was Jessica Haynard, but that's a very long time ago.'

'You've been here a while?'

Her smile lit up her face, making it suddenly beautiful. 'Since I was sixteen. All of thirty years. Yes, you might say I've been here a while.' She gazed hungrily at Adam. 'What a beautiful child.'

The beauteous one, I was delighted to notice, had gone to sleep, lolling against his pillow in his usual abandoned manner, arms dangling over the edge of the box, legs splayed anyhow. Sister Apollonia made once more to leave the room.

Some instinct made me detain her.

'I daresay you're pleased to see the old graveyard –' I jerked my head in what I hoped was its general direction – 'put to some good use at last, now that Mayor Foster's bought the ground.'

A slight frown creased the sweet face and she hesitated before replying in her soft voice, 'One wouldn't, of course, wish to rob the poor or begrudge them any alleviation of their lot through Master Foster's generous foundation...'

'But?' I prompted.

She sighed. 'But I could have wished him to find land for his almshouses and chapel somewhere else.'

It was my turn to frown.

'But why?' I asked. 'My understanding is that the graveyard has never been used for the purpose for which it was intended. There are so few of you now – only three Sisters in all, I believe – that, when the time comes for you to exchange this world for the next, burial can be arranged by your families elsewhere.'

The little nun nodded her agreement. 'Oh, yes. That's true. And the money paid by John Foster can be, and will be, put to good use. But –' she lowered her voice to an awed whisper, so that I had to incline my head to catch her words – 'the graveyard, you see, was the site of the nunnery's miracle.'

'Miracle!' I exclaimed, so sharply that Adam opened his eyes in surprise and stared solemnly at me for several seconds before falling asleep again. 'What miracle, Sister? I can't say I've ever heard tell of one.'

'Oh, it was a long time ago,' Sister Apollonia told me. 'Twenty years or maybe more. As you get older, time passes so quickly that much of it flows together in one great stream. But yes, now I think carefully about it, it must have been twenty years, for it was just after Sister Walburga entered the nunnery as a postulant, and that, she tells me, is the length of time she has been here.'

'What was this miracle?' I asked.

'One of our other Sisters, Sister Justina, had fallen very ill. Her life was despaired of. She had received the last rites, and two of the lay Brothers from Saint Michael's had dug the grave ready for her, in the graveyard. But she was – indeed, still is – very dear to me, and I determined that all prayer could do to save her should be done. I prayed night and day, barely sleeping. And –' the little face was suddenly aglow with an inner light – 'God heard me. In spite of what the doctor said, Sister Justina recovered, and has remained in good health until this day.'

'But...but that's hardly a miracle,' I cavilled, loath to throw a rub in the way of such simple faith. 'Even the very best of physicians has sometimes been known to be wrong. People do recover from illnesses from which others have expected them to die.'

Sister Apollonia became animated, waving her hands about like two little white butterflies (albeit calloused ones) and her naturally gentle voice even sounded a note of impatience.

'No, no! Of course I'm not so foolish as to call that the miracle. Although, in its way, it was one, I assure you. But no, the miracle was that the grave which had been dug for Sister Justina filled itself in overnight – the night of her recovery – and was completely invisible by the morning.'

My heart was pounding in my throat as the full implication of what Sister Apollonia was saying hit me. For a moment I was unable to speak and let her chatter on, her shyness forgotten. At last, however, I interrupted.

'Sister, can you remember exactly which night the grave was filled in?'

'I've already told you.' She was reproachful. 'It was the night Sister Justina regained consciousness and started on the long road back to health.'

'What sort of night was it?' I persisted. 'What had the day been like? What time of year?'

She looked astonished by my urgency and the fact that I had actually seized her by the arm and was shaking it. Another woman, Sister Walburga for example, would have given me a sharp set-down, but Sister Apollonia was too sweet and kind for her own good, and wrinkled her forehead in an effort to oblige me.

'I think the time of year was early spring,' she said. 'March, I believe, and nasty, inclement weather. Yes, yes I remember now. We had had several days of wind and rain. I recollect listening to both while I was sitting beside Sister Justina's bed and thinking of the poor sailors trying to bring their ships up that treacherous river from the Avon mouth. Now, fancy my recalling that after all this time.'

My palms were sweating. 'Sister,' I begged, 'try to remember some more. It's important or I wouldn't ask it of you. When exactly did you discover that the grave had been filled in? Are you certain it was the very next morning after Sister Justina had begun to get better? Or was it a day or so later, when you and the other nuns were finally convinced that it would no longer be needed?'

'It was the following morning.' She was indignant, or as indignant as one of her gentle nature could be, to think that I could doubt her word. 'I've told you; it was a miracle. It was a sign sent by God, in answer to my prayers, that Justina was going to recover. Because even then, fully conscious at last and managing to drink a little broth, who could have said that she might not relapse into her former state? But as soon as one of the lay Sisters informed me that the grave had disappeared, I knew for certain that God had spoken. Sister Justina would live out her full span of years. And she has!' The little nun was quietly triumphant.

'Did the other Sisters regard the closing of the grave as a miracle?'

'Of course! What else could it have been?'

I shook my head, waiting for my companion to make the connection between the 'miracle' and the discovery, over a week ago now, of Isabella Linkinhorne's body. But Sister Apollonia merely smiled serenely at me, her faith unshaken. The raising of the door latch made her turn.

'Ah! Here is Sister Walburga. Sister, you have a visitor. In fact, two,' she added, gazing down fondly at Adam, who had not stirred. 'I trust you found Goody Lewison on the road to recovery?'

'Better,' was the terse reply. Sister Walburga

151

eyed me suspiciously. 'What are you doing here again, Chapman? You had all the information I could give you concerning my cousin last time you called.'

'The Sister here has been telling me about the nunnery's miracle,' I said pointedly.

I felt sure that the significance of the recent find in conjunction with this story could not have been lost on Sister Walburga, but she waited until Sister Apollonia had fluttered happily out of the room before closing the door and saying, 'You think the grave was used to bury Isabella's body?'

'Don't you?'

'The thought has crossed my mind in recent days.'

'I'm right in believing that the two events tallied?' I asked, making certain of my facts. 'I mean the disappearance of your cousin and the recovery of Sister Justina.'

Sister Walburga drew down the corners of her mouth. 'I'm afraid so. I had not long entered the nunnery when the "miracle" happened. It never occurred to me to connect it with Isabella vanishing like that.' She shrugged. 'Indeed, why should it? It never occurred to me, either, that any harm had come to my cousin. The miracle seemed just that – a miracle!'

'You didn't mention it when I was here four days ago.'

'I'd forgotten the incident. As a matter of fact, it was only yesterday, when Apollonia was bemoaning what she sees as the desecration of the graveyard, because of the miracle, that I suddenly saw that it had been no miracle at all, but a gift from the Devil to my cousin's murderer.' She spoke with great bitterness, and I noticed that there were unshed tears in her eyes.

I asked, more gently, 'Who would have known about the grave? The nuns themselves, obviously. I don't know how many of them there were in those days.'

Sister Walburga put a hand to her forehead. 'No more than at present, I fancy. Another joined the order some years later, Sister Jerome, but she left suddenly some three years ago. Just ran away. I forget the circumstances.'

I knew all about the woman who had been called Marion Baldock and the reason for her sudden flight.

'You can discount Sister Jerome,' I said and, ignoring my companion's raised eyebrows, went on, 'Apart from the nuns, then, who else would have been aware that a grave had been prepared for Sister Justina?'

'The men who dug it, one would suppose. But it's no use asking me who they were. I had not long arrived here, as I said. The names of people attached to the nunnery in a lay capacity were unknown to me in those days.'

I sighed. I was at a standstill again, but at least one question that had been worrying both Adela and myself was answered. The difficulty of how anyone could dig a grave, even after dark, without attracting attention had been solved. But, as so often happened, a solution posed yet more queries. How did the murderer know of the grave? How did he (or perhaps she) convey the girl's body to the top of Steep Street? From which direction did he or she come; up from the city or down from the heights above?

I told myself severely not to be greedy, but to be grateful for one problem the less. I turned to thank Sister Walburga and found her standing by the door, holding it open, impatient for me to be gone. I took hold of the handle of Adam's little cart and, with a 'God be with ye' to my companion, took my leave.

But as I made my way home, trundling my still sleeping son behind me, I couldn't help reflecting that there had been something more than impatience in Sister Walburga's manner. It was almost as though she had been afraid of me – of what I might find out if I was allowed to probe any further. Did she know more than she had so far admitted about her cousin's death? Or was I, as I was so often accused by my wife of doing, simply letting my imagination run away with me?

But there was no time to pursue these thoughts, for the present at any rate. Some uneven cobblestones jolted Adam suddenly awake, and he did what he always did when he considered that an unspeakable outrage had been committed on his person; he screamed with annoyance at the top of his voice, and continued screaming all the way to Small Street.

'Have you ever heard of the miracle of the Magdalen nunnery?' I asked Jack Nym.

It was a beautiful morning, spring having at last decided to favour us with her undoubted

154

presence. One would have dared hazard that winter had gone for good (or at least for the next four or five months) except that no Englishman would be so foolish as to wager on such a likelihood, experience having taught us that one can swelter in April and freeze in July. 'Island weather,' as people used to say.

Jack, together with his cartload of soap, which he was to drop off at Gloucester before continuing further afield to pick up a consignment of Cotswold wool, had called for me at the crack of dawn, wanting to make good progress before dinner. He had been none too pleased that Hercules was to accompany me (furious at being forcibly separated from his lady love) but when I whispered to him that Adela insisted, he accepted the explanation without further argument, merely uttering the word 'Women!' under his breath. He knew all about strong-minded wives.

An hour later, we had left the city behind, climbing up out of Bristol, past the windmill, in a north-easterly direction. Trees, like gilded statues, rose out of the mist ahead of us as the sun rose to full glory over the horizon. The white light of dawn had been replaced by glass-green distances, shot through with shadows of blue and plum; and the rippling and lapping of a boulder-studded stream had given Jack's old nag the chance of a much needed drink, and ourselves the opportunity to alight and stretch our limbs. It was while we were doing this that I asked my question.

'Miracle?' Jack queried as he climbed back on

to the seat of the cart and once again took up the reins. 'What miracle?'

I told him the story as Sister Apollonia had told it to me, and when I had finished, he at first shook his head very decidedly, but then had second thoughts.

'Mmm. Maybe I do recall some talk among the older folks about summat that'd happened at the nunnery. P'raps that was it. But nothing much could've been reckoned to it because it never, so far as I know, made much of a stir. And if it'd been summat as us Bristol folk could've made money out of, it wouldn't't've been let drop, as you well know, Chapman.'

I laughed. 'Come on, Jack! As someone not having the privilege of being born in the city, you don't expect me to agree with you, do you? You'd cut my head off.'

It was his turn to laugh, displaying his broken and blackened teeth. 'True enough. We don't generally take to strangers. You've been lucky to be as well accepted as you are. But this 'ere miracle you'm talkin' about. Are you thinking it's got summat to do with this Issybelly what's-'er-name?'

Jack, I admitted to myself, was no fool. He could put two and two together better than most men.

'I'm thinking it might. Indeed, I feel certain of it. Sister Walburga, Isabella Linkinhorne's cousin, confirmed that both events – the murder and the filling in of the grave – happened at around the same time.'

'And nobody thought of one havin' anything to

do with the other?'

I shook my head. 'Jonathan Linkinhorne and his wife were so sure that Isabella had run away with one of her lovers.'

'And one o' these men you think lives in Gloucester?'

'He did, according to Goody Purefoy. Whether he does now is another matter and something I have to find out. If he's still there, he's a goldsmith and his names may begin with the letters R and M.'

Jack considered this, his head a little to one side. The horse plodded along at a steady pace, while Hercules whimpered and grunted and shifted around in the back of the cart, letting me know that he was not enjoying the ride. Sacks of soap made uncomfortable bedding.

'Not an impossible task,' my companion eventually decided. 'Not, that is, if the man's still livin' in Gloucester, not if 'e's still a goldsmith and not if his names do begin with the letters R and M. But take away one o' those three and it ain't goin' to be so easy. Take away two and you're in trouble.'

'I know it,' I answered glumly.

We stopped and ate our dinner – bread and cheese with raw onion and a flagon of cheap wine, provided for the two of us by Adela – in the shadow of a little copse, where the ground was damp and slippery with recent rain. But the sun overhead was now growing so warm that we were glad of the shade. Hercules ran around, barking and upsetting the horse, who was munching in his nosebag, found a small stream to lap from, scared a water rat back into its hole, and finally finished any food that Jack and I had been foolish enough to leave.

We spent a night on the road, in a flea-bitten inn huddled in the lee of Berkeley Castle, and arrived at our destination late in the evening of the second day just before Gloucester city gates were shut against us.

After some discussion, and after I had made it plain that I would pay Jack's shot as well as my own, we made our way to the New Inn, not far from the abbey. Although still called the New Inn, the hostelry had been built some thirty years previously to house the ever growing number of pilgrims who wished to visit the tomb of the second Edward (his murdered body having been buried in a splendid marble sarcophagus in the abbey's north ambulatory).

The inn was, as usual, uncomfortably full, but Jack and I were allotted a small but perfectly clean chamber opening off the gallery that ran round the main courtyard. For a generous extra payment the horse was stabled and fed, and the landlord undertook to see that the cart and its contents were safely bestowed in a neighbouring barn. Hercules was provided with a large ham bone and some clean water to drink and allowed to share our room, and Jack and I enjoyed a supper of baked carp (it being Friday) followed by apple fritters and a jug of good ale. Jack smacked his lips and had second helpings of everything, on the principle that as he was not paying, he might as well make a pig of himself – although that didn't stop him grumbling indig-

158

nantly when he discovered that Hercules insisted on sharing the bed with us.

'Can't you make this pesky animal sleep on the floor?' he demanded irritably after the dog had wormed his way between us and laid his head on the pillow. (His breath was atrocious.)

'No,' I answered shortly, remembering the amount of money, on top of what I had already paid, that mine host had pocketed for our supper. 'Lie still and he won't bother us.'

There was silence for perhaps ten minutes or so while I drifted towards sleep; my face turned well away from Hercules. I thought vaguely of 'Melchior' and how, when I had parted company from Jack in the morning, I must start making enquiries for a city goldsmith. Melchior, Caspar and Balthazar; the names swam around aimlessly in my head like three fish in an abbot's fish pond...

'Chapman! I say, Chapman! Are you awake?' Jack's voice cut across my slumbers.

'I am now,' I answered crossly. 'What d'you want? If you're going to complain about Hercules again...'

'No, no, it ain't that.' With a muttered oath, Jack heaved himself into a sitting position to avoid the animal's stinking breath. 'You remember I told you that I'd once seen that Issybelly what's-'er-name with a man in All Saints' porch?'

'What of it?' I was fully awake and listening now.

'I said I didn't see 'is face.'

'That's right. He was in shadow, you said.'

159

There was a silence while I could almost hear Jack's brain working. 'Go on!' I exclaimed impatiently.

'We-ell,' he continued after a second or two, 'I s'pose I must've seen more'n I thought I did, because...'

'Because what? For the sweet Virgin's sake, spit it out, man!'

'Because – well – I've seen a face recently that makes me think it might've been 'im.'

'Whose face?'

'Dunno. That's the trouble. Can't remember.'

Ten

I, too, sat up in bed with a furious jerk that disturbed the bedclothes.

'What do you mean?' I demanded, incensed. 'First, you tell me you never saw the man's face. Then you say you've seen him lately, but you can't remember who he is! You might as well be speaking Portuguese for all the sense you're making.'

Hercules, recognizing that I was angry, but not with him, quietly farted in support and thumped his tail. Jack and I, as one man, covered our noses.

'Hell's teeth!' Jack exclaimed. 'What's 'e been eating?'

'Never mind that,' I retorted. 'Just explain

160

what it is you're trying to say.'

Although my eyes had by now grown accustomed to the darkness of the shuttered room, my companion's face was still more or less invisible, but he sounded unhappy.

'I wish I could explain...'

'Try!' I commanded. 'Because you won't get to sleep until you do.'

Jack called me by a name I prefer not to repeat before stigmatizing me as a tyrant. But finally, after much head scratching, he did his best to make things plain.

'S'far as I know, I didn't see the man with Issybelly what's-'er-name in All Saints' porch that day. His face were in shadow. I saw 'is hands, mind. They were all over 'er. But the point is, I must've seen something, 'cause on Wednesday, walkin' across the bridge, going home to Redcliffe, minding me own business and thinking about nothin' in particler except what my good woman had managed to burn for dinner –' Jack's wife was a notoriously bad cook – 'I suddenly found meself thinking 'bout Issybelly, jus' like she was there beside me.'

'We had been talking about her the day before,' I reminded him.

'Everyone's been talkin' about 'er for best part of a fortnight,' Jack pointed out, 'ever since they discovered 'er body at the beginning o' the month, but I ain't felt like that afore.'

'Like what, exactly?'

'I told you! Don' you listen? Like she was there, with me. Or like I was back in the porch of All Saints' with 'er, all those years agone. So,

161

bein' an intelligent sort o' fellow, I ask meself why'm I feelin' this way.'

'And what answer did your mighty intellect come up with?' I asked spitefully, but sarcasm was always wasted on Jack.

'I decided summat must've jogged me memory, recent-like. But then I recollected seein' a face sometime earlier in the morning, and yet not seein' it. If you know what I mean.'

'A familiar face?'

My bedfellow considered this while Hercules scratched for fleas, a few of which, no doubt annoyed at being disturbed, hopped into the bed in search of fresh company. Clad only in our shirts, Jack and I had also been scratching ever since we lay down.

'Must've been,' Jack said at last, in answer to my question. 'I'd've taken notice of a stranger, wouldn't I?'

Probably. Bristolians were used to foreign sailors in their midst and tolerated them as a necessary evil. But landlubbers were a different matter, and unknowns were immediately re-marked upon and treated with suspicion until they had either established their credentials or were vouched for by an inhabitant. Mind you, most cities I had ever visited were the same, a wariness of outsiders being always prevalent.

'All right. So this wasn't a stranger you saw,' I agreed, endeavouring to make sense of what Jack was trying to tell me. 'It was someone you recognized, but without actually registering who it was you were looking at. Well, I suppose that has happened to all of us at one time or another.

We catch a glimpse of someone so familiar that we don't really see him. Probably most of the people you met on your way home to dinner were like that, unless you stopped and spoke to them. So what makes you think that one of those faces prompted your memories of Isabella Linkinhorne?'

Jack was tired and growing weary of the conversation. He lay down again, sticking his elbow so firmly into the dog's ribs that Hercules gave an angry snarl and took himself off to sleep at the bottom of the bed, curling up by my feet.

'I dunno,' he grunted sleepily. 'It jus' felt like summat I'd seen made me think of her that day in the porch of All Saints' Church.'

'And you thought that, after all, maybe you had caught sight of the man she was with, and had just seen him again. Is that what you mean?'

But a loud snore was my only answer.

With the coming of morning, my companion was even less inclined to discuss the matter further. He was by now thoroughly bored with the subject and obviously regretted having mentioned it in the first place. He was anxious to be off to deliver his cartload of soap and to set out for Stowe as soon as possible.

'Then promise me this, Jack,' I said, as we swallowed a breakfast of bacon collops and oatcakes and emptied tankards of small beer, 'that if you ever remember whose face it was you saw – this face that prompted all these memories of Isabella – you'll let me know.'

He grunted and I had to be content with that.

But we parted on the best of terms and with expressions of mutual goodwill, he going off to the stables to collect his horse and to the barn to retrieve his merchandise, while I went in search of the landlord to enquire if he knew of any goldsmiths in the city.

'Goldsmiths, is it?' that worthy echoed, grinning. 'Thinking of buying something for the goodwife at home, are you?' He enjoyed the joke, shaking with silent laughter. 'Well, I daresay you'll find a trinket or two in Goldsmiths' Row, lad.'

I thanked him in as dignified a way as I could manage, ignoring his unseemly mirth, and set off, following his directions. Hercules trotted behind me, the belt buckled around his neck thwarting him in his attempts to fight every stray cur who crossed his path and to chase each new and enticing smell that tickled his nose.

'We haven't the time,' I told him severely.

Goldsmiths' Row, however, turned out to be a disappointment. There was no master in any of the workshops who was anywhere close to the correct age for 'Melchior', who must now, I reckoned, be around forty. Most of them were elderly, grey-haired, wrinkled men, all, with one exception, nearing sixty by my calculations. Nor did they own to any sons of the right age, but, like the good people of Westbury before them, grew steadily more suspicious of my intentions. And indeed who was to say they were wrong to be on their guard? A shabby stranger with a scruffy dog, I could hardly have inspired any confidence in workshops where I was surrounded by gems and precious metal. Nor did any one of the greybeards own to having any knowledge of Isabella.

The one exception was a Master Cock-up-spotty who had, as far as I could gather, inherited a thriving business from his recently dead father and was now hell-bent on exploiting his new-found importance by making the lives of his apprentices and workmen as miserable as possible, giving and countermanding orders in quick succession in a way that demonstrated all too clearly his ignorance of a business which must have been a part of his existence from childhood. His dress proclaimed the man, reminding me of a young popinjay I had known in Bristol who had come to an unfortunate end. Parti-coloured hose and tunic, long pikes to his shoes and a codpiece decorated with silver tassels. A self-satisfied youth of perhaps some twenty summers, he listened to my enquiry with a condescension that made me grind my teeth and long to hit him on his superior nose. And I noticed that his workmen – one hammering away to turn a thin sheet of the precious metal into gold leaf, another engraving a piece of amber – looked as if they would be pleased to see me try. A third, lovingly polishing a silver chalice with a rabbit's foot, grimaced at me behind his master's back.

When I had asked my question, Master Cock-up-spotty shook his head dismissively.

'There are no other goldsmiths that I know of in Gloucester except my neighbours here in the Row.'

'Do your workmen know of any?'

I could see that I was beginning to irritate, as well as worry him, but he cast a quick look at the bench behind him, raising his thin eyebrows as he did so. The men immediately stopped what they were doing and concentrated on the problem as though their lives depended on an answer. They knew that would annoy him.

'All right! Get on with your work!' he shouted when it became obvious that no reply was forthcoming. He turned back to me. 'I'm sorry, my good fellow, but nobody here can help you.'

At this point, the elderly man who had been attending to the furnace dropped his bellows and came forward, wiping his sooty hands down the front of his leather apron.

''Scuse me, Master, but there were Goldsmith Moresby. He had the workshop right at the end of the Row until ten years or so ago when he got sick and gave up the business. Master Flint, who lived next door, bought it from him, knocked down the inner walls and made the one big workshop. I don't suppose you'd remember. You weren't much more'n a boy at the time. But I recollect old master – yer father – and the others getting very disgruntled about it.'

'So I should think!' boomed Master Cock-up-spotty. 'Flint's always been a conniving old so-and-so, stealing a march on his neighbours. I wonder my father and the others...'

'What happened to Goldsmith Moresby?' I hurriedly asked the bellows man. 'Do you know?'

He nodded. 'Went to live with his niece, over

166

by the abbey. She looks after him now.'

'And how old would Goldsmith Moresby be?'

My informant pondered the question, ignoring his master's growing impatience, manifested by a tapping foot and a face like a thundercloud.

'Well,' he said at last, 'older'n you, but younger'n I. He were young when 'e started out. His father died, like the Master's here, when he weren't so very advanced in years, and he were quick to learn.' I thought I heard a faint note of accusation, or maybe contempt, in his tone as he cast a fleeting glance at his own unsatisfactory employer.

'Would you reckon him to be forty now? Or a little older?' I queried.

The bellows man bit a grimy fingernail before replying.

'Ar, I reckon so,' he finally agreed.

'You say he lives with his niece. Has he no children of his own?'

'Not that anyone knows of. Not that he knows of. He never married.'

'Do you know why not?'

But at this, Master Cock-up-spotty exploded with wrath.

'How much longer are these questions going on? If it comes to that, how much longer do you intend wasting my workmen's time? You're costing me money, whoever you are! What's this Goldsmith Moresby to you?'

I drew myself up to my full height and flexed my not unimposing chest and shoulder muscles, hoping that this display would be sufficient to counteract the glories of piked shoes, parti-coloured hose and nattily adorned codpiece. It seemed to work. Master Pomposity appeared somewhat deflated.

'I am making enquiries on behalf of Mayor John Foster of Bristol,' I announced, and left it at that. I didn't feel that I owed him an explanation.

Meanwhile, the bellows man answered my question as if there had been no interruption.

'There were some talk – mainly tattle, as these things generally are – about an unhappy love affair. Some maid as he'd wished to wed who'd none of him come the time of askin'.'

I took a deep breath. 'What was Goldsmith's Moresby's baptismal name? Did you ever hear it?'

It was one of the other men, the polisher with the rabbit's foot, who answered.

'It were Robert an' I remember right.'

Robert Moresby. R.M. It seemed too good to be true – and experience had taught me that it probably was. For a start, there was as yet no proof that this man was the 'Melchior' whom I sought. Secondly, even if he were, there was again no proof that R.M. was the murderer. And thirdly... Well, thirdly, a thought that had really only just occurred to me; how did I persuade a man to admit that he was a killer and run his head into a noose? Nevertheless, I could not ignore so promising a lead, for it seemed to me that I could safely wager on Master Robert Moresby, goldsmith, being one of the three men I was seeking.

I obtained the niece's direction from my friendly bellows man – learned, too, from him that her name was Juliette Gerrish – thanked him profusely and took my leave, Hercules trailing behind me. I had the distinct impression that my informant and his fellow workmen were sorry to see me go: I had not only provided them with a diversion, but had also managed to infuriate their master. He might vent his spleen on them later, but their half-grins and secret side-long glances at one another indicated that they considered his anger worth it.

As I approached the abbey it became obvious that someone of importance – or someone who thought he was important; not necessarily the same thing – was either just arriving or just leaving. The stamp and jingle of moving horses and the sharp, high-pitched clamour of the human voice were everywhere to be heard, bouncing back off the old grey walls and filling the surrounding alleyways with their echoes. Brothers and lay brothers, grooms and pageboys were scuttling across the abbey green like so many worker bees in a hive, so I hurriedly made myself scarce in case the hub of all this activity was someone with whom I had a nodding acquaintance from those days when I had performed some service for the Duke of Gloucester.

I had been directed by the bellows man to a small enclave of houses known as Cloister Yard on the north side of the abbey and, as instructed, knocked on the first door I came to. There was a moment's pause before it was thrown open and a laughing voice exclaimed, 'You're back early! What's happened? Wasn't Master Harvey in?' The words died away as the young woman who had answered my summons gave a little gasp and stood gaping up at me, an expression of ludicrous astonishment on her pretty face. 'Who...who are you?'

I tugged off my cap and smiled down at her. 'Mistress Gerrish?' I enquired.

She was of no great height, at least not by my standard, but she would probably have been regarded as a trifle short in most company. Standing beside me the crown of her uncovered head, with its profusion of copper-red curls, reached only an inch or so below my shoulders. But what she lacked in stature, she made up for in animation. Her large eyes, regarding me with such comical dismay, were the soft velvety brown of pansies, but there was a mischievous sparkle to them that belied their seeming docility and gentleness. At first glance I assumed her to be about eighteen, but a second, closer look informed me that she was not quite as young as I had supposed. In reality she was, I judged, somewhere in her mid-twenties (and she later told me that she had indeed seen twenty-five winters and would be twenty-six in August, on Saint Oswald's Day).

'Sweet Virgin!' she exclaimed now in mock alarm. 'A veritable giant! And what can I do for you, Goliath? If it's my uncle you're wanting, he's gone to visit a friend outside the city and won't be back until curfew.' At this juncture, Hercules made his presence known, sniffing the hem of her skirt, and she at once dropped to her knees, fondling his ears. 'What a dear little dog!' Never slow in recognizing a well-wisher,

Hercules licked her face.

'Ah!' I exclaimed, disconcerted. 'If your uncle is Master Robert Moresby, then yes, I was hoping to talk to him. You say he won't be returning until curfew? Perhaps, in that case, I'd better wait until tomorrow.'

'Do you live in Gloucester, Master Goliath?' she asked. Her eyes twinkled wickedly. 'I'm sure you don't or I should have noticed you, and so would every other girl in the city.'

'I live in Bristol,' I answered, and was about to add, 'with my wife and children,' but for some reason forbore to do so.

'And you've come all this way to speak to Uncle Robert?' Her eyes widened. 'It must be very important. What's it about?'

I was taken aback by this direct question. I could hardly say, 'I want to know if he murdered a young woman twenty years ago.' So, instead, I mumbled awkwardly, 'It...it's...a...a personal matter. I...I'm sorry.'

'There's no need to be,' she replied cheerfully. 'I shouldn't have asked. I've no doubt Uncle has his secrets, like everybody else. And whatever they are, they're not my business. But don't run away.' She held the door open invitingly. 'It will be dinnertime soon. Come inside and share mine. It's all right,' she added with that swift, winning smile of hers. 'You won't regret it. I'm accounted a very good cook. Indeed, I doubt if Uncle Robert would have stayed with me if I hadn't been. He's fond of his belly.'

I regarded her severely. 'Do you often do this with strangers? Invite them indoors when you're

171

on your own and unprotected? How do you know I'm not a robber or a murderer or a...a...?'

'Or that you'll rape me?' She finished my query for me. 'I hope I can read men's faces better than you give me credit for doing. I'm no green girl, you know, whatever you might think. Now, I can offer you pigeon pie, a slice of venison, apple and cinnamon coffins and some fine Rhenish wine from my uncle's cellar to wash it down with. And don't tell me that doesn't tempt you because I'd wager you'd be lying. A man of your size needs to be a good trencherman.'

She had taken my measure and nodded with satisfaction as I stepped past her into the house. I heard her shut the door behind me.

She was a kind woman with an especial fondness for animals, serving Hercules first with a bowl of clean water and a plateful of broken meats. He made short work of this and was ready to be a nuisance by the time my hostess and I sat down to table. But I knew him of old and had already asked Mistress Gerrish's permission to shut him in the kitchen.

It was a pleasant two-storied house with, on the ground floor, dining parlour, buttery and kitchen, all opening off a stone-flagged passage-way. There were two more doors which were closed, but obviously gave access to other rooms, making it a dwelling of commodious size and a fitting place of retirement for a successful goldsmith. Then I remembered that Master Moresby had gone to live with his niece, not the contrary.

Over our meal I probed, as delicately as I could, the household circumstances.

'I'm a widow,' Juliette Gerrish told me frankly. 'When he died five years ago, my husband left me wealthy and childless. But not lonely. My uncle had moved in with us four years before that, when he became ill and had no one to care for him.'

'You must have been married young,' I observed. 'Very young.'

She nodded. 'I was barely fifteen, but no younger than many girls. Mind you, I don't advocate it. After my miscarriage, I was never able to conceive again.' Her foot found mine under the table, whether accidentally or not I wasn't sure at the time. 'But,' she added cryptically, 'such barrenness has its advantages.'

I ignored this, although, deep in my mind, a warning bell rang, but not loudly enough it seemed.

'You've had visitors in Gloucester today,' I remarked thickly, through a mouthful of excellent pigeon pie. 'Abbey Green is humming with activity.'

My hostess smiled and helped me to a large and succulent slice of venison, at the same time adding another helping of pie to my laden trencher.

'The Duke of Gloucester's men as I understand it, raising men and money for the coming war with Scotland.' I raised my eyebrows in query and she went on, 'Oh yes! Hadn't you heard? It seems King James has broken the truce yet again. He and his army are over the border

173

and harrying the northern shires. Prince Richard is going north this summer, as soon as the weather is warmer, at the head of an English force.'

'King Edward doesn't go himself?'

Juliette Gerrish frowned. 'Rumour has it that he's too sick to undertake the task and relies entirely on his brother. But there!' She shrugged. 'How much you can rely on gossip is always a vexed question. All the same, I wonder you haven't heard of this in a place as big as Bristol.'

No doubt the news had reached some quarters of the city, but my old friend, Timothy Plummer, always maintained that Bristolians were too wrapped up in their own affairs, and in those of their southern Welsh and Irish neighbours, to pay much attention to what was going on in the rest of the country, especially in the north of England and Scotland; two territories that seemed as alien to them as the lands of the Great Cham of Tartary or the realms of Prester John.

'I've been out of the city for a day or two,' I said by way of extenuation, 'on my way here.' I refused a second slice of venison, patting my already bloated belly. 'I shan't have room for those apple and cinnamon coffins you promised me.'

These turned out to be as good as the rest of the meal, and the wine was undoubtedly as excellent as Mistress Gerrish claimed, but its savour was lost on me. I had been brought up on ale and small beer, and had no palate for anything better. I didn't own as much, however, permitting my fine glass goblet to be refilled more than once. A mistake; my head was beginning to spin.

'Do you have no one to help you in the house?' I asked. One of her hands lay close to mine on the tabletop. I succumbed to temptation and patted it lightly. It felt soft to the touch, unlike Adela's work-roughened skin.

'No, it's just my uncle and myself. I do all the cooking and the work. I buy a special ointment, made up for me by the local apothecary to keep my skin soft.' Her hand quivered slightly under mine. She turned her head and regarded me frankly. 'Are you betrothed Roger?'

'N-no,' I stammered. 'Not betrothed.' I was beginning to sweat.

Juliette laughed softly. 'Married, perhaps?'

I hesitated, appalled to find how close I was to lying; how much I wanted to disclaim my family shackles. But I had been brought up to be honest (well, fairly honest; we all lie on occasions). I nodded reluctantly.

But my admission did me no harm. My companion seemed in no hurry to withdraw her hand from under mine, merely remarking sagely, 'I thought you were.'

I was nettled. Too many people in the past few years had told me that I had the look of a married man. I was now the one who lifted my hand from hers.

'Why do you say that?' I demanded.

She gave that soft, sweet laugh that made the hairs rise on the nape of my neck.

'Don't be offended,' she chided gently. 'It was meant as a compliment. Anyone as handsome as

175

you are is almost certainly bound to be married. Are you faithful to your wife?'

'Of course.'

She rose from her seat and began to stack the dishes. 'There's no of course, Roger. Lust may be one of the seven deadly sins, but it's a sin practised in the very highest places. The King, I've heard, has many mistresses and when he tires of them, he passes them on to his friend, Lord Hastings. Is that true, do you think?'

I knew it was true, but refrained from saying so and turned the conversation into less dangerous byways. The day wore on and my hostess and I, by tacit consent, sat well apart from one another, on opposite sides of the parlour, making general small talk and watching the shadows lengthen. Twice, I took Hercules for a walk around the nearby streets and alleyways and on each occasion considered the advisability of returning to the New Inn and not going back to Cloister Yard. But neither time could I bring myself to be so discourteous to Mistress Gerrish. (Or, at least, that was what I told myself.)

Four o'clock came and with the hour supper-time, a meal every bit as appetizing as dinner had been. Curfew was called, candles were lit and still Robert Moresby had not returned.

'Uncle must be staying the night with Master Harvey,' Juliette said at last. 'But don't go, Roger. You can have his bedchamber. It's foolish to pay good money when there's room to spare here.' She added with a mischievous twinkle in her beautiful brown eyes, 'There's a bolt on the inside of the bedchamber door. You can lock

176

yourself in if you wish.'

I knew very well that I shouldn't stay, that I should insist on leaving, but somehow or another, I didn't have the will to do so. I even concurred with her suggestion that a bed of some straw and an old blanket should be made for Hercules in the kitchen. It was, under duress, where he slept at home, and although he gave me a reproachful look and a protesting bark, he nevertheless settled down and let me retire without further ado.

At the top of the stairs, Juliette wished me a prim goodnight before entering her own room and firmly closing the door. I did likewise in Master Moresby's chamber, but after contemplating the bolt for several seconds, turned away and stripped off my clothes, shaking them thoroughly to get rid of the dust and fleas and dirt they had gathered along the road. A ewer of water and a basin had been placed on the chest alongside the big four-poster bed, with its crimson velvet hangings, together with an 'all-night' of bread and cheese and ale. I washed and fell into bed, sleep beginning to claim me almost as soon as I was engulfed by the goose feather mattress.

But not for long. I was drawn back from the borderland of sleep by the sound of the door latch being lifted. A soft voice spoke out of the darkness.

'Roger?'

I rolled on to my back and stretched out a hand. Juliette slid into the bed beside me.

Eleven

Daylight brought guilt, rolling over me in great waves, as well as a feeling of satiety and pleasure. It was the first time in nearly four years of marriage that I had been unfaithful to Adela. I turned my head on the pillow and found Juliette already awake and staring at me with those large velvety brown eyes, brimful of penitent laughter.

'Oh dear!' she said, raising herself on one elbow and kissing me gently between the eyes. 'I can see by your expression that you're already regretting last night. And it was all my fault. I'll be perfectly honest and admit that I was determined to seduce you the moment I saw you, but I really didn't think it would cause you such grief.'

'Not grief,' I protested gallantly. 'And I wouldn't like you to think that it was anything but the happiest of experiences. Moreover, it wouldn't have happened if your uncle had returned, as you expected...'

She laid a finger lightly on my lips.

'I knew he was absent for the night,' she admitted. 'He never intended coming home until this morning. I lied to you, Roger, I'm afraid.' She gave a rueful, lopsided grimace. 'Are you very angry with me?'

The trouble was that I couldn't find it in my heart to be even mildly annoyed. I felt guiltier than ever. Later on, I would have to come to terms with these feelings and decide whether or not I was going to tell Adela the truth, but for the moment all I was aware of was Juliette's soft body close to mine and the desire to make love to her again. She knew even before I did what I wanted and was in my arms almost as soon as the thought had formed in my mind. The rest was inevitable.

It was well past dawn and the lifting of curfew when we finally got out of bed and Juliette returned to her own chamber. She brought me hot water to shave with and directed me to the pump in the walled enclosure behind the house, and by the time I had finished dressing, a tempting smell of bacon and fried wheaten cakes was coming from the kitchen. Following my nose, I found Juliette with a skillet in one hand and a wooden spoon in the other, standing over the open fire, her cheeks delicately flushed, while Hercules sat up and begged in what he knew to be his most engaging fashion.

'Ignore him,' I advised. 'He's quite capable of foraging for himself if you're plagued with rats or mice. If not, any old scraps will do.'

She shook her head, laughing, and cut a collop of meat in two, throwing him the larger portion.

'Like master, like dog,' she said, piling a thick trencher of stale bread with bacon, flanking it with wheat cakes and bringing it to the table. 'You both have good appetites.' She sat down opposite me and started to eat her own breakfast.

'Mistress Gerrish,' I began, then realized how ridiculous such a mode of address sounded in the circumstances. 'Juliette...' I paused, uncertain how to continue.

She glanced up and regarded me with that glinting smile of hers.

'It's all right, Roger. You've nothing to worry about. I don't make a habit of hounding the men I seduce and making their lives miserable. I shan't come to Bristol to find you and stir up difficulties between you and your wife. It's just that I've been a widow for a long time now and have to take my pleasures where I can find them. You're not the first man I've lain with and you won't be the last. That shocks you, I can see, but it shouldn't. Women need men in the same way that men need women, although I know most men don't like to think so. Men are different, isn't that what you all believe?'

She was right. I was shocked; shocked and more than a little aggrieved if the truth be told. I was wounded in that most vulnerable of spots: my vanity. I had crassly assumed that she had found me irresistible, not that anyone passably good-looking and in possession of all his limbs (and, of course, other working parts) would do just as well. I suddenly felt extraordinarily sheepish.

She put down her knife, sucked her fingers clean, got up and came round the table to drop a kiss on the top of my head in much the same way as a mother humours a troubled child. Then she fetched me more bacon before resuming her seat.

'Uncle Robert said he would be home in time for dinner,' she said, wiping her mouth free of grease on the hem of her sleeve. 'And as he likes his food as much, if not more, than you do, I can rely on his word. It would be best to let him think that you haven't long arrived, don't you agree?' I did, fervently. Juliette nodded and continued, 'Couldn't you give me a hint of why you wish to speak to him?'

I realized with even greater clarity that after last night, to tell her the truth would be impossible. She would find out soon enough when I had gone, and the discovery would probably make her take me in instant dislike. For some reason, this upset me. I could only hope that Master Robert Moresby would be able to exonerate himself to my satisfaction, so that I should have no further cause to suspect him.

'I'd...I'd rather not,' I answered.

Once again, my companion accepted my reluctance without demur, as, I guessed, she accepted most setbacks in life. She was plainly not an argumentative woman, and I reflected sadly that she was wasted looking after an elderly relative when she would make some man such an excellent wife. She blew me a kiss and collected the knives and other dirty utensils together.

'Wait in the parlour,' she told me. 'I'll let Uncle know you're here as soon as he arrives. Will you stay to dinner?'

'I don't know,' I admitted. 'It depends.'

Once more she refrained from asking on what, merely handing me Hercules's belt and advising

181

me to walk him around the neighbouring streets for a while. I did as I was bidden, then tried to settle down to wait for Master Moresby's return.

It being Sunday, the town was quiet except for the ringing of bells summoning people to worship. Cloister Yard was silent as the grave, only the spasmodic shuffling of feet or a voice imbued with Sabbath hush penetrating the unshuttered window of the parlour. By the time I eventually heard the clop of hooves outside, followed by the raising of the front door latch and a man's deep tones, answered by Juliette's affectionate lighter ones, I had almost persuaded myself to return to Bristol and report failure on this entire case to Mayor Foster. It was all too long ago, and the possible disruption to innocent folk's lives too great a risk to take.

On the other hand, murder was murder whenever it had been committed, and only the previous year I had helped to clear my own half-brother of a crime that had been perpetrated many years before. Isabella Linkinhorne's ghost demanded equal justice. What had passed between me and Juliette Gerrish the night before should not, must not, be allowed to prevent that.

Time passed. Someone – obviously the new arrival – went out again and led the horse away, presumably to the stables. I heard Juliette's voice upraised in song while she clattered pots and pans in the kitchen. The palms of my hands were sweating. Some of my unease must have communicated itself to Hercules, causing him to whimper and twitch, even in his sleep.

The parlour door opened, making me jump, and Robert Moresby came in.

He had to be over forty, a fact attested to by the wings of grey hair at his temples, but he moved with all the sprightliness of youth. There was nothing now to suggest that he had ever been so ill that he had been forced to give up work and go to live with his niece and her husband. Juliette's ministrations had plainly made him a hale and hearty man again.

I knew at once that 'Melchior' must be the one of the three suitors who had been described to me as handsome. He still retained his good looks in the long, aristocratic nose and high arched cheekbones. His eyes, of clear Saxon blue, were evenly spaced, while the lips, neither too full nor too thin, parted to reveal excellent teeth. A determined jawline completed the picture. He paused just inside the door, regarding me curiously.

'My niece says you have business with me, Master...?' In addition to his other attributes, he had a most pleasing voice. It was difficult to see why some scheming Gloucester spinster or widow had not managed to lead him to the altar by now. It would not be for want of trying, I was sure. And yet, according to the bellows man, Robert Moresby had never married.

I got to my feet. 'Roger Chapman,' I said. 'At your service.'

He eyed me up and down, taking in my well-worn tunic and mended hose. I was not the sort of person he normally had dealings with, at least not in his niece's parlour. I looked what I was; a ragamuffin of the road, to be met with at back

183

doors and in kitchens, peddling my wares.

'And what can I do for you, Master Chapman?' He motioned me back to my chair and seated himself in another with arms and an abundance of soft cushions, which I had not dared to defile with my plebeian buttocks. 'My niece tells me that you are making enquiries on behalf of Mayor – Foster, is it?' I nodded. He continued, 'Mayor Foster of Bristol. As far as I am aware, His Worship is unknown to me.'

I took a deep breath, hesitated, then plunged.

'Master Moresby, I believe I am right in thinking that many years ago, you were acquainted with a Mistress Isabella Linkinhorne.'

He stared at me, his mouth falling slightly open, half-rising from his chair. This was the last thing he had expected, this sudden confrontation with the past, and he seemed, for the moment, too shocked to answer.

'Isa...Isabella L-Linkinhorne?' he manage to gasp out finally. Indignation replaced astonishment. 'Sweet Virgin! That was twenty years or more ago! What about her?'

'You admit you did know her then?'

'Yes, I knew her.' He spoke with sudden venom, as though the memories conjured up by the name were bitter. 'What, in God's name, is this all about?'

'How well did you know her, Master Moresby?' The handsome features were suffused with a rush of blood, and I hastened to avert his very natural wrath. 'Forgive me, but these are not idle questions. When I explain the reason for them, I hope you'll understand.'

'In that case, you'd better hurry up and give me an explanation,' he snapped, but then went on without waiting for it, 'I don't scruple to tell you, Master Chapman, that Isabella Linkinhorne was a flirt, a cock-teaser, a woman who had no hesitation in breaking her given word. So, are you going to tell me what this is about? Or are you going to waste more of my time?' A thought seemed to strike him. 'Has she sent you?'

The question sounded genuine enough; but if Robert Moresby were the murderer, and had guessed what my probing was about, it might be just a clever ploy to put me off the scent.

'Isabella Linkinhorne is dead,' I said starkly, adding, 'And I've already told you that I'm here on behalf of Mayor Foster of Bristol, on whose land her body was found.'

Master Moresby's anger drained away. He sat staring at me with a puzzled expression. 'What do you mean, her body was found?' he asked after a moment.

'She was murdered,' I said. 'Twenty years ago.' And I went on to explain the circumstances of the discovery and John Foster's interest in it.

But I doubt if my companion heard much of the latter. He was sitting like one stunned, as pale now as he had been red before. 'Dear God, dear God,' he kept whispering to himself over and over again. And then, suddenly, in what appeared to be an agony of remorse, he began rocking himself to and fro. 'I've wronged her! All these years I've wronged her. I thought she'd led me on, promising to marry me, and then deliberately, callously breaking her promise. Oh,

God in heaven!' He buried his face in his hands and burst into tears; hard, racking sobs that shook his whole body.

I tried steeling my heart, although it was difficult. But I could not yet afford to let it be softened by this display of emotion, because a display might be all it was. 'Melchior' could simply be a very crafty dissembler.

I waited for the sobs to subside a little, then said, 'You say that Mistress Linkinhorne had promised to marry you. How long were you betrothed?'

Slowly he straightened up in his chair and gradually controlled his bout of weeping. After perhaps a minute or two, he once more had himself well in hand.

'We were never betrothed in the formal sense,' he said thickly. 'That last morning I ever saw her, she finally promised to marry me. She had refused me time and time again, saying she wasn't sure, she didn't know, she couldn't leave her parents, who were both elderly. Whether that was true or not, I had no means of telling. I never met either of them.'

'It was perfectly true,' I interrupted. 'That they were elderly, I mean. Her father, Master Jonathan Linkinhorne, is still alive. He's eighty-five. He and his wife were both over forty years of age when Isabella was born. But please, go on.'

He shook his head sadly. 'There's not much more to tell. She promised to run away with me the following day. She said it had to be a runaway match or her father would try to prevent it. I protested that if matters stood like that, we should go at once and be wed before her parents had time to find out that she'd fled. My mother was still alive in those days and she would have looked after Isabella and kept her safe, and been glad to have done it for my sake. I was always her favourite.' He was lost for a moment in a haze of reminiscence.

'But Isabella wouldn't agree?' I prompted.

'No. She said she had to go home to collect her clothes. I said not to be so foolish. I would buy her everything she needed when we got to Gloucester. But I couldn't persuade her. She apparently had many gowns she was fond of. And then there was her jewellery, some of which I'd given her. I promised her more and better, but to no avail. She was adamant. So we arranged that I would wait for her the following day at a house a little north of our usual trysting place, where I had a very good customer. But she never came. I have to admit my pride was hurt as well as my heart. I had been made to look a fool in front of other people. Or so I thought at the time.' He drew a deep breath, almost a gasp. 'Now, of course, I know differently.'

'You used to meet at Westbury village,' I said. 'That much I have discovered. The last day you saw her was, I believe, a very cold day of wind and driving rain.'

Robert Moresby shook his head. 'No, that was the following day; the day she was to meet and come away with me.' Some expression on my face must have made him suspicious. 'I never saw her that day. What makes you think I did?'

I avoided answering the question, merely

frowning as though I had not quite understood what he had said.

'You mean you waited all day at the house of this customer, but she didn't come?'

'I've just told you, haven't I? It was a terrible day, lashing wind and driving rain from morning till night. I got to my friend's house early – for you must understand that he and his wife, as well as being excellent customers, had also become friends over the years. Indeed, it was while spending a day or two with Sir Peter and his lady the previous spring, while I was out riding in the surrounding countryside, that I first met Isabella. So they knew all about her from the start, knew of my desire to marry her, of her reluctance to abandon her elderly parents. When I confided in them the preceding day that Isabella had finally agreed to run away with me, and begged leave to use their house as our rendezvous – confessed that in fact I had already taken the liberty of asking Isabella to meet me there – they were all complaisance. They even suggested that I should remain with them overnight, rather· than go home to Gloucester, only to return again the following morning.'

'That would have seemed the logical thing to do,' I commented. 'Why did you refuse?'

'I wished to prepare my mother for the reception of her future daughter-in-law. Also my brother and his wife, who were still living with us at that time, above the workshop in Goldsmiths' Row. My niece, whom you've met, was then a child, some five years old.'

The house would have been fairly crowded,

then, especially when servants and apprentices were included in the count.

'Mistress Linkinhorne knew of your family circumstances, I suppose?'

Robert Moresby stared at me as though I had asked an indecent question.

'Of course she knew! I never had secrets from Isabella. But nothing mattered to her except our love,' he added triumphantly. 'She once told me she could live in a hovel so long as I was by her side.'

The girl was a liar, so much was obvious. Not only was she deceiving him with two other men, but everything I had so far found out about her convinced me that she was not the sort to be happy in cramped quarters, let alone one of a crowd. Provided that my companion was telling the truth, his first estimation of Isabella, as a flirt and a cock-teaser, was closer to the real woman than the suddenly rose-coloured picture he entertained of her now.

I wondered why – again if his version of what had happened was the correct one – Isabella had agreed to run away with 'Melchior' when subsequent events suggested that she had had no intention of doing so. Perhaps she had grown tired of his importunings and decided to put an end to them once and for all by teaching him a humiliating lesson. But on the other hand, perhaps she had had every intention of eloping with him to Gloucester, but had met someone else on her way to the rendezvous; someone who had persuaded her to change her mind. (Who? And what argument was used?) Then again, maybe the whole story was a farrago of nonsense, a pack of lies, thought up over the intervening years just in case one day the truth was discovered and Robert actually found himself confronted by an accusation of murder. And if the latter, it was quite possible that he had come to believe what he had made up. I had known this to happen.

'These friends of yours,' I said, trying to look like a poor peasant, easily impressed. 'You mentioned Sir Peter just now.'

Robert Moresby's chest expanded a little. 'Sir Peter and Lady Claypole.' The chest expanded even further. 'Araminta to her friends.' He enlarged no further, allowing me to draw my own conclusion; that he was included in this circle of the elite. My heart hardened against him.

'Sir Peter and his wife live in or near Westbury?' I asked, but tentatively, as one just enquiring out of curiosity. I had no wish for 'Melchior' to divine my real purpose; namely, to call upon the Claypoles in an attempt to discover if his story were true.

Such was his conceit, however, in the importance of this acquaintance, that he saw nothing suspicious in my catechism, merely a yokel's natural interest in his betters.

'They had a manor house near Hambrook,' he informed me. 'Lady Claypole became interested in my wares after a visit to Gloucester with Sir Peter, when she happened to stumble across my workshop in Goldsmiths' Row and preferred my work to that of any of my neighbours. Later in

190

the month, she sent a message for me to wait on her at Hambrook Manor and to take a selection of necklaces and rings with me.'

I thought, 'And you offered them to the lady at special prices, I'll be bound. Which is the only way you became a frequent and honoured guest.' But aloud I said, 'Sir Peter and his lady still live at Hambrook?'

Master Moresby flushed, looking suddenly uncomfortable.

'I...I don't know,' he admitted. 'I haven't seen either of them for many years now.'

It dawned on me that he had probably never been back to visit them since his humiliation at Isabella's hands. Or his apparent humiliation, depending upon the veracity of the tale he had spun me. 'I wouldn't know for certain,' he added, 'if they are still alive or not.'

'They were old?' I queried.

He stirred abruptly, as though beginning to be conscious that my curiosity might be seen as abnormal. I assumed what I could only hope was a bland, slightly oafish expression. At any rate, it seemed to satisfy my companion, who settled down again in his chair.

'They were a couple in the middle years of their life,' he said. 'Older than I was by many years, but not old enough to be stigmatized as elderly.' 'Melchior' preened himself a little. 'They had no children, and I rather think they came to regard me in the light of a son.'

I doubted this, having (quite unwarrantably, I had to admit) formed a picture of a self-conse-quential, but somewhat impoverished, couple

191

making use of people who, in turn, could be of use to them.

'Mistress Linkinhorne was wearing jewellery that you had given her when she was killed,' I said. 'It was still on her body when it was found last week. That was how her corpse was identified so quickly. Her cousin, Sister Walburga of the Magdalen nuns, recognized it. She didn't know your name or anything about you, saving that you were a goldsmith. I found out that you lived – or had lived – in Gloucester from Isabella's maid, Jane Honeychurch.'

This information seemed to distress him all over again. He gave a little moan and buried his face in his hands. After a moment or two, tears seeped through his fingers and ran down his cheeks. I waited, torn between genuine sympathy and cynicism, for the spasm to pass. Eventually he sniffed loudly, removed his hands and straightened his back.

'What was she wearing?' he asked.

'A gold and amber necklace, a girdle of gold and silver links with an amethyst clasp and several gold finger rings.'

He nodded mutely, and some seconds ticked away before he mastered his voice sufficiently to say tremulously, 'Yes, they were all my gifts. And there were others. No doubt she had them with her.' He rose from his chair and began pacing about the room. 'It shows she was on her way to meet me, to keep our tryst, when she was waylaid and killed.' He drove a clenched fist into the palm of his other hand. 'Or perhaps she never left home. Maybe her parents discovered

192

her intention and locked her up. Starved her to death and then disposed of her body.'

I shook my head. 'You forget I told you that she had been struck a fateful blow to the back of her head. And it had to be that day she was murdered. There was an open grave in the grave-yard. Later, it was found filled in.' And I ex-plained about Sister Apollonia's so-called miracle.

'Melchior' groaned yet again and stopped striding around in order to throw open a casement, breathing deeply as one in urgent need of air. Beyond the window, I could see a hawthorn bush just coming into flower, and a clutch of mulberry-coloured clouds above the rooftops opposite.

'I was told,' I said, 'that there was a tree near Westbury village with your and Isabella's initials carved into the trunk. Did you do it together?'

He shook his head, but without turning round.

'No.' He gave another sob, quickly suppres-sed. 'Isabella did it as a surprise for me. She had a little pearl-handled knife that her father had given her for eating and she must have used that. We couldn't always arrange the exact hour of our meetings. Sometimes I had to wait for her and sometimes she had to wait for me. So once, when I was later than expected, she used the time to carve our initials into a tree trunk, enclosed in a heart. I thought then that it was proof of her love for me. But then, of course, in later years, I considered it just another act of perfidy. Sweet Jesus, forgive me!'

'Sweet Jesus forgive you for what, Uncle?'

193

Juliette had entered the parlour without either of us noticing. She stared with a puzzled frown from one to the other.

'Unhappily, I've brought Master Moresby some very sad news about the death of an old friend of his,' I said, smiling reassuringly at her.

'More than a friend,' the goldsmith explained huskily, closing the casement and turning to face his niece. 'A lady I once asked to marry me, and who I subsequently believed had betrayed me, was in fact most foully murdered on the day we were to have run away together. Her body has only recently been discovered, twenty years on.'

'My dear uncle!' Juliette went towards him with outstretched hands.

Robert Moresby grasped them as though clinging to a lifeline, his eyes refilling with tears. Yet again, it struck me that he was either innocent or else a very fine actor.

Juliette reached up and kissed his cheek and, remembering how she had kissed me during the night, I felt a small thrill of desire, followed by immediate arousal. Hercules suddenly woke up and started barking loudly.

'Come and have your dinner,' Juliette said, tucking a consoling hand into the crook of Robert's elbow. 'You know good food always makes you feel better.' She was an eminently practical woman, in spite of her hot-blooded nature. (Although why the two shouldn't go hand in hand, I couldn't really tell you.) 'Master Chapman, will you honour us by joining us? After discharging such a harrowing mission, you too must be in need of sustenance.' Her eyes mocked me. 'Let me assure you that I am considered a very good cook. Is that not so, Uncle?'

'It is I who shall be honoured,' I answered formally. 'There is, however, the dog.'

'He shall be looked after. Indeed,' she added, as Hercules pushed past her and turned, without hesitation, in the direction of the kitchen, 'he seems to know his way about already.' Her lips twitched, but she forbore to tease me further. She squeezed her uncle's arm. 'Come and eat, dearest, and while we do so, if you feel like it, you can tell me all about it.'

Twelve

I took my leave of Master Moresby and his niece after dinner – a splendid meal of roast pork and apple fritters – in spite of Juliette's attempts to persuade me to stay.

'As you say you don't wish to travel on a Sunday, Master Chapman, why return to the New Inn and pay to be far less comfortable than you would be here? We have a chamber, right at the top of the house, under the eaves, to be sure, but clean and warm and private. At the inn you may well have to share, and I'm certain that the food will not rival mine.'

She looked intently at me as she spoke, conveying the message that there would be other comforts on offer as well as those she had mentioned. But that was the trouble. I knew that if I did as she wanted, I would be unable to resist the temptation of her company in bed, even though her uncle would be in the house. Had the quondam goldsmith added his entreaties to hers, I believe that in spite of my overwhelming sense of guilt and betrayal, I would have given in. But Robert Moresby remained silent; nor could I rid myself of the notion that he would be glad to see me go, although, if I were right, I was uncertain of his reason. Did he simply wish to mourn alone, to come to terms with the fact that for so many years he had vilified a woman he now – however mistakenly – thought to have been his one true love? Or was he afraid of revealing too much if he had to put up with my company for the rest of the day?

Of the two possibilities, the former seemed most likely, but there was no way I could be certain until I had paid a visit to Sir Peter and Lady Claypole at Hambrook Manor, and even then I might be none the wiser. They could both be dead by now and someone else in possession of the manor. Or their memories might not stretch back twenty years, at least not with any clarity. Recollections became muddled after a shorter period than that. But I should have to visit Hambrook to satisfy my own curiosity and find out what, if anything, there was to be discovered.

I could tell that Juliette was disappointed by my decision to return to the New Inn, and when she bade me farewell, she hissed the word 'Coward!' in my ear. But she blew me a secret kiss behind her uncle's back She'd soon forget me when the next opportunity to seduce a man offered itself, but I wasn't so sure that I'd as easily forget her.

Conscience told me that I should go to confess my sins, but I was bad at acknowledging my transgressions. (I always have been and always will be, I daresay, until the day I die; a day not too far off now, perhaps.) But, for the good of my soul, I did go to Mass later on, just one of the crowd of stinking humanity breathing down one another's necks in the abbey nave in the glory of that great and wonderful building. And I regret to say that my reflections were not on my own shortcomings, but on the fact that much of the glory was due to the burial there of the second Edward, a man condemned in his lifetime for his lack of martial qualities and his preference for male lovers, but whose murder had transformed him from reprobate into martyr, and made his tomb a place of pilgrimage. His hideous death in Berkeley Castle a century and a half previously had made Gloucester Abbey rich.

I returned to the New Inn in time for supper. Hercules, who had been left in the charge of the landlord, demonstrated his excitement at seeing me again by peeing down my leg, a feat which other drinkers found highly amusing, and I had to endure ribald comments for the rest of the evening until I eventually slunk off to bed.

It took me the better part of three days' steady walking before Hambrook Manor eventually came into sight in the late afternoon of the third

197

day; three days during which the increasingly warmer weather made it possible for the dog and myself to spend the second of two nights in the empty outhouse of a shuttered farmhouse, bedding down on a pile of hay. This was from choice rather than necessity: I have always enjoyed sleeping under the sky and the stars, watching the trees fade and disappear with the encroaching darkness until they are nothing but a faint lacy blackness against an even deeper black. And sunsets – when there are any worth looking at in this grey and murky island of ours – always fill me with a sense of well-being; the distant hills turning gradually to fire, saffron ribbons of light threading the western sky.

We ate well, too, for I still had plenty of money in my purse, thanks to John Foster's generosity. Where there was no wayside alehouse to satisfy our wants, there was usually a cottage or a landholding where the goodwife was pleased to meet our needs with bread and bacon and small beer. And Hercules never failed to ingratiate himself simply by being the obnoxiously thrusting, cocky little beast that he naturally was. He took his own importance so much for granted that everyone else took it for granted as well.

'It'll be a different story at Hambrook Manor,' I warned him. 'Sir Peter and Lady Claypole don't sound to me the sort of couple to extend a hearty welcome to a pair of scruffy travellers like ourselves.' Hercules wagged his tail confidently and barked. 'That's all very well,' I reproached him. 'However, we shall see.'

And see we did when we finally marched

198

boldly up to the door of the manor house and knocked peremptorily on the oak.

It was a pleasant enough building, surrounded by fertile meadowland and, at the rear, sheltered by a spread of trees that gradually thickened as it merged with the general woodland beyond. There were the customary outhouses and barns, pig and sheep pens, a flower and herb garden for the lady of the manor, and it should have presented a prosperous face to the world. And yet there was a faint air of neglect about the place, a broken down wall that need mending here, a hole in a roof there, and some very scrawny chickens scrabbling for food in the dirt alongside the well where a maid servant was hoisting up the bucket.

'What do you want, stranger?' she demanded as I drew abreast.

'I have business with Sir Peter Claypole,' I told her.

She laughed. 'Oh yes?'

'Yes,' I answered firmly.

'Well, you won't see him,' she announced with satisfaction. 'He's been dead these ten years and more.'

'Oh!' But it had always been a possibility. 'I must talk with Lady Claypole then.'

The girl lowered her bucket of water to the ground and put her hands on her hips. 'You must, must you? I doubt she'll want to talk to you.' She eyed me up and down, her top lip curling slightly.

'Appearances can be deceptive,' I retorted briefly, and continued up the path to knock on the door.

It was answered by a young page who, when I repeated my request, seemed inclined to argue the point.

'My lady don't see no one, at least not the likes of you. Kitchen door's round the side if you're selling summat. Although,' he added with a sniff, 'I don't see no pack.'

'Fetch the Steward,' I commanded, drawing myself up to my full height, expanding my chest until it hurt and trying to look as authoritative and menacing as I could.

The boy hesitated a moment longer, then shrugged his shoulders and disappeared.

It was several dragging minutes before a tall, lean man, carrying the Steward's wand of office and wearing a long robe made of either burel or brocella (both very coarse woollen materials and no longer made today, as far as I know) arrived to order me off the premises. His intention was writ large on his face, so I spoke quickly before he had time to open his mouth.

'I wish to speak to Lady Claypole. I'm here on the business of His Worship the Mayor of Bristol.'

'Indeed?' The thin arched eyebrows conveyed a world of scepticism. 'And what about the dog?'

'He's my assistant,' I replied tartly.

The man facing me was the last person I would have suspected of harbouring a sense of humour, but at this he threw back his head and laughed.

'I'll find out if my lady can see you,' he said. 'Wait there.'

It was a full five minutes by my reckoning before he returned, during which time Hercules and I had watched a ragged flock of sheep being penned for the night, and a couple of large, evil-looking boars being driven in from the forest to join the sow in the sty. One herdsman appeared to take care of all the animals; a broken-nosed, wall-eyed man who regarded me malevolently from a distance. I returned his stare with interest, but Hercules growled warningly.

'My lady will see you, Master,' said a voice in my ear, making me jump, and I turned to find that the Steward had returned. 'Follow me, but leave your assistant tied to that bench outside the door if you please.'

I grinned and looped Hercules's belt around the seat of the bench indicated.

'Lie down and be good,' I admonished him. 'I shan't be long.'

The inside of the house had the same slightly rundown appearance as the exterior, suggestive of the fact that there was just not quite enough money to keep things as they had once been, although Lady Claypole's solar, up one flight of stairs and at the side of the house overlooking the flower garden, was comfortable and well-furnished with an armchair, plenty of cushions, a spinning wheel and a small intricately carved chest on which stood a silver ewer and a tumbler made of fine Venetian glass.

The lady herself was a woman well past the first flush of youth – over fifty I guessed – who had once been pretty in a plump and fair-complexioned way, but whose pasty cheeks now sagged and whose blue eyes blinked short-sightedly from beneath lashes that were almost colourless. I noticed, too, that she had grown a little careless, the bodice of her red velvet gown stained here and there with food and splashes of wine.

'Well, my man,' she demanded, 'what is it you want? Master Steward has been babbling some nonsense about the Mayor of Bristol.' She snorted derisively. 'You don't look like a friend of His Worship to me. If I find you've been wasting my time...'

She didn't complete the threat, having had a moment or two to take in my size, and realize that she probably had no one capable of throwing me off her manor. I should have to be humoured if she wanted me to go quietly.

I glanced around for somewhere to sit, but there was nowhere, so I propped myself against the wall facing her and told my tale as simply and as succinctly as I could. Indeed, I was tired of repeating the story and made it as brief as possible for my own sake as much as hers. To her credit, Lady Claypole listened without interruption until I had finished, when her first question, somewhat to my surprise, was, 'He's still alive, then, Master Moresby?' A faint flush mantled her cheeks. 'How is he?'

'In good health, as far as I could tell. But not having met the gentleman before Sunday, I'm unable to say for certain. Lady Claypole, can you remember back twenty years to the last occasion on which you saw Robert Moresby? That day he waited here for Isabella Linkinhorne to join him.'

'Oh, yes. I recollect the day well and his bitter disappointment, his anger, when she failed to arrive. Both my husband and I tried to persuade him that he had been deceived in her, that she had never intended to go away with him.' My companion smiled thinly. 'I could have told him the truth, but I couldn't bring myself to do so.'

'The truth?'

Lady Claypole tittered. 'I had friends in Westbury. I was a good horsewoman in those days and often rode that way. I knew that this woman Robert had set his heart on was playing him false with at least one other man, most likely two.'

'You didn't feel it your duty to enlighten him?'

She shook her head. 'I know men better than that. When a man fancies himself as deeply in love as Robert did with her – that creature – he doesn't want to hear the truth. The only person who loses by it is the teller. And I had no wish to forfeit his friendship.'

I suddenly realised that Lady Claypole had been in love with Robert Moresby and jealous of Isabella Linkinhorne. But that was not my business. I asked, 'Can you recollect what the weather was like that day Master Moresby waited here for Isabella and she didn't come?'

'Easily. It was early March and the windiest, wettest day we had had for several weeks. Indeed, at first we all – myself, Sir Peter and Robert – thought it was the conditions that were delaying the girl's arrival. It was only as the day wore on and mid-afternoon was approaching, when the lashing rain and terrible wind had

203

eased considerably, that it began to dawn on us that she wasn't coming. After supper, Robert – er, Master Moresby,' she corrected herself, 'decided to ride out to look for Isabella. But it was getting dark by that time, and I think that in his heart of hearts he had convinced himself that she had never intended to keep her promise. It was what Sir Peter and I had thought all along. But now –' Lady Claypole sounded aggrieved – 'you tell me the girl had been murdered, so perhaps we were wrong.'

I didn't enlighten her as to the truth of the matter. And in any case, how did I know what the truth was? Maybe Isabella *had* been on her way to Hambrook Manor to keep her rendezvous with Robert Moresby when she had been waylaid by someone else (one of her other two swains?) with news or information that had caused her to change her plans. I heaved myself away from the wall and prepared to take my leave.

'Your ladyship has been most gracious...'

'You can spend the night here, if you care to, Master Chapman. The local hostelry is not one I would wholeheartedly recommend.' She must have noted my hesitation and added quickly, 'You would be doing me a favour. I have had little outside company throughout the winter, and I begin to feel cut off from the world.'

'There is a dog,' I said, 'at present tied up, but in general, no respecter of persons.'

That forced a thin smile from her. 'He can be fed in the kitchens and sleep by the fire. Will you stay?'

I told myself that it would be foolish to refuse, and found it hard to understand my reluctance to accept the offer. I bowed.

'I should be honoured, my lady.'

She nodded, taking this for granted, and summoned her Steward. I was handed into this gentleman's keeping and shown to a small chamber on an upper floor where, in due course, a ewer of hot water and a towel were brought to me by the young maid I had seen earlier drawing water from the well. Servants seemed to be in short supply at Hambrook Manor. I dropped my satchel on the bed – a large four-poster whose hangings had seen better days – propped my cudgel just inside the door, poured the water into a basin, then stripped and washed from head to foot, ridding myself of the dust and grime of the last three days' walk. I took my spare shirt from my satchel, shook it out and dressed again, cleaned my teeth with the willow bark I always carried for that purpose, combed my hair with an ivory comb I had brought with me from my pedlar's pack and sat down to wait until the Steward should reappear to conduct me to wherever Lady Claypole was taking supper.

I looked about me, at my surroundings. The chamber, as I have said, was a small one, but not so small as it seemed, on account of the size of the bed. This took up most of the floor space with just enough room left over for a carved oak chest on which stood the basin, a candle in its holder and a tinderbox. There was a single window, at present unshuttered, the pale, late-afternoon sunlight filtering through the oiled parchment panes. The bed curtains and counter-pane, no doubt once vibrant with colour, were all faded to a uniformly greyish hue so that it was almost impossible to make out what story they had once depicted. However, I managed to trace with one finger what looked like a head on a plate and guessed it to be that of Salome and Saint John the Baptist.

For some reason I was unable to fathom, I felt a strange sense of unease. The whole house depressed me and I discovered, to my consternation, that I was shivering. Was I ill? I didn't think so. My cheeks were cool, my heart beat as strongly as ever. I sprang up and went for a walk along the corridor outside the chamber. This led to a flight of steps at the far end, which in turn led to an unbolted door opening into the garden. Somewhere close at hand I could hear the grunting of the boars and sow. I returned to my room and once more waited for Master Steward to fetch me to supper.

'And you say,' Lady Claypole remarked, picking delicately at a curd flan, which was short on cheese, butter and saffron to my way of thinking, 'that Mayor Foster, when he has built his alms-houses, intends also to build a chapel dedicated to the Three Kings of Cologne. Surely that will prove to be most unpopular with the good citizens of Bristol? Does he not know that Cologne is part of the Hanseatic League? Does he not appreciate that the Rhinelanders are poaching much of England's trade? You see that I am not entirely unaware of what is happening in the world outside these walls.'

'You are very well informed, my lady,' I flattered her. 'But Mayor Foster is a great admirer of the Rhinelanders, although not, I hasten to add, of the League itself. He knows perfectly well the damage that is being done, particularly to Bristol's fish trade with Iceland. But I think he is a man who will not let prejudice cloud his judgement. He wishes, in his own fashion, to pay a small tribute to what he considers to be one of the finest buildings in Europe: Cologne Cathedral.'

My hostess snorted and speared another piece of curd flan on the tip of her knife, inspecting it from all angles until she finally put it in her mouth.

'I doubt very much if your fellow townsmen will see it in that light. The people of Bristol are noted for their parsimony.'

I smiled. 'Indeed they are. I am not myself one of them, coming as I do from the town of Wells, at the foot of the Mendips, but my wife was born in the city and knows how to hoard the pennies.'

But speaking of Adela, I was once again overcome with shame and panic. (Well, not shame perhaps, that was the trouble, but certainly panic.) I had little doubt that she would be able to prise my guilty secret from me if I lowered my guard for a single instant. And if I managed not to lower my guard, she would sense the tension and grow suspicious that something was wrong. I was caught in the jaws of a trap.

I became aware that my companion was offering me more tart, which I declined, claiming a full belly. But the truth was that the food at Hambrook Manor was of the same quality as the rest of the place. The pork which had comprised the first course had been swamped in a green sauce – *sauce vert*, as my former mother-in-law liked to call it when she was trying to put on airs. But green sauce, as I knew very well, made as it was from mint, parsley and other strong-tasting herbs steeped in peppered vinegar, was mainly used to disguise meat or fish that was not quite fresh, and in some cases downright stinking. And the dried pea puree that had accompanied the pork had also been of a very poor quality. It struck me forcibly before the end of the meal that financially matters at Hambrook were worse than I had at first thought them.

After supper, the table was cleared and I was invited to play at three men's morris with my lady until bedtime, but I could see by the way she was yawning that she was accustomed to early hours.

As the board was placed in front of us by the page boy who had answered the door to me on my arrival, Lady Claypole asked, 'Am I to understand that, in view of what I have told you, you have eliminated Master Moresby from the people you suspect of this poor girl's murder?'

'I think so,' I said.

And indeed I was almost certain that I could acquit the goldsmith of being Isabella's murderer. He seemed not to have spoken to her on the day she was killed. He had been here with the Claypoles from early morning, when he had arrived from Gloucester, until it was almost dusk, when he had ridden out in the forlorn hope that she still might be on her way to keep their assignation.

'You *think* so?' My hostess caught me up short.

'Very well,' I smiled. 'I exonerate him.'

I thought she suppressed a sigh of relief. 'He isn't married?' was her next question.

I reassured her on that point, and saw a faint, predatory gleam in the short-sighted eyes. I wondered how soon after my departure my lady would suddenly find it imperative to pay a visit to Gloucester.

She yawned again, more pointedly than before and missed an obvious move with her counters that might have prolonged the game. So I, too, gave a good imitation of a man who could barely remain awake and waited for her suggestion that we should retire and seek our rest. This was not long in coming, but she insisted that we first take some wine.

'It will help us sleep,' she said, ringing a small handbell that stood on the parlour table.

Now, I don't know if it was the speed with which this was brought by the Steward, as if he had been waiting for the summons, or the fact that it was this worthy himself who brought it, and not the page, or the fact that this whole burst of hospitality seemed out of keeping with the generally straitened circumstances of the manor, but my sense of unease increased. I took a sip or two from the glass Lady Claypole handed me, then managed to pour the remainder back into the ewer while my companion's attention was momentarily elsewhere. I then wished her a deliberately slurred goodnight and took myself off to the chamber that had been allotted to me.

As I closed the door behind me and made for the tinderbox and candle on top of the chest, I heard a slight noise from the direction of the bed. The hairs rose on my scalp and I groped for my cudgel which, thank God, was still where I had left it, leaning against the wall, just inside the door.

'Who's there?' I hissed, trying to sound menacing and praying that my voice didn't quaver.

A short, snuffling bark answered me, and the next moment something cold and wet was thrust against my hand.

Hercules!

I picked him up and hugged him, almost squeezing the breath out of the poor animal, I was so pleased to see him.

'How did you find your way here?' I demanded. 'You're supposed to be spending the night in the kitchen.'

But however he had made his escape and discovered my whereabouts, I had no doubt that he had done so because he, too, was unhappy and ill at ease. He also had his doubts about this place and had come to tell me so.

'You're right, my lad,' I said. 'I think I'd prefer to sleep under a hedgerow than spend the night in this place. And it seems you feel the same.'

He whimpered and licked my face. I set him down on the bed while I lit the candle and started to pack my satchel. Not that there was much to pack; only the shirt I had discarded after washing, my willow bark and the sharp, narrow-bladed knife I used for shaving. Then I inched open the door of the bedchamber and glanced up and down the corridor. It appeared deserted.

'Right,' I whispered. 'I know a way out of here without disturbing the rest of the household, so let's go.'

There was a sudden low rumbling sound and the floorboards began to shake. Then came a grinding noise as of slightly rusty cogs engaging and disengaging. Wheels began to whir somewhere, but whether above my head or beneath my feet I couldn't be certain. Then, as a terrified Hercules sprang clear of the bed, it began to tilt until the base was almost vertical, revealing a gaping black pit underneath. A terrible stench arose as the bedclothes and mattress disappeared into its depths, and I realized that, most probably, had I drunk that wine as I had been intended to do, I should have been too befuddled to know what was happening to me. I should have been smothered in the darkness below. Even as I watched, with yet more grinding and whirring, the bed righted itself.

I had heard of these contraptions for the unwary traveller to be murdered and robbed, but never thought to see one. The originals, I had been told, came from somewhere far away in eastern Europe, on the borders of Muscovy, but craftsmen in France, England and Spain had soon learned to copy them, and it was known that in some of the wilder parts of the country certain inns possessed these beds. So seriously was this menace taken that owners suffered the full rigours of the law, being pressed to death between two great stones.

But to find such a machine in a respectable country manor was beyond belief. I had no doubt that the motive in my case was robbery. I had guessed that Lady Claypole had fallen upon hard times, and I had no doubt let my tongue run away with me as usual when speaking of Mayor Foster's generosity. One thing was certain, however: I had no intention of remaining in this house a moment longer than I had to. I grabbed Hercules, my satchel and my cudgel, and was out of the room, along the corridor, down the stairs and through the door at the bottom faster than I had ever moved before in my life.

Thirteen

Someone was ahead of us, on the path that led to the outer palisade and gate, barring our passage. I gripped my cudgel and prepared to do battle, but Hercules was ahead of me. He launched himself forward, barking like all the fiends of hell, seized the man's right arm between his jaws and hung on for dear life, swinging several feet above the ground. He had performed this trick on at least two previous occasions when he and I had been in a tight situation, and it never failed to work. The person attacked tried vainly to shake him loose, but without avail. Hercules had jaws of iron.

As I closed with the man myself, I recognized the shadowy features of the herdsman. He looked just as ugly a customer in the dark as he did in daylight, and I had no compunction in hitting him a hefty thwack about his ears with the weighted end of my cudgel. He fell like a stone. Having, very briefly, assured myself that he wasn't dead and would probably suffer no more than a nasty buzzing in the head all day tomorrow, I ran for the gate, Hercules racing along beside me, his tail erect with all the pride of a dog who had done his duty. Which, of course, he had, and there would be no living with him for the next few days.

The gate, as I had expected, was locked and there seemed to be nothing for it but to climb the palisade. I didn't much care for the look of those nasty, pointed palings and realized that I could do serious damage to an essential part of my anatomy if I wasn't extremely careful. Suddenly, however, I came to my senses, of which panic had temporarily bereft me, rummaged in my satchel for my shaving knife – a long thin blade, keenly honed – and proceeded to pick the gate lock with the greatest of ease. This was a skill I had been taught in my youth, while a novice at Glastonbury Abbey, by a fellow postulant, and one that had stood me in good stead on more than one occasion in the past. The gate creaked open, Hercules bounded ahead of me and I followed without any further delay.

* * *

We put as much distance between ourselves and Hambrook Manor as was possible in the darkness, and spent the rest of the night in a sheltered ditch which had retained a fair amount of last year's dead leaves. These kept us warm and, to some extent, dry; but while Hercules snuffled and snored, none the worse for his adventure, I found it almost impossible to sleep for any length of time. I kept waking with a start, then spent the next half hour or so wondering what I ought to do. This pattern repeated itself throughout the night, but when dawn rimmed the distant hills, I still had not made up my mind.

I knew that as a good citizen I should report Lady Claypole's possession of the tilting bed, but at the same time I knew very well that I should not be believed. Put the word of a lowborn pedlar against that of a gentlewoman – and a defenceless widow with a title, to boot – and there was no doubt whose word would be accepted and who excoriated as a liar. I supposed I might go to Mayor Foster, but I had a feeling that he, too, would not wish to know. He was a busy man, both privately and publicly at present, and would hesitate to interfere, however obliquely, in the affairs of a lady of quality. Besides which, I had no idea how these beds worked, where or how the mechanism was hidden, whether or not it could successfully be concealed from prying eyes. And in this particular case, Lady Claypole's outraged protestations of innocence would most likely be sufficient to reassure any official sent to investigate my claim. So, after much heart-searching, I decided to let the matter go.

I salved my conscience with the conviction that the rustiness of the clanking and whirring sounds I had heard indicated that the bed was rarely used for any purpose other than sleeping – and perhaps not often for that. I doubted if Hambrook Manor had many visitors, and the important ones would certainly be missed, and enquiries made, if they were to disappear. As for itinerant beggars and pedlars like myself, in general they would not be worth the robbing – as I wouldn't have been if I had just kept my mouth shut about John Foster paying me for my services and probably giving an exaggerated impression of how much money I carried in my scrip. I had never, in the past, thought of myself as a braggart, but this wasn't the first time I had landed myself in trouble because I was too free with my tongue. I made a solemn vow to be more modest in the future.

'Your master's a coward,' I told Hercules when he finally emerged from his leafy covering, shook himself and looked around to see what there was to eat.

And I was going to be an even bigger coward when we finally reached home and I had to look Adela in the eye. It was just as well then, I decided, as the dog and I strode out, keeping an eye open for a cottage where we could beg some breakfast, that I should have to set off again almost immediately for Bath to look for 'Caspar', the second of Isabella's three swains. And he would not be so easy to locate. This time, I had no occupation by which to recognize my 'king', and I had already identified the R.M. whose initials Isabella had carved into the tree. It would be a game of blindman's bluff, stumbling around in the dark.

We arrived in Small Street before dusk and for once I was greeted with rapture by all my family. Well, rapture may be an overstatement, but Adela threw her arms about my neck and kissed me soundly, Adam embraced my knees (nearly bringing me down, but his intentions were good) while even Nicholas and Elizabeth forgot to ransack my person for whatever goodies I had brought them before standing on tiptoe to give me a hug. My burden of guilt increased.

'Sit down,' my wife urged me, pulling forward a stool and placing it by the kitchen table. 'We've had our supper, but it was only lentil stew and there's plenty left.' She ladled spoon-fuls of the savoury-smelling broth into a bowl as she spoke. 'And then, when you've finished, you can tell me what happened. Oh, Roger, I am glad to see you again. It feels as if you've been absent for a month instead of a week.'

'That's right, God,' I thought to myself. 'Punish me! Make me feel the weight of my sin.' Aloud, I said, 'And I'm glad to be back. But I haven't found poor Isabella's murderer, so I'm afraid I'll have to be off to Bath in a day or so.'

'At least that's not so far,' Adela said, sitting down beside me. 'It won't take you so long.'

When I had eaten my fill, I swallowed a beakerful of ale, pushed my stool back from the table and recounted my story with one serious omission. I wasn't aware of any change in either

216

my countenance or my voice when I mentioned Juliette Gerrish, and it was probably nothing more than my guilty conscience that made me think Adela looked at me a little more keenly at that point in my narrative. So, in order to distract her attention, I told of my adventure at Hambrook Manor with the tilting bed.

Nicholas and Elizabeth were thrilled, and immediately wanted to know where such a contraption could be obtained – no doubt with plans to use it on Adam – but my wife was appalled.

'You must report it, Roger,' she urged me, horrified.

But when I had discussed with her all the likely pitfalls attendant upon such a course, she did finally agree that it might be better to say nothing and, for now at least, keep my own counsel. It was some little while, however, before she could stop shaking.

'You could have been dead and buried,' she kept saying, 'and I would never have known what had happened to you.'

'Not buried, I fancy. I suspect I would have been fed to the swine.'

She gasped in dismay, but the two elder children's eyes lit up once again.

'Couldn't we keep pigs?' my daughter asked. 'There's room for them in the yard, and Nick and I would look after them.'

Her stepbrother nodded agreement, but I was tired and had had enough of their aggravating company, so I drove them off to bed, ignoring their howls of protest. Adela, sensing my irritation, seized Adam and bore him off as well, and by the time the city churches rang their bells for Compline, peace reigned throughout the house, Hercules was snoring under the kitchen table and my wife and I were able to relax in each other's company, seated together in the parlour. Except that neither of us was really at ease.

Adela was still brooding on what I had told her.

'I think you should tell someone about this place, Roger,' she said at last. 'Oh, I know that I agreed with you a while ago that perhaps you should say nothing, but I've been thinking while I was putting Adam to bed, and it seems to me that that's the coward's way out. You could tell Richard.'

'No!' I exclaimed violently. 'Certainly not Dick Manifold! Can't you just imagine how he'd laugh and make fun of me? He'd swear I'd dreamed it all.'

Adela shifted uncomfortably in her chair. 'You really don't like him, do you? Don't deny it! I know you tolerate his company for my sake, because he's such an old friend, but I can see that it's always an effort for you to be civil to him. And yet, in spite of his – I'll admit – patronizing ways, he doesn't bear any animosity towards you. When you're not here, he speaks of you almost with affection.'

'Does this mean he's been here again in my absence?' I demanded, jealousy, however un-justified, scorching my throat and burning like a flame in my chest.

'He came once to supper. Margaret brought

him,' my wife replied with quiet dignity. 'I could hardly turn him away. It would have been an insult to her as well as to him. I knew you wouldn't like it, Roger, but I had no choice.'

Of course she didn't; the laws of hospitality would have been breached. But I wasn't prepared, for the moment, to be understanding. My own conscience was riding me too hard.

'And you talked about me!' I sneered.

'Amongst other things.' Guilt was making Adela keep a tight rein on her temper, I could see. 'I'm afraid,' she went on, 'that Margaret revealed the reason for you being away from home. She told him all about the work you're undertaking for Mayor Foster, and also the fact that His Worship is paying you for your pains. I...I fancied that Richard was not well pleased, and muttered something I didn't quite catch about encroaching ways. But his annoyance was directed at John Foster, not at you. He feels, I think, that his territory has been invaded. Unexplained deaths are his preserve, and he should be left to continue with his enquiries without other people butting in.' Adela sighed. 'I wish I hadn't mentioned it. I can see that I've angered you, and as a consequence, you'll be awake half the night with bile and wind.'

This picture of myself – uncomplimentary though it might be, but true nonetheless – forced a sudden crack of laughter from me that put my ill humour to flight. I was still angry that Richard Manifold had been made a party to my business, but for once I could appreciate his point of view, and had to admit that none of it was Adela's fault. Besides, what right had I to be angry with her about anything, with my own sin hanging like a millstone round my neck?

The candle finally guttered and went out, leaving the usual smell of smoke and melting tallow lingering on the air. So we went to bed. I knew that Adela was waiting for me to make love to her after a week apart, but I pleaded tiredness and pretended to fall asleep almost at once. But in reality, it was a long time before I slept, the face of Juliette Gerrish and the memory of her perfume interposing themselves between me and my slumbers. I knew that tomorrow I must go and be absolved of my sin before I could touch Adela again, as I longed to do. She deserved a better husband than me, I scolded myself; and drowning in a tide of self-reproach, I even went so far as to wonder if she would not have done better to marry Sergeant Manifold. Self-immolation could go no further, however, and under this penitential weight my eyes finally closed. And the next thing I knew, it was morning.

My mood didn't change with the coming of day, and when I woke to find Adela curled into my side, in the same way she so often did, I put my arm around her and gently kissed her. She opened her eyes so quickly that I realized she was probably already awake, and I was suddenly afraid that her expectations would echo those of the previous evening. But she shook herself free of the lingering remnants of sleep and raised herself on one elbow, looking down into my face.

'I've been thinking, sweetheart,' she said, 'that, as I told you yesterday, you must tell somebody about Hambrook Manor. If you won't confide in Richard, go to Mayor Foster and find out what he has to say to your story.'

I shook my head. 'He has too many civic duties to attend to at present. Deep down, he might be convinced, because he trusts me, but he won't really want to know. He won't wish to offend Lady Claypole any more than any other dignitary in the city would. Believe me, it will be wisest to keep a still tongue in my head for the present.'

Adela made no reply, merely asking when I would be setting out for Bath and if I would be taking Hercules with me.

'Tomorrow,' I said, giving her another kiss which, I hoped, held a world of promise in its meaning. 'Today I must patch my boots, fill the water barrel and fetch more kindling for you from the Frome Backs. In short, I mean to be a model husband, if only for a while.'

That made her laugh. 'I shall believe it when it happens,' she said, scrambling out of bed. But then her laughter faded and she stood staring at me, looking worried.

'How will you set about discovering this man in Bath?' she asked. 'Even supposing he's still alive, still lives there, you have nothing whatever to go on this time.'

I nodded. 'I realize that, my love. "Caspar" is going to be a far greater problem than "Melchior". Even the initials R.M. are of no use to me now. Robert Moresby proved to be the owner of those. And then of course there's "Balthazar". Who was – or is – he?'

My wife threw a pillow at my head.

'I can't keep up with all these names,' she protested, holding up a hand. 'Pray don't bother trying to explain.'

She stripped off her night rail before dropping her undershift over her head and I felt a sudden urge to possess her there and then. But I controlled myself. I must expiate my sin first. Consequently, as soon as I had finished breakfast, before the streets had really sprung to life, I made my way to Saint Giles and purged my troubled conscience with confession. I can't remember what penance I received, except that it was nothing severe; not as severe as I felt that I deserved. (There was a general slackness in the behaviour of churchmen at that time, as I recall: many of the priesthood themselves were probably fornicating daily.) At any rate, I emerged into the April sunshine feeling vaguely dissatisfied, as though I still owed Adela something, and recollected her desire that I speak to John Foster concerning the tilting bed at Hambrook Manor. So I returned to Small Street and, a few minutes later, was knocking on the door of his house.

The same maid admitted me, but seemed put out by the earliness of the hour. His Worship the Mayor, she informed me, was still abed, and enquired if the reason for my visit made it worthwhile to disturb him. I admitted that it didn't, but just as she was about to show me politely out again, John Foster, with a much rubbed blue velvet robe cast hurriedly over his nightshift, and worn leather slippers on his feet, descended the stairs.

'I thought I recognized your voice, Master Chapman. What have you to tell me? Oh, don't stand here in the hall, man! There's a draught from that street door that I shall have to fix one day, when I have the time. Come into the parlour.' And he led the way, deaf to my muttered protestations that really it was nothing that couldn't wait. 'Sit down. Sit down,' he urged, but remained standing himself. 'Now, have you discovered that poor girl's murderer yet?'

'I–I'm afraid not,' I stammered. 'Not that I've been wasting my time,' I added swiftly. 'Indeed, only yesterday I returned from a journey to Gloucester.' I saw the disappointment in his eyes and hastened to tell him of Robert Moresby and why I felt convinced of that gentleman's innocence.

'You've checked his story with this Sir Peter and Lady Claypole?' the Mayor asked, a trifle brusquely I thought.

But it gave me the opening I needed to recount the details of my sojourn at Hambrook Manor, including my precipitate departure after nearly being smothered alive in the tilting bed.

John Foster frowned. 'I've heard of such things, of course, but they're unlawful. There are severe penalities for possessing one.' The frown deepened. 'You're certain you didn't imagine this, Master Chapman? You didn't dream it?'

His scepticism was no more than I had expected, but it annoyed me just the same.

223

'No,' I answered shortly. And left it at that.

This curt reply appeared to impress him far more than a protracted and indignant denial would have done. He regarded me closely for a moment or two, then sighed deeply and at last sat down opposite me, on the other side of the empty hearth.

'This allegation of yours should be investigated, it goes without saying. A statement must be taken from you by a notary public before anything else can be done, and then any enquiries should be undertaken with the utmost caution and tact. If your allegations prove to be untrue... All right, Master Chapman, I'm not accusing you of lying, but people, as we well know, are crafty at concealing things they don't want to be found. Moreover, even if the mechanism for the bed were to be discovered – revealed by Lady Claypole herself – how could we prove that you had been an intended victim? It would be your word against hers. No, no! This needs very careful consideration. I can do nothing in a hurry. And I am hard pressed with civic duties just at present.' He shot me a harassed glance. 'There is more trouble with the Hanseatic towns. The city merchants have just raised their bid for stockfish to the Icelandic fishermen, but only yesterday we were informed that members of the League have almost doubled their offer per barrel. The Council is meeting in emergency session with the Fishmongers' Guild this very morning and I am afraid we are in for a stormy session. And I very much fear that when I finally make known my intention to build a chapel dedicated to the Three Kings of Cologne, I'm likely to meet fierce opposition. However,' he continued, squaring his shoulders, 'I intend to carry my point. I admire the Rhinelanders and, above all, I love Cologne and its cathedral. I do not intend to be deterred. But if I can offer people a solution to this murder which has so disturbed them, well...!' He let the sentence hang, giving an eloquent shrug of his shoulders.

'I should hardly think you need worry about your almshouses and chapel yet awhile, Your Worship,' I remarked acidly. 'If the masons work at the same pace as the workmen clearing the ground, you'll be fortunate to see them built in your lifetime.'

John Foster gave a crack of laughter and the worry lines disappeared momentarily from his face.

'I hope for better speed than that, Roger. I'm not so old as you pretend to think me. And in their defence, I must protest that our English workmen may be slow, but they are thorough. I learned early on in life that my fellow country-men cannot be hurried, but if left alone and not hassled, they will do their best. In the meantime, I cannot conceal my intentions from our good citizens; and the longer they have to reconcile themselves to the notion of a tribute to Cologne, the more they will accept it. And now I must go and get dressed. I have a long and strenuous day ahead of me. But don't think that I shall forget what you have told me about Hambrook Manor. I shall mull the problem over carefully. And what, if I shall give no offence by asking, is your

225

next destination?'

'Bath,' I said. 'I am hoping against hope that someone may still be living there who might be able to shed some further light on the final hours of Mistress Linkinhorne.'

He nodded and rose to his feet, offering me his hand. I also got to my feet and clasped it warmly. John Foster was one of the few people I knew who regarded all their fellow men as equally deserving of respect and courtesy.

'Are you in need of more money?' he asked, glancing towards the little chest with its carving of acanthus leaves, standing on top of the larger one.

I attempted to reassure him, but, the idea having once entered his head, he insisted on sending the young maid upstairs for the key, then unlocking it and filling another small leather bag with coins.

'I wouldn't have you think me ungrateful for all your pains,' he said, pressing it into my reluctant hand and dismissing my stuttered thanks with a wave of his own. 'Go to Bath and when you return, come to see me again.'

I returned home to find Margaret Walker installed in the kitchen on one of her all too frequent visits. But what could I say? She kept Adela company during my absences.

'You're off again then, I hear,' was her first remark as I entered, knocking my head, as I often did, on the bunches of dried herbs and vegetables hanging from the ceiling. A few scraps of onion skin floated, like autumn leaves,

226

to the floor.

'Off again,' shouted Adam from the shelter of his mother's lap. 'Always off again!'

My wife told him to be quiet but was unable to prevent the trembling of her upper lip, and burst into peals of laughter when I grinned. My former mother-in-law got up, adjusting her cap and reaching down her cloak from a peg on the wall. She delivered a short but pithy homily to us both on the correct way to bring up children and was about to take herself off when I stopped her.

'Is Jack Nym back from Stowe yet, do you know?'

'I haven't seen him. Why do you ask?'

'He might just have managed to recollect something that he was trying to remember for me, that's all.'

She was intrigued, but when I refused to part with any further information, took herself home to Redcliffe in a huff.

'You shouldn't upset her,' my wife reproached me, but smiled nevertheless. 'I really don't know how I'd do without her when you're away.' She grew serious. 'Margaret says someone told her that you were seen coming out of Saint Giles earlier this morning. It's not like you, Roger, to be so diligent in your devotions. Was there a special reason?'

Oh, wonderful! Thank you very much, God! There would just happen to be someone who knew someone who was a friend of Margaret Walker loitering near Saint Giles as I was leaving. Mind you, there was no reason why a man shouldn't feel the urge to go to church now and then without being suspected of ulterior motives. But I could see at once that Adela was suspicious.

'I went to confession,' I answered lightly. 'What's for dinner?'

'Oyster stew,' was the terse response. 'It's Friday.' A pause, and then, 'Was there anything in particular you needed to confess?'

Now was the moment to make a clean breast of things; to clear my conscience once and for all; to grovel abjectly and be forgiven. But somehow or another I failed to grasp the opportunity: the hour did not seem propitious.

'It's just that I haven't been for some while and I thought it time. That's all.' But I found it impossible to meet her eyes, and as we sat down to table – Elizabeth and Nicholas having been summoned from whatever game they were playing in their upstairs fastness – Adela's air of suspicion was palpable. I carefully assumed a mask of innocence, realizing as I did so that deception becomes easier the more it's practised. I began talking about my next day's journey to Bath.

The hours until supper were occupied as I had foreseen. I patched my boots (one of the soles had worn right through), paid several visits to the well to fill our water barrel and used Adam's little push-cart to get wood from the city stockpile near the bottom of Steep Street. On the last occasion, I walked up to see how the work was progressing on the clearing of the graveyard and discovered that it was now at least three quarters free of large stones and tangled briars.

Neither Hob Jarrett nor the man called Colin were in evidence, only the tall fellow, leaning on his spade and regarding the site with a lugubrious air.

'Hob not here?' I called.

'Bad back,' was the terse reply.

I grunted and turned away, not even bothering to enquire after Colin. Had I done so, no doubt I should have received the same answer.

I devoted myself to Adela for the remainder of the day, but not too obviously or her already simmering suspicion would have boiled over. As it was, I insinuated myself further into her good graces by suggesting that I wait until Monday before setting out for Bath as I would probably only reach as far as Keynsham by the end of the following day and would not wish to travel on the Sabbath. So we had three nights together instead of one, and although the Church forbade love-making within a certain period either side of going to Mass, I managed to persuade her, although much against the workings of her conscience, that what the eye couldn't see, the heart couldn't grieve over. Consequently, when I said my goodbyes on Monday, after breakfast, there was a spring in my step and a sparkle in my eye that hadn't been there for some time, and the name of Juliette Gerrish had (almost) been erased from my memory.

Fourteen

I left by the Redcliffe Gate and took the opportunity to call on Jack Nym as I was passing. His evil-smelling little dwelling was in Saint Thomas's Lane, close to the church, stinking, as it always did, of burned food, mouse droppings, unemptied chamber pots and stale, unwashed clothes. His slatternly wife was standing in the doorway, watching with dull eyes while Jack loaded his cart with bales of cloth from Master Adelard's weaving sheds.

'You're up and away early, friend Roger,' he grunted, stooping to heave another roll of some dark green stuff from the cobbles, where its edge was beginning to muddy on account of the shower of rain that had fallen overnight, mixing with the dust and grime of the road.

'I'm off to Bath,' I said, nodding briefly in Mistress Nym's direction, receiving nothing but a blank stare in return. No doubt she would recollect who I was in her own good time. 'There's no chance, I suppose, that you might be going that way?'

Jack shook his head. 'I'm off up to Tewkesbury. Pity, but there it is. I could have done with some company again. Not got the dog with you today?'

'Just my satchel and my cudgel, as you see. I thought the poor fellow needed a rest.' I patted the horse's nose as he stood patiently between the shafts. 'What I want to know, Jack, is if you've had any further ideas about who it might have been with Isabella Linkinhorne that day you saw her in the porch of All Saints'.'

Jack heaved the last bolt of cloth on to the cart and rubbed his nose.

'To be truthful,' he admitted, 'I haven't given it another thought. I'd forget about it, Roger. After twenty years, I don't suppose I'm likely to remember now.'

'You said—'

'I know what I said. But I were half asleep at the time. Must've been dreaming.'

'Nonsense! You were wide awake. Well, awake enough.'

'Look, it ain't come back to me. All right? What I've said all along was c'rrect. I didn't see the man she was with. Just leave it, eh? It's too long ago. Raking over cold ashes never does no one any good.' He climbed on the cart and took the reins, blowing a perfunctory kiss to his wife from what seemed a safe distance. I didn't blame him. My guess was that Goody Nym smelled as bad as her house.

I watched Jack drive off in the direction of Bristol Bridge and the Frome Gate before pursuing my own course to the Redcliffe Gate where I was caught up in the flow of incoming early morning traffic as animals, cartloads of vegetables, sea coal, butter and milk churns flooded into the city at the start of yet another week, the

231

drivers, without exception, swearing at the tolls they had to pay and holding up the outgoers like myself until we were all cursing one another roundly. Eventually, however, I was through the gate and heading eastwards, towards Keynsham.

The April morning was hazy, giving the promise of warmth later in the day. Distant hills floated like clouds against a pale blue sky and daisies (the day's eyes) were already opening to the sun. Other travellers gave me a 'Good day!' or a 'God be with you!' as they passed, but although I answered cheerily my mind was elsewhere, partly on the difficulties that lay in store for me once I reached my destination, but also on Jack Nym.

Looking back on our conversation, it struck me more forcibly with every step I took that Jack had been evasive. At the time, it had seemed no more than the natural irritation of a man interrupted in his work and no doubt suffering pangs of indigestion after one of Mistress Nym's breakfasts. But a period of quiet reflection brought the growing conviction that he had thought about the matter and had come to some sort of conclusion about the face he had seen in the crowd; the face that had jolted that memory of twenty years ago. But if that were so, why then was Jack so reluctant to reveal the name of the person to whom the face belonged? It could be, of course, that he had simply decided he had made a mistake; that this person could have had nothing to do with Isabella Linkinhorne and it had been merely a coincidence that he had begun to think about her shortly after noticing him. On the other hand, it might be that he had reason to fear this man – yet who that could be and why, I had no idea. Jack, independent and responsible to no one as his master, was unafraid of anyone as far as I was aware. Although I supposed there were secrets in everyone's life.

These unsatisfactory musings lasted some miles and it was past ten o'clock and dinnertime when I passed the manor house at Keynsham and knocked on a cottage door to ask for sustenance.

'I can pay,' I said hastily, chinking the coins in my purse.

The goodwife, who looked as if she had been about to direct me to the abbey and the charity of its kitchens, suddenly beamed and invited me inside. In no time, she had produced bread, broth and small beer and was pressing me to a second helping of each. As her portions were generous, I declined, but asked her if she had any knowledge of Bath and its inhabitants.

'Dear life, no,' was the amazed reply. 'It's all of seven miles from here. I did go to Bristol once, when I were a girl, for the Saint James's fair. Great big place. Took my breath away, it did.'

I thanked her, paid what she asked for the victuals and set out again in the hope that I might, with a little expedition, accomplish my journey in one day instead of two. I had covered the five or so miles to Keynsham in better time than I had expected, having set out at the crack of dawn. I was used to peddling my wares as I went and journeys generally took me much

233

longer, so I had miscalculated the length of time necessary to reach Bath. I suddenly realized that there was indeed a possibility of getting there before the gates were closed against me at dusk if I continued at the same brisk pace.

But what exactly was I going to do when I got to the city? How was I going to set about looking for a man of whom I knew nothing – not his name, nor his occupation, nor his initials? I didn't even know that he still lived there, nor if Jane Purefoy's information were correct. In the end, I decided that there was nothing for it but to complete my journey, find a comfortable alehouse or inn somewhere and then wait to see what happened.

'If Your hand is in this, God,' I said, addressing the sky, having first made certain that there was no one in the immediate vicinity to hear me, 'You'll need to give me a bit of help. I don't think I'm capable of doing this on my own.'

There was no reply. As I have said more than once before, there never was.

I decided to follow the course of the River Avon as it meandered on its way between the thickly wooded hills that rose on either side of it. Local lore said that the valley floor had once been dotted with Roman villas as the population of the settlement at Aquae Sulis had spread beyond the city boundaries. But any trace of these opulent homes had long gone, erased for ever by the tramp of Saxon hordes as they claimed these western lands for their own and drove the Celtic tribes, abandoned by their Roman protectors, ever further west into the fastnesses of Wales.

With the sun now almost directly overhead, the day was fulfilling its early promise of warmth and my brisk pace was starting to flag. Once or twice, I was forced to sit down in order to rest my aching legs and to scoop handfuls of water from the river to quench my thirst. By following the river bank I had left the main track to Bristol and consequently found myself alone in the landscape except for a lone figure on the far horizon behind me, plodding along at a steady rate, but too far away to catch up with me. It did cross my mind that I might wait, for my own company was, for once, beginning to pall, but I was a long way ahead and if I was to stand any chance at all of reaching Bath before dusk, I had to press on.

But even my stamina eventually gave out. Twelve, maybe thirteen, miles in a single day proved too much for the fittest body without the rest and ease normally provided by cottage and farm or manor house kitchens and their attendant offers of refreshment. My third stop along the river bank resulted in my falling sound asleep in the lee of some rising ground and not waking up again for several hours.

I knew I must have slept for a long time because the sun, which had been just past its zenith when I closed my eyes, was now sinking slowly westwards, its rays beginning to strike the distant treetops, tipping them with gold. I woke with a start and a snort and a feeling of chill in my bones that set me shivering. The heat of midday had evaporated leaving a freshness in

235

the air to remind me that April could be a treacherous month, pretending to be summer one hour, but then reverting to a cold and bitter spring the next.

'You been asleep a fair long time, Chapman,' remarked a voice close to my left ear. 'I thought you was never goin' to wake up.'

I jumped, my heart pounding, and slewed round, at the same time reaching for my cudgel which lay on the ground beside me. A most unwelcome sight met my eyes.

'Jack Gload?' I must have looked as incredulous as I sounded. 'What in heaven's name are you doing here?'

Richard Manifold's henchman did his best to appear offended, but only succeeded in looking vacant, as usual.

'Why shouldn't I be here? I've got as much right as a pedlar to walk anywhere I choose.'

'I never reckoned you or Pete –' Peter Littleman was his fellow lawman and best friend – 'cared for the countryside.'

He considered this with a slight frown creasing his brow, not quite sure of my meaning.

'Goin' t' see my daughter,' he announced after a momentary silence. 'She lives in Bath.'

I made no effort to conceal my surprise.

'I didn't know you had a daughter, Jack. I didn't even know you were married.'

'I ain't. Not any more. Not for a long time, come to that. My goody died when Cecily were born. She's married now – Cecily, I mean – to a baker. He has a stall not far from the North Gate. Don' know why she couldn't have married a decent Bristol man,' he grumbled. 'Plenty of 'em. 'Stead, she has to go off to Bath to live. No thought for me, left all on me ownsome. But that's children for you, as you'll find out afore you're much older, I daresay.'

I thought that if I'd been Cecily Gload I too would have seized the chance to escape and put twelve miles between myself and Jack. If she was a person of any spirit, the idea of spending the rest of her life with her father must have been daunting in the extreme.

Jack went on, 'I been following you, but you was too far ahead for me to catch up. Good job you fell asleep when you did, and for as long as you did. I'd never have been able to overtake you otherwise.'

I wished I could share his enthusiasm and began to cast about in my mind for ways to shake him off. His next words sent my heart plummeting. 'We can go the rest of the journey together.'

'We won't make it into the city tonight,' I said. 'It will be sunset soon and the gates will be closed. I'd guess we have another two or more hours' walking.'

'More like three,' he answered cheerfully. 'But the North Gate – where my daughter lives, like I told you – has a little gate for people on foot alongside it. That door's not always locked for a few hours after sundown. Lots of folk use it for getting in and out o' the city after dark. Or if 'tis locked by any chance, there's one or two places where the walls are broken down and ain't been mended for a while. There are gaps in the stonework easy to get through, same as at home.'

Probably the same as every other city in the land, I reflected. Unlike our less fortunate neighbours across the Channel, long centuries free from the threat of invasion had made city authorities everywhere more than a little slack when it came to keeping up their towns' defences. It seemed a waste of good money that could profitably be spent on other things (preferably the Mayor and Council).

'I don't fancy walking in the dark unless it's necessary,' I cavilled. 'There's sure to be somewhere – a barn or cottage or even a dry ditch beneath a hedge – where I can lie up for the night.'

'Never thought of you as a coward, Chapman,' Jack Gload scoffed. 'Big fellow like you ain't afraid o' the dark, are you?'

'Not at all,' I retorted, nettled, then heaved a quiet sigh as I accepted that there was no way to shake off my unwanted companion without sacrificing my reputation. I made one last throw of the dice. 'But perhaps your daughter and her husband won't want a stranger, as well as yourself, cluttering up their house.'

The lawman guffawed. 'They won't care. They got four children, two cats and a dog, so they'm pretty crowded already. Two more – even two more as big as us – ain't goin' to make no difference. There's plenty o' room in the bakehouse and it's warm by the ovens.'

My heart sank at the prospect before me, but I could see no way of refusing Jack's invitation, only stipulating that if either his daughter or son-in-law made the slightest demur about housing me, I was to be allowed to depart in search of other lodgings without any rub thrown in my way by him. Reluctantly he agreed, and it crossed my mind to wonder why Jack Gload of all people was suddenly so anxious for my company. We had never been friends and, at times, had been positive enemies. And I must surely have offended him on many occasions by my lack of respect for both himself and his office. However, he seemed determined at present to stand my friend, and I could only hope that I might find a means of escape before we reached Bath.

But luck was not on my side. After what seemed an interminable walk in the steadily gathering gloom, which deepened into a profound darkness before a half-moon rose to light our pathway, the walls of Bath, twenty feet or so high in places, crumbling in others, rose up before us. We had left the river bank some time earlier and now skirted the walls and the West Gate until we came to the north of the city, where, as my companion had told me, there was a small arched portal set alongside the main gate, the latter by then being locked and barred. And he was correct, too, when he had said that this postern might still be open, although we were not a moment too soon. As we pushed our way through, the night porter was approaching from the opposite direction with his bunch of keys.

He greeted the pair of us with a nod and a grunt and the remark that Jack's youngest grandchild was giving his lungs an airing.

'Heard him,' he said, 'as I passed the bake-house not two minutes since. Fact, you could hear 'im right down the bottom of the market-place.'

'Ay, he's a grand little fellow,' Jack replied proudly.

My heart sank even further, but by the time we had gone a little way down the high street, peace reigned in the two-storey house next to the baker's shop (now boarded up for the night) and bakehouse with its funnelled chimney.

Mistress Cecily Baker was a surprisingly handsome young woman of perhaps some twenty summers, short and a little on the plump side, but with thickly lashed brown eyes, a sweet, full mouth and a neat, straight nose. I realized at once that she must favour her mother, for she was nothing like Jack. Her husband, Thomas, was as tall as she was short, a thin streak of a man with untidy brown hair, blue eyes and the white, floury complexion of all men of his calling. I soon learned that he spoke seldom but when he did, it was to state his opinions with all the dogmatic forcefulness of the totally uninformed.

My hope of being denied their hospitality was doomed to disappointment. Nothing could have exceeded my hostess's pleasure at seeing me, and as she obviously ruled the roost, her hus-band extended an equally warm welcome to both his father-in-law and myself. The dog was inclined to take exception to the presence of strangers, but once he had sniffed Hercules's

240

scent on my clothes, he seemed to accept me as a friend. The cats, of course, ignored us, as cats the world over do, and continued pursuing their quest for mice and rats, pouncing at every rustle in the straw covering the kitchen floor.

The baby, a fat, red-faced infant of, I guessed, about six months, was breathing wheezily in his cradle which had been brought downstairs and placed next to the hearth, and which Cecily was rocking with her foot. Of the other three children there was no sign, although, now and then, a thump from the upper floor and a quickly suppressed shout of laughter indicated that they might be in bed, but were not yet asleep.

Jack Gload introduced me as his friend from Bristol (a description I secretly took great exception to) and as such I was given the best seat in the room – a simple armchair which I suspected really belonged to the master of the house – and offered two helpings of everything when Jack and I eventually sat down to a very belated supper. Thomas then took himself off to the bakehouse to set the dough to rise for the next day's bread, while his wife ushered her father and myself into a snug back parlour where she joined us after she had cleared away our dirty dishes. Jack was instructed to fetch in the cradle, the children upstairs were shouted at and threatened with dire consequences if they did not immediately go to sleep, and then father and daughter settled down for a cosy gossip to catch up on family news. I naturally could take no part in this and soon found myself nodding off, drifting in and out of a dream in which I found myself standing on the edge of the great gorge in Bristol, overlooking Saint Vincent's rocks, and arguing with the hermit about something or another. Unfortunately, although I recognized myself as the taller of the two men, I was also detached from him and unable to hear a word of the conversation. I shouted at myself to speak up – and woke with a cry on my lips that made my two companions start.

'You been dreaming, Chapman, and no mistake,' Jack Gload said, grinning, while his daughter looked at me reproachfully as the noise had disturbed the baby, who was beginning to grizzle, flailing his little arms which he had tugged free of his blanket. Fortunately some vigorous rocking from his mother soon quietened him again, and I pulled myself up straight on the narrow window seat on which I was sitting, shaking my head to clear it of the cobwebs of sleep.

'S'pose you wake yourself up by telling us what you're doing in Bath,' Jack continued, the grin becoming slightly more malevolent. 'It's got something to do with that there old murder, hasn't it? That body that was turned up in the nuns' graveyard.'

Dame Cecily immediately clamoured to know what her father meant by this, and to be told the full story, so I was spared the necessity of replying for the moment. Jack at once puffed out his chest and in his capacity as one of (in his opinion) Bristol's most important law enforcers told what he knew – which, I was relieved to discover, was no more than, if as much as, I knew myself. I should have hated to think that Dick Manifold was as diligent or as clever as Roger Chapman. On the other hand, honesty compelled me to admit that so far I had found out very little.

'And you, sir,' my hostess enquired, turning to smile at me. 'Do you also work with my father and the Sergeant?'

'No, 'e don't!' guffawed Jack. ''E's nothing but a common pedlar!'

Cecily Baker coloured uncomfortably and glanced askance at her parent, obviously distancing herself from his boorish manners.

'But you do have some interest in the matter, Master Chapman?' she urged.

So, reluctantly, I divulged my part in the enquiry and, battered into submission by a volley of questions from father and daughter, Mayor Foster's interest in the affair, plus a little of what I had discovered and the reason for my visit to Bath.

'Although,' I finished lamely, uneasily aware that I had perhaps said even more than I had intended to, 'I expect very little success here. "Caspar" has no name, no face, no identification of any sort. Even the descriptions I have for the remaining two of Isabella Linkinhorne's swains could apply to hundreds of men. Furthermore, I have no proof that "Caspar" is living or dead, nor whether, if the former, he is still here in Bath.'

I could tell by Jack's puzzled expression that he was having great trouble following the bit about the Three Kings of Cologne and was unable to understand my reason for giving the three – now two – unknown men these out-landish names.

'It helps Master Chapman to identify them in his own mind, Father,' Cecily explained kindly in the same indulgent tone she might have used to one of her children. 'Don't tease yourself about it,' she added, patting his arm. (She had to take after her mother for intelligence, as well as looks. How on earth, I wondered, had Jack Gload managed to attract such a paragon?) My hostess turned back to me. 'I fear you have very little hope of success, Master Chapman. Indeed, I'd go so far as to say none at all.'

During the past ten minutes or so, her husband had returned from the bakery and joined us in the parlour, settling himself alongside me on the window seat, sitting down with a thump that sent a fine cloud of floury dust up into the air where the motes whirled around in the candlelight like a miniature snowstorm.

'Shouldn't be encouraging the League,' he announced, fastening on to the one point he had really understood. 'All this talk of Cologne. Trade with the Rhineland should be outlawed. The King and Council should see to it.'

'Yes, my love,' his wife agreed pacifically. No doubt her early years with her father had equip-ped her for dealing with men of limited intellect without losing her temper. 'But we weren't really discussing the Hanse towns. Master Chap-man here has a problem.' She smiled faintly. 'He's looking for someone he knows nothing about.'

'Nonsense! He must know something. He wouldn't be such a fool as to come searching for a man of whom he knows nothing.'

'Always thought you was an idiot, Chapman,' Jack remarked conversationally. 'Now I'm sure of it.'

I ignored this jibe, addressing myself to Dame Cecily.

'The only course open to me, as far as I can see, is to make enquiries around the town for anyone who knew Isabella Linkinhorne in his youth. As this is likely to take me some days – and even then, I doubt I'll have much success – is there a clean, but cheap hostelry you can recommend, Mistress? Somewhere where the food's good and the fleas don't bite too much.'

She laughed. 'There are one or two. But you'll spend tonight with us. We keep a spare mattress for my father in the little room under the eaves. He won't mind if you share that with him.'

'Shan't mind at all,' Jack agreed. 'I snore and fart a bit, Chapman, but then I believe you do, too.' He grinned more malevolently than ever. 'At least, you do according to Sergeant Manifold.'

His meaning was clear. Dick Manifold had got the information from Adela and shared the information with his two henchmen. I could feel my temper rising and had to clench my hands in my lap to stop myself from hitting Jack.

Dame Cecily, although ignorant of the cause, was immediately conscious of the rising tension between us, and hurriedly turned the conversation by asking her husband, 'Is the list of deliveries ready for the boy in the morning? Our apprentice,' she explained for my benefit, 'lives nearby and goes home to sleep at nights with his widowed mother. But he's here at daybreak and needs to know which homes to take bread to before Thomas opens the stall. Some people are too old or crippled to come themselves.'

'Or too lazy,' her spouse supplemented. 'Or think they're too important to make one of a crowd.' He snorted indignantly, adding a trifle obscurely, 'Just because his sister married above her station.'

'Who's that, then?' Jack demanded.

The baby woke up and started to cry again. Cecily lifted the child out of the cradle, loosened her gown and put it to her breast. The noises from upstairs had long since died away.

'Ralph Mynott,' she said in answer to her father's question. 'Lives opposite the monks' burial ground, over towards the East Gate.'

'Who'd his sister marry then, that he thinks himself too good to come to the stall?' Jack persisted.

'Oh, some baronet or another,' his son-in-law snorted. 'No one of any great note. A Sir Peter Somebody-or-other. No one from around here. I fancy they live somewhere northwards of Bristol.'

I had been listening with only half an ear, brooding on what Jack Gload had hinted at a little while before, knowing full well that it had been nothing more than malice on his part, yet feeling a great surge of anger with Adela for discussing me with Richard Manifold and laying

246

me open to his ridicule. But suddenly, all that was temporarily forgotten. It was as though a bright light had penetrated the dim corners of my mind.

'This Sir Peter,' I said, a trifle breathlessly. 'He wouldn't happen by any chance to be called Claypole, would he? Sir Peter Claypole?'

'That's it,' Thomas Baker confirmed. 'That's the name. Although I fancy someone told me that he'd died some time ago.'

'Ten years,' I said. 'And you say this Ralph Mynott is Lady Claypole's brother?'

The baker nodded, asking austerely, 'And how do you come to know her ladyship, Chapman?' as though a pedlar had no right to be on speaking terms with a member of the nobility, however minor.

But I didn't answer him. I was too busy sending up a silent prayer of thanks to God. He hadn't, after all, failed me. I had found 'Caspar', I was convinced of it.

Everything suddenly began to fall into place.

Fifteen

This man, this Ralph Mynott, was brother to Lady Claypole and would no doubt have visited both her and Sir Peter at Hambrook Manor on many occasions in the past. Twenty years ago, he might well have encountered their visitor and friend, Robert Moresby of Gloucester, and, through the latter, met Isabella Linkinhorne. He had been struck by her beauty, she liked him and was by no means predisposed to attach herself to just one man. So somehow, unbeknownst to Robert, they had arranged to meet when he was not by, Westbury being just as convenient a place for their rendezvous as it was for him and Isabella. Oh, yes, the more I thought about it, the more I was convinced that I had – with a little help from the Almighty, of course – found my 'Caspar'.

'Oi! Chapman! Thomas is talking to you.'

Jack Gload's voice interrupted my musings and made me jump.

'I beg your pardon, Master Baker,' I apologized. 'You were saying?'

He repeated the question I had only half-heard, and out of politeness I was forced to explain my dealings with Lady Claypole the week before. Fortunately, this seemed to satisfy my host, once he had established that I was not a friend of her ladyship but merely the instrument of someone else's bidding (and that person being His Worship, the Mayor of Bristol). I could tell that he was somewhat confused by my tale, having missed the greater part of it while working in the bakehouse. Nor was he really much interested, and was soon holding forth again on the trials of being a baker with a growing family to feed, until he suddenly decided that the candles had burned low enough in their holders and that it was time for bed.

Jack conducted me outside to a small lean-to privy at the back of the house and then, when we had relieved ourselves, lit the way by the flame of a flickering rushlight up the narrow, twisting staircase to the tiny garret room under the eaves, where a mattress, furnished with blanket and pillows, occupied nearly all of the available floor space. Here, I stripped off my outer clothing only, not caring to sleep naked with Jack Gload, but I need not have worried. Jack himself fell into bed just as he was, not even bothering to remove his boots. I edged away from him as far as possible.

I had expected, after my day's exertions, to fall asleep almost at once, but excitement at having found 'Caspar' would probably have kept me in a state of wakefulness even if Jack had not suddenly felt the need to talk.

''E's not pleased with you, you know, Chapman. Not at all pleased. 'E feels you're treading on his toes.'

'Who?' I demanded peevishly, although I

could guess the answer without being told.

'Sergeant Manifold, o' course. 'E don't like you being hand in glove with Mayor Foster. Says it undermines 'is standing in the city. Makes 'im look a fool, like he's not able to find this Isabella's murderer on 'is own account. Don't know why you've been dragged into it in the first place.'

'I should have thought he'd have been glad of a little help,' I snapped, rolling on to my back and staring up at the low ceiling a foot or so above my head. It seemed to be pressing down upon us like the ceilings of those torture chambers one hears about (and hopes never to encounter). 'It's not easy trying to find a killer after a lapse of twenty years.'

'You don't seem to be doing so bad,' Jack Gload pointed out. 'Not if all you says is true.' He managed to force a little scepticism into his tone. 'But you don't share what you've found out with the Sergeant, do you? Tha's what 'e don't like.'

'He's never jibbed before when I've been making enquiries into other matters,' I objected, frowning into the darkness. 'Why should he take umbrage this time?'

'Dunno, but 'e 'as. Daresay it's to do with Alderman Foster takin' an interest. Now 'e's the Mayor – Foster, I mean – Sergeant Manifold feels it more. I tell you what, Chapman, I'd back off if I were you. Tell His Worship you ain't able to go on working for 'im. The Sergeant could be a powerful enemy if 'e put 'is mind to it.'

'I'm not afraid of Dick Manifold,' I snorted

crossly. 'He's too fond of getting his great feet under my table for me to have anything to fear from him. Too fond of my wife, as well,' I added darkly. 'He won't risk upsetting Adela.' A sudden suspicion crossed my mind. 'He didn't put you up to this, did he?'

'Up to what?' Jack sounded defensive.

'Coming to see your daughter because he'd found out that I was coming to Bath?'

'Course not!' The denial was unconvincing.

'He did, didn't he?' I persisted. 'It's not a big place, and even if you hadn't fallen in with me on the road, you could easily have sought me out. With a valid reason for coming here, Sergeant Manifold sent you to warn me off.'

'You'm talkin' moonshine.' Jack turned over and humped his back towards me, indicating that our conversation was at an end. Then he decided on one last warning.

'I could see the way your mind was working downstairs. This Ralph Mynott's name means summat to you. But I'd forget it, whatever it is. You go straight home tomorrow morning and tell Mayor Foster you don' want no more to do with this murder. You leave it to Sergeant Manifold and me.'

The 'and me' really made me laugh, but fortunately my companion was too sleepy by this time to take offence – I doubt if he even heard me – and was snoring, with a distressing whistling accompaniment, almost immediately. I rolled once more on to my side, facing away from him, and by burying one ear in the pillow and pulling the blanket well over the other, I was able to fall asleep far quicker than I had expected with that din filling the tiny room.

It was daylight when I opened my eyes again, and a thin, watery sun was just managing to rim the shutters of the window under the eaves. Jack's snoring had stopped and he was lying sprawled on his back, dribbling profusely from an open mouth, one booted leg and foot free of the blanket, most of which he had dragged off me during the night and now lay in a tangled heap at the foot of the mattress. It was no wonder, I reflected, that I was feeling cold. Annoyed, I scrambled to my feet and flung the shutters wide, letting the chill early morning air stream in on my bedfellow in the vindictive hope that it might rouse him. But he was still slumbering peacefully when, having hastily pulled on my clothes, I descended the stairs to the kitchen.

This seemed to be full of children and animals, three of the former – two boys and a girl – chasing one another round the table and screeching with laughter while their mother, ignoring their antics with practised ease, spooned hot oatmeal into a row of wooden bowls. One of the cats was sharing the baby's cradle while the other was eating, together with the dog, from a plate of scraps and managing to grab more than the lion's share. Eventually, however, order was restored from chaos. The children were persuaded to sit down on the floor and eat their oatmeal, the two cats were shooed out of doors and the dog was consoled with a large mutton bone. Of Thomas Baker there was no sign – he was, presumably, in the bakehouse or opening up his stall – so my hostess and I sat quietly at the table, eating our own oatmeal and drinking small beer. For the moment, peace reigned.

When, finally, I had eased my hunger and slaked my thirst, I said, 'This Ralph Mynott whom you mentioned last night, Mistress, I think you said he lived near the East Gate, opposite the...er...the monks' graveyard. Was that it?'

Cecily nodded. 'Go to the bottom of the marketplace and turn left. You'll see the grave-yard on the other side of the road, in front of the abbey. Master Mynott lives in the third house from the gate, and the gate itself, in case the information is of any use to you, gives access to the monks' mill ferry and the track to Bathwick.'

I thanked her but said that if Ralph Mynott turned out to be the man I was seeking, I should be returning home as soon as possible. I also begged her not to reveal my plans to her father and she smiled understandingly. I then offered her payment for my night's lodging which, after a furtive glance around to make sure her husband had not silently entered the kitchen without her knowledge, she refused.

'Any friend of Father's can always be sure of a welcome from me.'

I felt I was accepting her hospitality under false pretences, but could hardly tell her so. Then, having shaved and collected my satchel and cudgel, I took my leave of her, burdened by guilt. I could only hope that, knowing Jack as well as she appeared to do, she was not altogether deceived.

The city was coming alive as I walked to the bottom of the marketplace, where some stalls were already open, while masters and apprentices were busy raising the shutters on others, and where various livestock were being driven into pens. But it was still a little too early to call on a respectable citizen who might be eating his breakfast, so I wandered around the streets for a bit. These were made from neatly laid, well compacted cobbles of limestone with a central band of iron slags to take the heavier traffic. The houses were mainly timber, but here and there a stone one, three or four storeys in height, indicated the home of a wealthier citizen, and there were a number of prettily laid out gardens to be seen amid the dwellings and almshouses, churches and workshops that cluttered the town. The abbey with its attendant buildings, including the bishop's court and palace, occupied much of the ground below the East Gate, and water was piped into the city by a conduit that passed over the Avon Bridge and in through the South Gate, where there was also a public fountain. The chapel of Saint Laurence, halfway across the bridge, offered the weary traveller the chance of a moment's peace and reflection before plunging into the noise and bustle of the crowded streets.

The sun was, by now, well above the horizon and the din of the traders' cries was becoming deafening. I made my way back to the East Gate, which, like the other three, had a single, low tower atop it, counted back three houses from the archway and knocked.

It was one of the more imposing houses, three storeys high and made of stone with a gabled front. And the maid who answered my summons was not the usual flyaway Moll or Nell, but a neatly dressed, ruddy-faced young country girl, her hair tucked beneath a linen hood and a spotless linen apron covering her dress of brown burel.

'Is Master Mynott at home?' I asked. 'Master Ralph Mynott.'

'Which one?' the girl replied, while dubiously eyeing me up and down. 'Old master or young master?'

Did this mean Ralph Mynott had a son or an elderly father? On the whole, I rather thought the former.

'The older master,' I said. 'He'd...he'd be about forty. Perhaps a little more or a little less.'

The girl's suspicion increased. 'And what would be your business with him?'

'Who is it, Ruth?' A more authoritative voice cut into the conversation. The maid was shouldered aside and a tall woman in a dark blue woollen gown trimmed with budge took her place; a thin-faced woman with a pair of piercing blue eyes, sharp nose and an uncompromising mouth. 'Who are you and what do you want?' she demanded.

I repeated my request, which was greeted with so haughty a stare that, to my chagrin, I found myself stumbling over my explanation that it was on the business of His Worship, the Mayor of Bristol.

'A likely story,' she snorted. 'Off with you, or I shall have you handed over to the Watch.'

Fortunately, this annoyed me so much that I recovered my nerve, drew myself to my full height, had a flash of inspiration, and announced that unless I was allowed to see Master Mynott immediately, I should be forced to summon the Sheriff's Officer who had accompanied me from Bristol and who was only a street or two away at the home of his daughter.

My luck was in: I had convinced the woman that I was someone of importance. Grudgingly, she stood aside and let me enter.

'Tell the master he's wanted,' she told the girl, who promptly vanished into the back regions of the house.

The hall where we were standing spoke, if not of great wealth, then at least of a comfortable living. The beams and door posts were elaborately carved and painted in shades of blue and red with, here and there, a touch of golden yellow. A fire burned on the hearth, for the April morning was chilly, and the furnishings comprised two fine oaken chests, two armchairs, a corner cupboard containing the family silver and a bench on which were scattered some half-dozen red and green cushions. The walls, it was true, were bare of any coverings, but my impression was that Master Mynott did not suffer from a shortage of money.

The lady whom I presumed to be Mistress Mynott vouchsafed no further word, in spite of a half-hearted attempt on my part to engage her in conversation, staring down her nose at me with a disapproving gleam in her cold blue eyes. She turned with something like relief as the door at the back of the hall opened and a man in a long furred bed robe appeared.

'Ah, here you are, my love,' she said sharply, her tone belying the affectionate form of address. 'This gentleman –' the word had a pejorative ring to it – 'wishes to talk to you. He says –' again she threw scorn into her voice – 'that he is on the business of His Worship, the Mayor of Bristol.'

I could see at once that Ralph Mynott, if he had indeed been one of Isabella's swains, must be the one described as 'ordinary'. Of middling height, with brown hair, now greying and going more than a little thin on top, eyes of a nondescript blue, he might have been any one of a score or so men I passed in the street every hour of every day. He must have been the same when young, without any distinguishing feature to mark him out from the crowd; not remarkably good-looking, but not necessarily displeasing either.

He blinked at me several times before saying mildly, 'I'm sorry, I don't understand.'

'I'd like to speak to you alone, Master Mynott,' I suggested tentatively, anticipating furious opposition from the lady.

She did look daggers at both me and her husband, but to my utter amazement, when Master Mynott said in his quiet way, 'Very well. Alice, my dear, will you please leave us,' she flounced out of the hall without another word. I began to revise my first impression of 'Caspar'.

He might look downtrodden, but it was plain to me that his wife was a little afraid of him – which, in the circumstances, interested me very much. Was Ralph Mynott capable of violence?

Once we were alone, he motioned me to one of the chairs and himself took the other.

'Now,' he enquired calmly, 'what is this all about? Suppose you start, young man, by telling me your name.'

'Roger Chapman,' I said, but hurried on, 'Before I go any further, sir, did you, twenty years ago, know a young woman by the name of Isabella Linkinhorne?'

He looked shocked, blinking rapidly again. 'Sweet Virgin!' he murmured. 'After all these years to be reminded of her!' He took a deep breath to steady himself. 'Yes, I knew her. It would be incorrect to say that I had forgotten her, but I haven't thought about her in a very long time.' His voice tailed off and he sat staring in front of him for several moments, lost in a reverie. Then, pulling himself together, he repeated, 'What is this about? And whatever it is, what has it to do with the Mayor of Bristol?' He added, 'Isabella must be my age by now and, I should imagine, long since married.'

'She's dead,' I announced baldly. 'She has been for twenty years.' And I proceeded to tell my story.

Master Mynott listened in silence, only twice interrupting me with a question. When at last I had finished, he said nothing for a while, sitting with his hand to his mouth, his gaze unfocused, looking at nothing in particular. Finally, he uttered the one word, 'Murdered!' before lapsing into silence again. I would have been ready to swear that his dismay was genuine, but as yet I didn't dare let myself believe it.

'Yes, murdered,' I confirmed.

'You're certain?' he asked, suddenly sitting up straighter in his chair and regarding me fixedly. 'You're sure the body found was Isabella's?'

Slowly, I went over the story yet again; the evidence of the jewellery she had been wearing when she met her death; the testimony of the various people I had talked to, including Robert Moresby. 'I think you must have been acquainted with Master Moresby,' I added. 'He was a friend of your sister and brother-in-law, Sir Peter and Lady Claypole.'

Ralph Mynott nodded, confirming what I had already suspected. 'It was through Robert that I got to know Isabella. I often rode to Hambrook Manor in those days and was introduced to him by my sister. He was in fact no more than an itinerant goldsmith,' he added somewhat dismissively, 'whom Araminta and Peter had chosen to befriend. And then one day, on my way from Bath to Hambrook, on the downs above Bristol, I met Master Moresby out riding with this beautiful girl. He introduced her, not without some prompting from me, I might say, as Isabella Linkinhorne.' Once again, Ralph Mynott breathed deeply. 'I thought her quite simply the most lovely creature I had ever set eyes on.'

'You got to know her,' I suggested, 'when Master Moresby wasn't present?'

'She told me herself that she went riding on the downs every day, and after that...' He broke off, shrugging. 'After that, whenever I could be spared from my father's weaving sheds, I rode north in the hope of meeting her. There were many occasions, of course, when I was disappointed, but she was often to be found in or near Westbury, on the River Trym, where she had a cousin living.'

If Ralph Mynott's father had been a master weaver, it explained the family's affluence and how the daughter of the house had been able to ensnare a baronet. Bath was as famous for its cloth as its neighbour, Bristol.

'You fell in love with Isabella?' I asked.

He lowered his voice a little, indicating by a gesture of his hand that I should do the same.

'Yes, I fell in love with her. She was so lovely and so unhappy, like one of the heroines in the romances that my sister used to read. I wanted to rescue her. To take care of her for the rest of her life.'

'Did she know how you felt? Was she in love with you?'

'I asked her to marry me. She promised to consider my offer. She told me she returned my affection, but could not leave her tyrannical old parents for the present. I tried to make her see that she couldn't waste her life and mine waiting for them to see reason or to die. I told her that when my own father died, I would inherit the weaving sheds; that I was able to take care of her, even then, in comfort for the remainder of her days. She knew that my sister was married to

Sir Peter Claypole and that I was not unconnected. But she was as good as she was beautiful; a kind, dutiful daughter, mindful of the Church's teaching to honour her father and her mother...'

'That her days might be long upon the earth,' I couldn't help interjecting ironically. 'But they weren't.'

Ralph Mynott smiled sadly and I saw tears start in his eyes. Either he was pretending, or, like Robert Moresby, he had never understood Isabella's true nature. He had had the money, his rival the good looks. So what quality had 'Balthazar' possessed?

But that was a problem yet to be tackled. For the moment, my interest lay with Ralph Mynott.

'When was the last time you saw Isabella, sir?' I enquired, trying not to make it sound like an interrogation. It was plain that he had not yet grasped the significance of my visit or of my questioning.

He furrowed his brow. 'Does it matter?' But without waiting for my reply or trying to work it out for himself, he continued, 'I think it must have been springtime, but early. There weren't many flowers about as I recall. A few primroses, sweet violets, wood anemones perhaps, so it must have been March, but to the best of my recollection the weather was stormy and cold. However, I'm unable to tell you more than that.'

I pressed him harder. 'But there must have been an occasion after which you never saw her again. Do you have no memory of when that was?'

Ralph Mynott said slowly, 'Yes. Of course, you're right. I remember riding that way throughout one spring and summer in the hope – in the expectation at first – of seeing Isabella, but she had simply vanished. I asked a number of people in and around Westbury if she had been seen, but the answer was always the same: no one recalled seeing her and her horse for...well, weeks to begin with, then months. Eventually I gave up looking for her.'

'What did you think could have happened to her?'

A rush of blood suffused his sallow face. 'My sister finally admitted to me, months afterwards, that Isabella had been planning to elope with Robert Moresby. It was a blow to my pride that she could prefer that fellow to me, so I stopped thinking about her after that.'

'But Lady Claypole must also have told you that on the day appointed, Isabella failed to arrive at Hambrook Manor to keep her rendez-vous with Master Moresby.'

My companion chewed his thumbnail, then nodded agreement.

'True,' he said. 'But I could see no reason why Isabella should not have changed her mind yet again later on, and ridden to Gloucester to join him and become his wife. Indeed, the longer I thought about it, the more convinced I became that this is what had happened. There were, after all, a number of reasons why she might not have been able to reach Hambrook on the day arranged. That some violent fate might have overtaken her never so much as crossed my mind.'

I waited a moment or two before speaking again to allow him time to master what appeared to be a very natural grief. But when he seemed to have his emotions under control, I said, 'On the morning Mistress Linkinhorne should have joined Robert Moresby at your sister's house, she was seen talking to a man near Westbury village. His face was hidden by his hood, which was drawn well forward, concealing his features, it being an extremely wet and windy day. That – forgive me – that wasn't yourself by any chance?'

A suspicion as to where my questioning was leading suddenly seemed to strike him and once again he coloured up, but this time with anger.

'As I don't know which day it was, I cannot say for certain that I was not the man. But if, Master Chapman, you are implying that I might have murdered Isabella, I must ask you to leave my house immediately.'

Ralph Mynott had risen to his feet and was now glaring down at me, his pale eyes flashing with anger. He had a temper all right; and for a man with normally so meek and mild an appearance, he could look surprisingly dangerous when roused. It did nothing to reassure me that he was telling the truth and that I could rely on his word. Moreover, I was forcibly reminded of his sister's tipping bed at Hambrook Manor. The Mynotts were a family to be wary of, I decided. On the other hand, it didn't mean that Ralph had murdered Isabella.

For a start, even had he done so, I had not a

263

scrap of proof to link him with the crime, and there was always the difficulty of how he could have put the body in the grave in the nuns' graveyard. How would he have known about it? How would he have managed to transport the body there? This didn't mean that I was entirely convinced of his innocence, but the more I considered the facts, the more I realized that at the back of my mind, for some time past, I had been nurturing the growing conviction that, where knowledge and opportunity had been concerned, 'Balthazar', the man who was said to have lived in Bristol, was most likely to be the killer.

I uncoiled my length from the chair and towered over my host. Two could play at being threatening. Ralph took a step backwards, his angry expression changing to one of uneasiness. Beneath his mild exterior, he was a bully, and in my experience, bullies are easily intimidated.

'Master Mynott,' I said quietly, 'are you prepared to swear to me, by Christ and all His Saints, that you did not murder Isabella Linkinhorne?'

He blinked. I supposed it was a nervous habit. But there was no other hesitation, not so much as by a second.

'I swear,' he said, adding, 'I loved her. I couldn't have harmed her.'

And on reflection, if what he had told me was the truth, Ralph Mynott had not known of Isabella's perfidy until many months after she was dead. *If* it was the truth...

I sighed to myself. It seemed to me that there probably never would be a satisfactory answer to the question of who had killed Isabella Linkin-horne. It was too long ago. But for my own pride's sake, I had to keep trying.

I took my leave of Master Mynott and wondered if he would tell his wife about my enquiries. I rather fancied that he wouldn't. She didn't look the sort who would take kindly to the tale of a long lost love. But what next? I asked myself as I shouldered my satchel and made my way across the town to the West Gate. And to that question there was only one answer. I had to find 'Balthazar'. But how to locate him? Except that he had reddish hair and probably still lived in Bristol, I knew as little about him as I had known about Ralph Mynott.

But then, suddenly, with a flash of inspiration, I wondered if that were really true.

Sixteen

'So here you are, Chapman,' said a most un-welcome and slightly breathless voice behind me. 'Off home, are you? I suppose you thought you'd given me the slip.' The tone was re-proachful.

I turned my head. Jack Gload was only a pace or two behind me.

'I had no intention of giving you the slip,' I retorted. 'Why would I want to do that? I was under the impression that you were spending some days with your daughter. I left you sleeping like a baby and it would have been a shame to wake you.'

'Well, I ain't,' he said. 'Spending a few days with Cecily, that is. Children and animals, I can't abide 'em. Besides, can't be spared for long,' he added importantly. 'Too many villains in Bristol for the Sergeant to do without me, and I'm 'is right-hand man. Pete – Pete Littleman – 'e's all right. A plodder, but 'e don't have my brains. Leastways that's what Sergeant Manifold says.'

I had no doubt that Dick Manifold said precisely the same thing to his other henchman. He had enough guile to keep them both happy and subordinate to his authority by playing them off against one another. But my heart sank at the prospect of Jack Gload's company for my return journey to Bristol and, moreover, I was suspicious of his motive for accompanying me. Fortunately, he had no subtlety and asked almost at once, 'You been to see this Ralph Mynott, then?' He didn't wait for my assent, but continued, 'What did 'e have t' say for 'imself?'

As we had reached the West Gate, I was able to postpone my answer until we had negotiated our way through against the incoming tide of traffic, exchanging some good-humoured badinage with the gatekeeper and a few bad-tempered words with a carter, who seemed to think that his load of iron ore for the city foundry entitled him to hog the entire width of the road and drive pedestrians to the wall. And by the time we were out in the open countryside, I hoped that my companion might have forgotten his question.

266

A forlorn hope, however.

'So?' Jack urged. 'What did you find out?' And when I did not immediately reply, he pressed again, 'What did this Ralph Mynott 'ave to say for 'imself?'

Such persistence confirmed me in my steadily growing belief that Jack had been sent after me by Richard Manifold to question me and discover what, if anything, I knew.

The Sergeant could have found out from any number of sources – Adela amongst them – that I was on my way to Bath, and, knowing that Jack Gload had a daughter and son-in-law living in the town, despatched him on the most natural of pretexts to follow me.

'Master Mynott was certainly acquainted with Isabella Linkinhorne,' I admitted grudgingly, but without volunteering anything further.

'And?' the lawman prompted impatiently.

'And what?' I knew how to play stupid when required.

'Is 'e guilty of 'er murder, or not?'

'Impossible for me to say with any certainty,' I confessed. 'But on reflection, I should hazard the guess that he is not.'

'Mmm.' Jack shot me a sideways glance. 'So that leaves this third fellow you were talkin' about. You gave 'im some fancy name.'

'Balthazar.'

Jack showed me the whites of his eyes.

'But you don't know 'is real name, do you?' he asked. 'If truth be told, you don't know nothing whatsoever about 'im.'

'I didn't know anything about "Melchior" and

"Caspar",' I pointed out, with the purpose of confusing my dim-witted companion, adding with some satisfaction, 'But I found them, all the same.'

Jack, however, had a simple philosophy; ignore everything you don't understand and hammer on with what you do.

'You was lucky with this Ralph Mynott, though. Sort o' luck you ain't likely to run into twice. As for the other, the one what lives in Gloucester, you said you knew 'im to be a goldsmith. That were summat to go on in a town that size. Bound to lead you to 'im in the end.'

'In twenty years, he might have died or moved away.'

'But 'e 'adn't,' Jack pointed out. The argument was unanswerable, so I didn't attempt it. He continued inexorably, 'What I'm saying is, Chapman, you know nothing – absolutely nothing – about this third man and it'd be too much to expect that you're goin' to strike lucky again.'

'True,' I agreed gloomily, trying not to smile. I had no intention of sharing with Jack Gload the one clue to 'Balthazar's' identity that I thought I might have; that little flash of inspiration that had come to me like a sudden ray of light penetrating an otherwise Stygian darkness.

Robert Moresby, Ralph Mynott. Both had the same initials: R.M. And at the same moment that this realization hit me, I recollected Jane Purefoy's revelation of finding the piece of paper on which Isabella had written three sets of initials, every set the same, with a question mark against each. At the time, I had assumed it was the sort

268

of idle repetition that indicated a preoccupied mind; that she had been thinking of one man, and one alone, and whether or not to marry him. But now it suddenly occurred to me that, by one of those coincidences Fate throws up every now and then, all three men – 'Melchior', 'Caspar' and 'Balthazar' – had baptismal names and surnames beginning with the letters R and M. So the man I was looking for, the final one of the three, most probably was also an R.M. And, if my memory served me aright, he had reddish hair.

I suppose I should have seen the truth, which was staring me in the face, right away, but I'm ashamed to admit that I didn't. I was feeling too smug and pleased with my brilliant deductions to pursue them further, and was wallowing in a veritable sea of self-congratulation.

'You've thought o' something,' Jack Gload accused me. 'I can see it in your face.'

'That's just indigestion,' I told him. 'Your daughter gave me too much breakfast. Which reminds me,' I added, glancing up at the sky, 'it'll be dinnertime soon. I intend stopping at the nearest cottage and buying whatever the goodwife can spare me. Furthermore, Jack, I have no intention of trying to complete this return journey in one day. I was exhausted yesterday evening by the time we entered Bath.'

But if I had hoped to shake off my unwanted companion, I was again to be disappointed.

'Couldn't do it, Chapman,' he agreed. 'Didn't start off early enough today, not after you'd been to visit Master Mynott and Cecily had rolled me

269

out o' bed. Take our leisure, that's what I say. Sit down and admire the view sometimes. The Sergeant ain't expecting me back until tomorrow. And I know a neat little tavern this side o' Keynsham where we c'n rack up for the night. Belongs to a friend o' mine.'

My heart sank, but I could think of no way to rid myself of him. Whatever ploy I tried, I could tell that he was going to stick closer to me than a burr to a sheep's fleece. There was nothing for it but to accept the inevitable and guard my tongue against Jack's probing questions.

But, somewhat to my surprise, he seemed to have accepted defeat on this point; and while we ate a dinner of black bread, goat's cheese and buckrams (or bear's garlic, as some country people call it), washed down with a cup of homemade ale, all provided by a cottager's wife while her man toiled in a nearby field, Jack did no more than quiz me on various problems I had solved in the past. I was, of course, only too happy to provide him with the details. (Well, I'm only human, after all, and what man can refrain from boasting now and then, especially about past success?) And by the time the soft April evening began to draw in, the sun slowly sinking amidst streamers of pale rose and gold, I was almost in charity with him. We had pursued a leisurely course along the valley floor, stopping to exchange greetings with anyone who spoke to us, and learning such snippets of news as the fact that the Princess Mary had become betrothed to the King of Denmark (not an item of much interest to either Jack or myself, but something for me to tell Adela, nonetheless) and now we were pleasantly tired and ready for our beds.

'And here's the alehouse I was telling you of,' my companion remarked suddenly, indicating a small hostelry set back from the main Keynsham track by perhaps a dozen yards or so.

It appeared clean and wholesome enough with a general chamber behind the taproom where travellers could sleep for an extra charge on the price of a meal, and more again for the hire of a blanket and pillow if they didn't fancy a night spent only on straw. The food, too, was well enough: a rabbit pottage with boiled orache and rampion added to the vegetables already in the stew. Jack chose a rough red wine to drink, but I stuck to ale; then, it by now being dark and both of us being extremely tired, we adjourned to the back chamber, where we were the only two wayfarers staying overnight.

We didn't bother to undress. I stowed my satchel beneath my pillow, placed my cudgel where it was ready to hand should I need it, bade Jack a sleepy goodnight and knew nothing more until morning.

It was a cock crowing somewhere, answered by the bark of a dog, that woke me. The early light of dawn was seeping through a very small window, set high in the wall behind my head, but the thing that struck me most forcibly was how quiet the room was. There was no sound of breathing but my own, and none of the snores and gurgling noises that I knew from the previous night's experience Jack could make. I sat up and turned my head. The straw mattress was empty, the blanket tossed to one side, but while the pillow still bore the impression of my erstwhile companion's head, of Jack Gload himself there was no sign.

I heaved myself to my feet and went into the ale room, where the owner, stretching, scratching and yawning, had just entered by a side door leading from his cramped living quarters overhead.

As soon as he saw me, he grunted, 'Your friend's gone. Roused me before it was even light to say he had to be on his way. Said you'd pay.'

For several moments, I was rendered completely speechless, taken aback by Jack's unexpected duplicity. Although I had never liked him, I hadn't thought him capable of playing such a mean and low-down trick. Then uneasiness set in. The more I thought about it, the more out of character it seemed. He was a law officer: he wouldn't want it spread around Bristol that he was a cheat and a sponger, even if it was only my word against his. There were, after all, plenty of people only too ready to believe the worst of anyone in authority.

The solution to the problem, however, eluded me for the present and I told the landlord that I was ready for my breakfast. Dried herring, stale oatcake and a pot of even staler ale did nothing to improve my temper, and I called for the reckoning as soon as I had finished this unsavoury repast.

It was then that I discovered my purse was

missing. The thongs which attached it to my belt had been cut through as neatly as you please while I slept and I hadn't felt a thing. I hadn't even missed its weight since I got up, so busy had I been dwelling on Jack Gload's perfidy. My first reaction was that the alehouse keeper had purloined it, but my accusation was met with such a furious and resentful denial that I believed him. Foolish, perhaps, but intuition told me that this was also Jack's handiwork. And still I couldn't see why.

'I can't pay you,' I told my host, showing him the cut thongs and explaining my predicament.

He took a little persuading that I was indeed telling the truth, but once convinced that it was so, he merely shrugged and said, 'Then you'll have to work for what you owe me.'

I protested vehemently, but he was adamant. 'That's my rule and I ain't altering it for no one.' And just to prove that he was serious, he locked the alehouse door and pocketed the key.

I considered him foolhardy for he was not a big man and someone of my height and girth could easily have overpowered him, but he was evidently a good judge of character and had gambled that I wouldn't offer him violence. I might bluster and threaten a bit, but he would come to no harm.

As it happened, I had already decided it would be a waste of time to resist in any way, and asked resignedly, 'What must I do?'

He jerked a thumb towards a trapdoor set in the alehouse floor.

'There are a dozen or so barrels of ale in the

cellar that want bringing up and standing along the back wall. I'm not an unreasonable man, and if you do that for me, I'm willing to call it evens.'

'I should just think you would be!' I exclaimed bitterly when I had lifted the trapdoor and surveyed the steep, almost vertical ladder that descended into the cellar's depths. But I had no choice. I stripped down to hose and shirt and began.

It was well past dinnertime – almost noon I guessed by the position of the sun, which I could see through the window – before I had finished this labour of Hercules. It had taken a good deal of cajoling – and a solemn promise not to escape – to persuade my host to open the shutters, and it was only when I genuinely appeared in danger of lapsing into unconsciousness from the heat that he finally agreed. But in the end, all the casks – and there were fourteen of them, not twelve – were lined up against the back wall of the ale room and I was at last free to resume my journey. I was drenched in sweat; every stitch I had on clung to me in such an indecent and revealing fashion that I hoped I should encounter no females for an hour or two until I was once again fit to be seen. (Mind you, I can't answer for the ladies. It might have given them the treat of their lives.)

To the landlord's credit, he had plied me with ale throughout my ordeal, and pressed another, final stoup into my hands just before I wished him farewell.

'I'd have a word with that so-called friend of

yours,' he advised me on parting. 'If what he did was meant as a joke, it's a mean sort o' trick, that's all I can say. He's been here afore and he knows my rules, cause he asked me once what I'd do if someone couldn't pay.'

'Oh, I shall be having a word with him, you needn't worry about that,' I responded grimly. 'I shall also be reporting him for theft.'

'I shan't be worrying,' my host chuckled as he held the door wide for a couple of dusty travellers (both men, thankfully) who were making their way up the grassy incline from the track. 'I'm darned grateful to him. Between you, you've saved me a back-breaking job. God speed you, friend.'

The warmth of the April day and a slight breeze dried my clothes faster than I had expected, and by the time I had passed through Keynsham, I presented a more or less respectable sight, but I was, of course, unable to stop for any refreshment, having no money. I did, however, pause in a sheltered spot on the banks of the little River Chew, strip to the waist and wash away the dust and sweat of the morning as well as I was able. After which, feeling somewhat better, in body at least, I settled down to walk the remaining five or six miles to Bristol.

I had ceased wondering what Jack Gload's game might be. Physical strain had taken over to such an extent that my mind felt numb, and all my effort was centred on putting one foot in front of the other. My cudgel saved me on more than one occasion from actually falling over, while my satchel felt as if it were packed with stones instead of the few necessities Adela had insisted I carried with me. Tomorrow, after a good night's sleep, I would seek out the errant law officer and lay a charge of theft against him. But until then, I had enough to cope with in my aching back and arms and my general fatigue.

This all-encompassing tiredness is the only excuse I can offer for the way I walked into the trap without even the smallest presentiment as to what was coming. The walls of the city were within sight, the din and the stench reaching out to fill my ears and nostrils as they do with every big town in the kingdom. I had approached from the east and could already make out, from certain vantage points of high ground, the people passing in and out of the Redcliffe Gate. Although I guessed it to be late afternoon, the days were lengthening apace and there was still plenty of traffic, both of the two-legged and four-wheeled variety, on the roads. But there were also those pockets of quietness which every traveller experiences, where both people and carts suddenly, and for no apparent reason, thin out, leaving one almost alone in the landscape.

This happened as I descended into a hollow with thick scrub on either side. I had deviated from the main track by some yards on to a narrower path where the going was softer for my aching body. As I dropped down between the banks of the hollow, I was aware of nothing except the overmastering desire to reach home; certainly not that I must have been followed for the last half mile or so. Normally, my senses would have alerted me to danger, but, as I said, my mind had ceased to function. I was thinking of nothing but a hot supper and one of Adela's concoctions of primrose leaves and honey which, applied externally or taken internally, would ease my joints and muscles of the worst of their pain.

A pair of heavy hands fell on my shoulders, nearly bringing me to my knees.

'I want a word with you, Chapman,' said a surly voice, and I was swung around with no more difficulty than my daughter had when she manhandled the bundle of grubby rags she called a doll.

To my utter astonishment, I found myself staring into the face of Ranald Purefoy, and what he could want with me I was unable even to guess.

'A word? What about?' I mumbled.

'What about? What about!' he shouted, the noise reverberating through my head almost as if I were recovering from a bout of drunkenness. 'Comin' the innocent won't help you, Chapman.'

Anger began to steady my nerves and make me forget my weariness.

'This is stupid!' I said, trying to turn away, but his big, shovel-like hands still held me fast.

'You been after my wife!' he exclaimed. 'Goin' t' my house when I weren't there and making up to her.'

The charge was so absurd that I was bereft of speech and could only goggle at my assailant for several seconds before bursting into laughter.

'Why in the name of all that's holy should I want to make up to Mistress Purefoy?' I managed to gasp at last. Then I made my fatal mistake by adding, 'She's as ugly as sin!'

His hands tightened their grasp. 'So now you're insulting her as well as trying to deflower her!' he stormed, and brought up his right foot to kick me in the groin.

Fortunately for Adela's and my future happiness, my instinct suddenly raised its hitherto dormant head and I twisted sideways just before his boot landed with a bruising thud against my hip. The impact, however, felled me to the ground, and he threw himself on top of me, rolling me over to lie face downwards and grinding my nose and mouth into the dirt. Next, he seized me by the hair – my hat having fallen off during the encounter – and started to bang my head up and down against some stones that had, over the years, accumulated in the hollow. I could feel blood trickling down my cheek. I recall wondering feebly where my cudgel was – I had dropped it as I fell – but had no means of groping for it, both my upper arms being pinioned to my sides by Ranald Purefoy's massive thighs and knees. Such was my weakened state after my morning's exertions that I began to lose consciousness.

'This'll teach you to leave my goody alone,' I heard him say, his voice seeming to recede into the distance. I even remember chuckling to myself in a stupid, hysterical, meaningless way as darkness threatened to close in around me.

But before it quite did, I received a blast of foul breath on one half of my face and up my right nostril as my attacker lowered his head to whisper in the ear that was uppermost. 'And you leave off askin' questions about that there Isabella Linkinhorne. D'you hear me? Jane don't like it. And there's others don't like it, neither. So you do as you're asked like a good fellow-me-lad and don't you go upsetting Jane no more!'

My hair was once more tugged at ruthlessly, my head was raised and crashed down on one of the larger stones, and the weight was finally removed from my back as Ranald heaved himself to his feet. But he hadn't altogether finished with me, landing me two hefty kicks in the ribs before pounding away to join the main Bristol track and make his way home.

I lay still, staving off an urgent desire to throw up and wondering how many ribs were broken. I was also afraid that I was about to pass out, but, as with the nausea, I managed to overcome it, fighting my way back to full consciousness by the sheer power of will. Slowly and cautiously I rolled on to my back and, even more slowly and cautiously, sat up. There was no sharp jab of pain, only a feeling of being black and blue all over, my general tiredness adding to my overall malaise. For a while, I was tempted to lie down again and wait for someone to find me, but two factors militated against this desire. The first was that very few people seemed to frequent this narrow sidetrack between the humps and hollows of uneven ground, and the second was that righteous anger was beginning to flood through me like a healing tide. Understanding, too, as I started to realize just what had been going on.

But there was a further realization, as well. In his eagerness to discourage me from discovering his identity, 'Balthazar' had made a number of very foolish mistakes, and upon reflection, I decided that this was typical of the man and only what I would have expected had I known who he was from the outset. R.M. Never as clever as he thought he was.

I dragged myself to my feet, using all my reserves of strength, and, leaning heavily on my cudgel – which I discovered a few feet away from where I had fallen – resumed my painful trudge towards the Redcliffe Gate.

'This job is becoming too dangerous,' Adela grumbled, rubbing me all over with her primrose and honey ointment and viewing the extensive bruising in the area of my ribs with deepest disapproval. 'You go to Bath for a couple of nights and come home looking as though you've been trampled by wild horses. I want you to give it up, Roger. Give Mayor Foster back his money – or what's left of it – and tell him that I don't wish you to continue with this investigation.'

'That makes two of you,' I said, submitting to having the growing lump on my forehead bathed with comfrey juice, and allowing the application of sicklewort ointment to the cuts and scratches on my face.

'Two of us? What are you talking about?' She

helped me pull my nightshirt over my head and put an arm about my waist as I lifted myself higher in the bed. Then she started to undress herself.

My bedraggled appearance, just before supper-time, had created a sensation among my nearest and dearest, but my wife, ever practical, had fed me first and asked questions afterwards. She had also, to their great disgust, packed the children off to bed as soon as possible, then waited while I fell asleep over the kitchen table before eventually rousing me and leading me upstairs with orders to strip while she assessed the damage. A sharp intake of breath had told me that it was as bad as I feared.

Now, however, I felt comforted and cared for and was ready to answer Adela's questions, so I started with the one she had just asked.

'There's someone else, my love, besides your-self, who wishes me to abandon this investiga-tion, and that's the man I have so far nicknamed "Balthazar". But at last I believe I know who he really is.'

And so I did. First of all, there were the initials R.M. and a conviction amounting almost to a certainty that, by an odd coincidence, all three of Isabella Linkinhorne's swains had had Christian and surnames beginning with the same letters. But whereas prayer and a certain amount of clever deduction on my part had led me to both Robert Moresby and Ralph Mynott, sheer, unalloyed stupidity by 'Balthazar' himself had revealed his true identity.

Who else would have detailed Jack Gload to

pay a visit to his daughter in Bath as soon as he had been made aware of my destination? Who else would have instructed him to keep me under his eye and find out what I knew concerning the three men in the murdered girl's life? And who else would have primed Jack to delay me on the road home so that he could get ahead of me, if he thought I knew too much, and deliver a warning? And who else would have tried to scare me off by employing the rough and ready tactics of Ranald Purefoy? Who else, indeed, would have been aware of any connection between the castle scullion and myself?

Who, in general, would have been so heavy-handed and lacking in subtlety?

Who else but Richard Manifold?

Seventeen

'Richard!' my wife exclaimed, when I finally spoke the name aloud. 'What do you mean, Roger? Are you saying that Richard is mixed up in this business?'

I rolled over on to my left side so that I was facing her, at the same time trying to ease my aching body. I felt as though there wasn't a sinew that hadn't been stretched to snapping point.

'I'm saying,' I answered carefully, 'that I believe Dick Manifold to have been the third man in Isabella Linkinhorne's life. How old would he have been, do you think, twenty years ago?'

Adela snuffed out the candle and climbed into bed. However, she made no attempt to snuggle down, but sat propped against her pillows, looking at me.

'Are you serious?'

'Yes. So? What age would he have been at the time of Isabella's murder?'

'Nineteen, perhaps twenty.' She regarded me through the gloom and wisps of candle smoke still hanging, like wraiths, in the air. 'I first became acquainted with him when I was about sixteen. He was ten years older. But Roger—'

'Listen,' I said urgently, 'his initials are R.M. I'm convinced, because of something Jane Honeychurch – Jane Purefoy – told me that all three "Kings" had the same initials. Yes, yes!' I continued impatiently as Adela made a move to interrupt, 'I realize it's a coincidence, but coincidences do happen. Furthermore, one of the three was reported as having reddish-coloured hair and so has Richard. It's going a little grey now,' I couldn't help adding on a note of satisfaction, 'but there's still a lot of the original colour left. And who would have known of my intention to go to Bath, if not Richard? He probably had the information from you. And if not from you,' I added hurriedly, as her bosom swelled in indignant denial, 'then from Mayor Foster. When I reported to him concerning the Hambrook Manor bed, he asked me what my next step would be, and I told him. I daresay he sees Richard daily in the course of his civic duties and could well have passed on the information had Richard questioned him regarding the progress of my enquiries.'

'Well, yes,' Adela agreed, 'but...'

I overrode the doubts she was obviously about to express.

'Knowing that Jack Gload has a daughter living in Bath, Richard sent him after me on the pretext of a paternal visit, but really with instructions to discover what I knew, how my enquiries were going and, above all, with orders to try and dissuade me from continuing with my investigation. But if Jack found it impossible – to dissuade me, I mean – he was to delay me by fair means or foul, leaving me stranded somewhere on the road, while he returned with all speed to Bristol and reported his failure to Dick. Our dear friend then came to an arrangement with Ranald Purefoy to waylay me – it wouldn't surprise me at all if money changed hands – and accuse me of trying to seduce his wife. Then Ranald could pummel me into a pulp and deliver Richard's warning at the same time.' I lifted my head from the pillow and regarded my wife with some severity. 'And what is amusing you so much, my dear?'

'I was remembering your description of Goody Purefoy,' she gasped. 'And to think that you could be accused of trying to seduce her! Oh, Roger! What a blow to your self-esteem.'

'Which just goes to prove how absurd the accusation was,' I answered austerely, 'and that it was a trumped-up reason for attacking me. I tell you, "Balthazar" is Richard Manifold.' I reached up and shook her arm, wishing she would lie down so that I could talk to her face to face in the darkness. 'Adela, think back to those early days when you first knew him. Did it ever strike you that there was some secret in his past that troubled him? Had there been other women?'

'Of course there had been other women,' she replied a little tartly. 'I've told you, Richard was twenty-six when I first knew him, and he was a good-looking man. Oh, not as good-looking as you, if that's what you want me to say,' she added with a laugh. 'But handsome enough to catch the eye of any number of women.'

I didn't much care for that laugh, but I ignored it. 'There wasn't one he mentioned especially?'

'He didn't boast about his previous conquests.'

Again, there was something in her tone that made me uncomfortable. And again, I dismissed it.

'You didn't marry him, though. Why not?'

She shrugged. 'I preferred Owen Juett. And in later years, after my return to Bristol from Hereford, I fell in love with you.'

'You sound as though you regret it,' I muttered anxiously, straining to glimpse her expression in the half light. 'Do you?'

'Do I have cause to?'

My heart began to thump. What did she know? Who could have told her? How could she possibly have found out? It felt as if the name Juliette Gerrish was burned in letters of fire into the darkness of the room. But no; there was no way Adela could have discovered my secret. It was woman's intuition. And yet I would have sworn that by not so much as a look or a gesture or a word had I betrayed myself. Here, however, was my chance to unburden my soul and confess my sin.

I decided not to take it.

'Of course you have no cause to regret loving me,' I answered, throwing as much self-righteousness into my voice as I could summon up without sounding defensive. 'And if you'll only lie down, instead of sitting up like a judge on his bench, I'll prove it to you.'

That made her laugh again. 'You're in no fit state for making love, Roger.' She was right, but she did finally lie down beside me and let me take her in my arms. 'So, what next?' she asked. 'You don't seriously believe Richard Manifold could be a murderer, do you?'

'Anyone can be a murderer if he or she is pushed to it,' I answered soberly. 'If I'm honest, I can't be completely certain that Robert Moresby and Ralph Mynott are innocent of the crime.' I sighed, a foolish action as it hurt my bruised and battered ribs. 'I have a feeling that this particular killing will remain unresolved. Mayor Foster will have to build his almshouses and his chapel dedicated to the Three Kings of Cologne without the satisfaction of bringing a murderer to justice.'

'It's not like you to give up,' my wife protested, shocked.

'Oh, I shan't give up just yet,' I assured her. 'I've got so far and must go a little further yet. Tomorrow morning I shall go and see Jack Nym before I confront Dick Manifold with any sort of accusation. And before,' I added grimly, 'I wrest my purse back from Jack Gload's thieving clutches.'

I was as good as my word, and cockcrow saw me up and about in spite of Adela's urgings to remain in bed and nurse my hurts. But I could tell that, breakfast over, she wasn't sorry to see the back of me. Two more days and April would be out. As well as all her other chores, it was time to be thinking of baking her Whitsuntide cheese cakes.

So I made myself scarce, walking slowly and carefully, so as to tax my bruised limbs as little as possible, through the awakening town and across the bridge to Redcliffe. But however early I was, Jack Nym was always up and about before me, and that morning was already loading his cart with bales of red Bristol cloth from Master Adelard's weaving shed, assisted by Jack Hodge. The latter's round, freckled face, so like his father's, was shiny with the sweat of his exertions, Jack being happier directing operations rather than actually lifting and heaving.

He became aware of someone watching him and swung round, a pugnacious expression on his narrow features, but which cleared when he saw who it was. He inspected my face curiously.

'Somebody been teaching you a lesson, Chapman?'

'Such as?' My tone was acerbic. My present delicate condition was no subject, I felt, for levity.

The carter grinned. 'Oh, such as keeping your nose out of other folk's business.'

'I'm in no mood for funning, Jack,' I retorted, and both he and Jack Hodge snorted with laughter.

'What do you want, then?' Jack Nym condescended to shoulder one end of a bale and help throw it on top of the others already in the cart.

'I want a word with you. In private,' I added, as the younger man's head lifted eagerly, scenting a secret or some scandal with which to regale his mother's ears when he got home.

'Well, it'd better be a quick word,' Jack agreed grudgingly. 'This lot –' he indicated the contents of the cart with the jerk of a grimy thumb – 'is bound for London, which means two or three days, if not more, on the road. And day after tomorrow, I'm sure to be held up by the May Day mummings. You'd best come indoors. No need to worry about my goody. She's still asleep.'

I had never been inside the Nyms' cottage before, and decided immediately that once was enough. I would try to avoid the experience in future. The air was redolent of a number of different smells, the least offensive of which were burned food and scorched fat. What the others were I didn't dare speculate as I felt my stomach heave. Goody Nym was indeed asleep, snoring and huddled against the far wall on a pile of straw that made small rustling noises. Fleas hopped merrily about the extremely stale rushes covering the floor, while a mangy cat sat in the middle of a table, one of whose legs was propped up with a block of wood, cleaning itself in places it would be better not to mention.

'Come on then, lad,' Jack said impatiently. 'What is it you're wanting?'

'You recall telling me, when we were at the New Inn, in Gloucester, that someone you'd recently noticed in a crowd had reminded you of an incident, twenty years ago – of seeing Isabella Linkinhorne in the porch of All Saints' Church with a man?'

My companion groaned. 'Sweet Virgin, you're not back at that again, are you? I told you on Monday that I can't remember nothing. Must've been dreaming at the time I said it. Hell's teeth, Roger, it were a long time ago. Now I must be off. This 'ere cartload o' red cloth's bound for the Aldermen of London. It's urgent and it's got to be delivered on time.'

I got between him and the door.

'Don't lie to me, Jack,' I said. 'You've remembered, haven't you? The face you saw on Bristol Bridge, or wherever it was, was Sergeant Manifold's, now wasn't it?'

He looked shocked, then started to bluster.

'No! O' course it weren't. No. No. Why should you think that?'

'Because I'm almost certain that Dick Manifold is "Balthazar".'

'Oh, for sweet Jesu's sake, don't begin on that nonsense again!' he exclaimed irritably. 'It makes my head spin. And shift away from that door. I got to get goin'.'

I stood my ground.

'When you tell me what I want to know,' I

289

said. 'Was it Sergeant Manifold's face that you saw that day and realized it was the one you'd glimpsed all those years ago with Mistress Linkinhorne?' I took one or two steps backwards until my shoulders were pressed close up against the wood. 'I'm not moving from this door, Jack, until you admit the truth.'

He sighed, accepting that I was in earnest.

'Very well,' he conceded. 'Yes, it were Dick Manifold I saw. But,' he added imperatively, 'that don't prove nothing. It don't mean it were him with Issybelly that day, and you can't make me say it was. You try and force me to say so in front of 'im, and I'll call you a liar to your face.'

'I'm not going to force you to say anything, Jack. In fact, I'm not even going to mention your name to the Sergeant.'

'Then what's all this been about?' he demanded belligerently.

'I just wanted to be sure that what I suspected was indeed the truth,' I answered, not being quite honest myself.

For while I had no intention of revealing Jack's name to Richard Manifold, I was not above hinting that I had a witness to that long ago meeting in the porch of All Saints' Church between him and the murdered woman.

'Well, now you know,' Jack said peevishly, 'so perhaps you'll let me get on with my business. And mind you, Roger,' he added as I stepped aside, 'I'm holding you to that there promise. I like to keep my nose clean. Don't like getting mixed up with the law unless I have to.'

'Do any of us?'

Jack snorted. 'Can't say it seems to bother you overmuch. You'll poke that big snout o' yourn into anything. What I say is that one day you'll regret it, you mark my words.'

I followed him out of the cottage (not without a sigh of relief) to where the younger man had finished loading up the cart and was feeding the horse a wisp of hay from its nosebag. Jack Nym jumped up on the seat and gave the animal the office to start. I watched until they had disappeared round the corner, then turned to bid farewell to Jack Hodge, but he had already gone back to his work at the weaving sheds.

So I went in search of yet another Jack; this time Jack Gload.

He was not in the Councillors' Hall near the High Cross, nor were Richard Manifold and his second henchman, Pete Littleman. Another of the Sheriff's Officers informed me – not without a secret snigger, I thought – that the three were holding a special meeting at the Sergeant's cottage to discuss their latest enquiry – into the theft of some jewellery from a merchant's house – in peace and quiet, away from the noise and bustle of the hall. I thanked him and made my way towards the castle.

Richard lived in an apartment in the outer ward, rent-free I fancied, a fact which had never endeared him to me, particularly when he was eating my food and drinking my ale or warming himself at my fireside. I asked a passing scullion – not, thank Heaven, Ranald Purefoy – which of the cluster of ramshackle dwellings was Dick's, and was directed to the one nearest the Barbican Gate, in somewhat better condition than the rest.

I entered without knocking.

The three were seated around a central table, a stoup of ale at each man's elbow, their heads inclined towards one another, deep in portentous discussion. But at my sudden and unannounced entry, the heads jerked up in surprise and three pairs of eyes stared at me in astonishment.

I dispensed with any sort of greeting, striding round the table and hauling Jack Gload to his feet.

'You thieving bastard!' I yelled, not mincing matters. 'Where's my purse?' I clamped both hands around his neck, my thumbs against his windpipe, and shook him like a dog shaking a rat. He made a sort of gurgling sound and cast a frantic look at his two companions.

Stools scraped against the flagstones and fingers clawed at mine in a vain endeavour to loosen their grip. But anger was giving me strength.

I heard Richard Manifold shout, 'Let him go, Roger! For God's sake, let him go!' But I took no heed. It was only when I noticed that Jack's face was turning from a rich shade of purple to a blotched blue colour that I finally released my victim. He staggered back to his stool, gasping for air and rubbing his throat, while Pete Littleman tenderly administered a few drops of ale.

'You could have killed him,' Richard Manifold accused me.

'I was only doing the hangman's job for him,'

I snarled. 'That villain stole my money.'

'I... It was a joke,' Jack croaked. 'I-I wasn't goin' t' keep it.' He delved into his own purse and flung a handful of coins across the table. 'Have that t' go on with. I'll fetch the rest when I go home. I'm sorry!'

I refused to be mollified. 'And what was the purpose of this stupid joke?' I made another threatening movement in his direction and had the pleasure of seeing him flinch.

'That'll do, Chapman,' Richard ordered, interposing himself between my quarry and me. 'All right, it was a foolish prank to play, I'll give you that. But Jack's apologized.'

I said nothing for a moment, then asked dulcetly, 'A prank, Sergeant? Are you sure that's all it was?'

My abrupt change of tone disconcerted him. 'Wh-what do you mean? Jack's just told you it was meant as a joke.'

'That's right,' Jack Gload confirmed, while Pete Littleman nodded in agreement.

'Really? A joke was it?' I regarded all three with narrowed eyes and what I hoped was an air of contained menace. 'Is that so? Well, perhaps it's escaped your notice that I have recently taken a beating, although somehow I don't think it has. None of you would miss a thing like that.'

'Thought your wife had given you a good hiding,' Pete Littleman muttered with a grin, but didn't get the response he was obviously hoping for.

'Be quiet!' Richard ordered sharply, while Jack Gload took a hurried gulp of ale without even so much as a smirk distorting his ugly features.

'How...how did it happen?' the former enquired solicitously. 'Who...who did it?'

'You know very well who did it,' I snarled, changing my tactics yet again and returning to the attack. 'Your friend and neighbour, Sergeant, Ranald Purefoy! How much did you pay him, eh?'

The shock of the question made Richard gasp and turn white, which only infuriated me more. Did he, in his arrogance, really think me so dim-witted that I couldn't piece together his pathetic little plot?

'What do you mean? What are you saying?'

'I'm saying,' I rasped, 'that you've been trying to persuade me to drop my investigation into the death of Isabella Linkinhorne. First, you sent Jack after me to Bath, on the pretext of visiting his daughter and her family, but really to convince me that it was foolish to pursue the matter.' I gave a derisive snort to demonstrate my contempt for such a piece of folly. 'But if he failed to do so – which the idiot was bound to do – he was instructed to detain me on the road home so that he could report back in good time for you to arrange some other, surer form of deterrent.' I laughed. 'Instead, all it did was to make me certain that what I was beginning to suspect was indeed the truth. That *you* are the man I'm looking for.'

'What's he mean, the man he's looking for?' Pete Littleman asked ponderously. He was brighter than Jack (not much, but a little). 'You told us it was to stop him gettin' in the way while we solved the Linkinhorne murder.'

'And so it was. Is,' Richard said quickly. He drew himself up, suddenly the superior officer. 'You and Jack can leave. Now. I want to talk to Master Chapman alone. You've caused enough trouble with your childish pranks.' I saw Jack Gload's mouth open in an O of astonishment, but Richard hurried on without giving him a chance to voice his indignation. 'Out! This minute! I shan't tell you again. You'll be charged with indiscipline.'

'All right! All right! We're going,' Pete muttered, but his expression was mutinous. 'Come on, Jack. I'll buy you a drink to ease that throat of yours.' He glared at his superior. 'We'll be in the Green Lattis when you've finished talking to the Chapman. Alone!' And he hooked a hand under his friend's elbow, hauling him to his feet.

When the cottage door had closed behind them, Richard sank slowly on to one of the vacated stools and waved me to another. He looked pale and dejected, but most of all angry with himself, as if he knew that he had bungled things. To my annoyance, I found myself beginning to feel sorry for him.

'I'm right, aren't I?' I asked, after several moments of profound silence. 'You knew Isabella Linkinhorne.'

Richard nodded. 'But I didn't kill her,' he added fiercely, 'if that's what you're thinking.'

'Then why have you tried so hard to conceal the fact that you were acquainted with her? Even to the extent of hiring a bully like Ranald Purefoy to beat me black and blue on the

295

insulting charge that I'd been attempting to seduce his wife. Goody Purefoy! Dear, sweet Virgin!' My temper was getting the better of me again, and I made an effort to be calm.

Even Richard was unable to suppress a fleeting grin, but it was gone almost immediately, like a glimpse of sun through clouds.

I said, 'You haven't answered my question. Why did you go to such lengths to prevent me finding out you'd known Isabella Linkinhorne?'

He threw me a glance of dislike. 'Oh, use your common sense, Chapman! I'm a man of the law. A well respected one, at that,' he couldn't stop himself adding, his natural arrogance reasserting itself. 'I didn't want to be mixed up with a murder, even one that will probably never be solved. Not even by you.'

'Especially not if you were the murderer,' I suggested, sitting down on one of the other two stools.

His head reared up at that, his jaw jutting angrily. He half rose to his feet.

'What exactly do you mean to imply by that?'

'I'm not implying anything. I'm simply stating a fact. It seems that one of Isabella's three swains killed her. It's just a question of discovering which one.'

Richard, instead of losing his temper as I had expected, suddenly looked discomfited.

'Until Isabella's body was found three and a half weeks ago and all the enquiries began, I wasn't even aware that there had been other men in her life. I really thought I was the only one. I

loved her,' he added simply, like a lost, bewilder-
ed child, so different from his usual air of self-
consequence that I felt as acutely uncomfortable
as if he had suddenly decided to strip naked in
front of me. 'I had absolutely no reason to kill
her or to wish her dead. You must be able to see
that, surely.' His natural conceit was beginning
to take hold again.

'But there's only your word for that,' I pointed
out. 'Supposing you'd found out about "Melchior" or "Caspar"—'

'Who? What in God's name are you babbling
about?' He was looking at me as though I had
lost my mind. Not, I suppose, without good
reason.

'Robert Moresby and Ralph Mynott,' I amended hurriedly. 'Just two nicknames I used for
them before I discovered who they really were.'
He was still eyeing me somewhat askance. 'You
must see that it was difficult not knowing what
they were called.'

I realized that he had forced me on to the
defensive and that, if I didn't take care, I should
lose the advantage over him. Once again, I
returned to the attack.

'As I was saying, if you had suddenly found
out about the existence of one, or both, of these
men, you might well have killed Isabella in a
rage. Particularly as you admit that you loved
her and had assumed you were the only one.'

'Well, I didn't,' he answered truculently.
'Sweet Jesu!' His anger exploded. 'I wouldn't
have laid a finger on her, you purblind fool! The
other man, perhaps. But not Isabella. She was

297

my sun, moon, stars! She meant everything to me. I worshipped the ground she walked on.'

'So what happened when she suddenly disappeared? What did you think? What did you do?'

Richard subsided on to his stool again, running a hand across his forehead.

'I didn't know what to think,' he said, more quietly. 'At first, I thought that terrible old father of hers had found out about our meetings and imprisoned her in the house. I went there, only to discover from the servants that she really had vanished. Run away. It didn't come as too much of a shock. I'd been urging her to leave home for months. A year, maybe. Almost as long as I'd known her, anyway. The only surprise was why she hadn't run to me. But then I told myself she wouldn't have wanted to have put me at risk from her father's anger. I had only just been enrolled in the Sheriff's Office and had my way to make in the world. Isabella understood that, and was protecting me. A father's rights over his children are the greatest there are. I could have found myself in serious trouble if I had been sheltering Isabella. I convinced myself that it was merely a matter of time before she got a message to me somehow or another. Then it would have been up to me whether I left Bristol and went to her or not.'

'But you must have heard what her parents were claiming about her,' I objected. 'That she had run off with a man.'

Richard Manifold shrugged. 'I knew what they were saying, of course. The whole city knew it eventually. I just didn't believe them. I thought it was spite; lies because they wouldn't, or perhaps couldn't, accept that their daughter hated them enough to run away.'

'But,' I insisted, 'as the weeks, months, then years went by and you still didn't hear from Isabella, what conclusion did you come to regarding her disappearance?'

Richard slowly shook his head. 'Eventually, gradually, as all hope died, I decided that she must have had an accident. Her horse must have thrown her, or she'd been set upon and killed by footpads somewhere in the forests. And in the end, of course, I stopped wondering. There was nothing I could have done. And she became lost to me. A dream. Other women came along: Adela, for one. I forgot her. That's all.'

There was silence between us. Then I asked abruptly, 'When was the last time you saw and spoke to Isabella?'

Eighteen

'The last time I...' He broke off, looking shocked, as though I had awakened him too abruptly
from a dream world to reality; as though, for a
few brief seconds, he did not know where he
was. 'The last time I spoke to Isabella?'

I nodded and said, 'Yes,' in confirmation. I
could see at once by the look in his eyes, by the
slightly shifty expression that lurked at the back
of them, that he remembered the occasion quite
clearly, but was reluctant to divulge it, so gave
him a helping hand. 'Was it the morning of the
day she disappeared?'

'It's...it's difficult to recall after all this time.
Twenty years seems like an aeon ago.' He gave
a nervous laugh that rang hollow. 'I was young,
I know that. A green youth in the throes of my
first great passion.'

I was unimpressed by this blatant bid for my
understanding and sympathy.

'It was a March morning of rain and wind,' I
said. 'You met her near your usual trysting place
of Westbury village. She was seen talking to
someone – a man, wearing a cloak with his hood
pulled forward over his face.'

'And why should you think that man was me?
It seems now that there were at least two other

men whom Isabella knew and was friendly with, so why should it necessarily have been me? Has someone claimed to have recognized me?'

'I told you, whoever it was had his hood pulled well forward, concealing his features.'

'Then why...?'

'Because Master Robert Moresby has a witness to the fact that, on that particular morning, he was elsewhere.'

'And the second man? Ralph Mynott, I believe he's called. If, that is, Jack Gload has the name aright. Can he, too, claim a witness as to his whereabouts that morning?'

'No,' I admitted. 'And if you asked me to produce evidence to exonerate him, I couldn't. It's just a feeling I have that he was not the man Isabella encountered on the downs that day.'

'A feeling!' Richard exclaimed scathingly. 'Feelings don't count, man, when you're searching for the truth. If you ask me, Roger, these mysteries that you claim to have solved – if, indeed, you have solved them and it's not just so much moonshine – have been more by luck than judgement.'

He was trying to goad me into losing my temper, and was very nearly succeeding. But I realized that the attempt was for a purpose and that to play his game was to hand him the advantage over me, so I suppressed my anger and answered coolly, 'You, yourself, have been witness to some of my successes. And if you have never been guided by your feelings – what women would call intuition – then I shall own myself very much surprised. Moreover, if you

301

claim otherwise, I shan't believe you. I recollect an occasion when you would have pinned a murder on me for no better reason than you disliked me for being Adela's husband. Fortunately, I had a witness to testify to my innocence.'

His eyes met mine for a moment, then dropped to study his hands, clasped on the table in front of him.

'Yes, you're right,' he said quietly. He began picking at a piece of loose skin around one of his thumb nails. 'It's true. I've always resented Adela's preference for you. Nor, I admit, have I ever understood it.'

He was, I realized, adopting another tactic: leading me away from the subject of Isabella Linkinhorne by trying to start a dispute between us over our rival merits in the eyes of my wife.

'Nor have I ever understood it,' I agreed, beating him at his own game. 'It is, moreover, undeserved,' I added with far more sincerity than he could possibly have guessed at. 'But all this is beside the point. I still think you were the man that Isabella was seen talking to on what proved to be the last morning of her life.'

Richard bit his lip. 'Oh, very well,' he admitted savagely after a moment's silence. 'Yes, the last time I ever saw her was on a very stormy morning early in the year. It might have been March. I don't really remember. But that it was the last morning of her life is more than I know. Or you, either, I fancy.'

'Perhaps. But it seems to be the last occasion on which anyone saw her alive. What did you talk about? How did you come to meet her? Had you arranged to do so, or was it by chance?'

He stood up suddenly, his face contorted with fury, his stool clattering to the floor behind him, his fingers gripping the edge of the table until the skin of his knuckles seemed in danger of splitting.

'Hell's teeth! Who do you think you are, Roger Chapman, to come here questioning me in this fashion? *Me!*'

I half expected him to order me from the cottage, and was preparing to retreat in good order. Instead, he began pacing up and down the floor, looking daggers at me, it was true, but also appearing to be debating with himself. Finally, he came back to the table, righted the stool and sat down again.

'I didn't kill Isabella Linkinhorne,' he said quietly, 'although it grieves me very much to have to say so. That anyone could think me capable of murder, least of all you, is shaming.'

'Why?' I demanded bluntly. 'Whatever face you choose to present to the world, Richard, I know you're quite capable of paying someone to beat me black and blue in order to protect yourself; capable, as I reminded you just now, of trying to arrest me for a killing I didn't do—'

'The evidence pointed to you,' he defended himself, and I was forced to admit that that was true. But spite had informed the attempt. And as though in sudden acknowledgment of the fact, he raised his head and looked me straight in the eye. 'All right,' he said, 'I met Isabella by chance that morning. We hadn't arranged a rendezvous, and when I saw what the weather was like, I doubted if even she would go out riding. Yet it was worth the risk. Little deterred her from taking those daily gallops across the downs. But by the time I'd reached the heights above Bristol, the wind and rain had increased twofold – threefold – to what they had been down here in the shelter of the city walls, and I had no real expectation of seeing her.'

'But you did.'

'Yes. I chided her for coming out in such weather, but she said she'd been unable to remain cooped up indoors.'

'Did she say why?'

My companion shook his head. 'She didn't really need a reason. She was wild, was Isabella. Headstrong. It was part of her great charm, at least for me. And she hated her parents. Perhaps hated is too strong a word, but she disliked them. She found their overwhelming love oppressive. It drove her, literally, I think, a little mad. She told me once that, when she was a child, she had attacked her mother with a knife, and only her nurse's timely intervention had prevented her from killing Mistress Linkinhorne. I longed to be able to free her by marrying her, but in those days I was in no position to support a wife.'

Once again, I was amazed by the inability of these men who had loved Isabella Linkinhorne to understand her. All three had wished to free her from her parents' tyranny by making her their wife; by removing her from one golden cage to what she would undoubtedly have seen as yet another; by rescuing her from her mother's and father's overwhelming love only to smother her with their own.

'What did you and she talk about that morning?'

'God alone knows!' Richard gave a sudden rueful grin, displaying one of his rare flashes of humour. 'And probably even He's forgotten.' He was immediately serious again. 'How do you expect me to remember after all this time?' He sounded testy. 'It wasn't the weather for idle chatter. I told you, I chided her for being abroad on such a morning, but what she said in answer or what I said after that I've not the smallest recollection.'

'She didn't say that she was on her way to meet someone? That she was going to another man?'

'No, she did not.' Richard's face was grim, as though the knowledge that this might have been the case, even after all those years, had the power to hurt him. 'You don't listen, Roger. I've explained that I had no idea, back then, that there was any other man – let alone two – but me.' He hesitated before asking, 'Are you telling me the truth?'

'If Robert Moresby was telling me the truth, then yes. But,' I went on quickly, 'I think it extremely doubtful that Isabella ever intended to honour her pledge to meet him at Hambrook Manor. If you can bear the truth, I think she enjoyed making fools of you all.'

'And what do you know of her?' Richard asked, rounding on me savagely.

'I've learned enough about her in these past

305

three weeks and more to work that out.' I softened my tone. 'Does it rankle so much?'

'I loved her,' he answered simply. 'And I thought she loved me.'

'First love is often like that, I suppose.' I rubbed my forehead, a sudden bleak feeling around my heart. 'It's the one you remember most.'

He glanced curiously at me. 'Adela wasn't your first love, then?'

I shook my head, recalling soft blue eyes, delicate, pale skin, lips that I had longed to kiss, but never had, a villainous father whom I had brought to justice, an act which made me her enemy and exiled me from her life...

I realized with a sudden shock that Richard and I were on the brink of becoming friends. Worse still, I was being unfaithful to Adela yet again, if only in my thoughts. With an effort, I pulled myself together and returned to the matter in hand.

But what else could I ask Richard Manifold? He had finally admitted to knowing the murdered woman; had acknowledged that he was the man seen speaking to her on the morning of the day she disappeared, and yet I was no nearer finding the killer than I had been at the outset of these enquiries. He could be any one of the three men I had spoken to, or none of them. If one, two, or all three were lying to me, how could I prove it after twenty years? Isabella Linkinhorne had, in some way, brought her death upon herself by her deliberate betrayal of the men who loved her. She had mocked their affection for her by abusing their trust and laughing at them

306

behind their backs. It would be all too easy to say that what had happened to her was no one's fault but her own.

But that would be to condone murder, to ignore the injunction laid on us by God: Thou shalt not kill. (Nor commit adultery either, whispered a voice inside my head, but I ignored it. I was finding it easier with practice.)

'Well?' Richard Manifold's voice cut across my thoughts. 'What have you decided, Chapman? Am I guilty of Isabella's death, do you think?'

I sighed and rose to my feet.

'The truth is,' I said, 'I don't know.'

'No, nor never will,' my companion sneered, also rising. 'The real truth is that you would have done better to heed my warnings to leave well alone. It's all too far in the past, and you and our Mayor between you have done nothing except open up old wounds, stir memories that are best forgotten and throw mud that all too readily sticks to the innocent as well as the guilty.'

'You'd prefer a murderer to go unpunished, then?' I asked, looking him straight in the eye.

If I'd hoped to shame him, I was disappointed.

'In this case,' he answered steadily, 'yes.' He added honestly, 'The reason for your visit here is bound to get out. Even a couple of dunderheads like Jack and Pete are capable of adding two beans to three and making five, and they are both incapable of holding their tongues. They won't mean to blab, of course. They just won't be able to help themselves. And as I pointed out to you a moment ago, mud, once thrown, has a nasty habit of sticking. What authority will I have, if people are wondering if I could possibly have murdered a woman?'

'I'm sorry, Richard,' I said. 'But if you hadn't tried so hard to put me off the scent, I might never have associated you with Mistress Linkinhorne. Anyway, it's too late for apologies now. There's nothing I can do about it.'

'Oh yes, there is,' he retorted, leaning towards me, his expression suddenly vicious. 'Just exercise those much vaunted, God-given powers of yours and find out who really murdered Isabella.'

I walked home for my dinner, tired and dispirited. I was never going to solve this mystery, I could feel it in my bones. And, indeed, although acknowledging that I had experienced a similar sensation more than once in the past, I had never done so with such conviction as at the present. As I had already told myself that morning, there was no way that I could say for certain whether my three 'kings' were lying or telling the truth.

The jostling crowds, impeding my progress, seemed suddenly inimical, my path constantly barred by sellers of hot pies, jellied eels, spiced wine, all plying their wares with what appeared to be unusual aggression. A gaggle of women and young children were chasing a hurdle on which an unfortunate baker was strapped as he was dragged to the stocks, pelting him with his underweight loaves and hurling abuse at his shamefaced head. And although he undoubtedly deserved his punishment, the sight nevertheless depressed me even further.

I received my customary welcome from my family. Adela gave me a quick, distracted peck on one cheek while she ladled broth into five bowls, prevented Adam from tipping his chair over backwards and cracking his head on the kitchen floor, and called yet again for Nicholas and Elizabeth to come to table. My son gave me a fleeting smile and continued banging his plate with his spoon, while my stepson and daughter, when they did finally deign to appear, ignored my presence completely. Only Hercules was pleased to see me, but as he seemed to have mistaken my left leg for a bitch on heat, I had to detach myself from his embrace with greater roughness than his affection warranted.

As we finally settled down to the business of eating, Adela said, 'A message came for you from Mayor Foster while you were out this morning, Roger. He sent that maid of his to say that he would be pleased if you would call on him – at his house, not the Councillors' Hall – when you've eaten your dinner.'

I groaned.

My wife eyed me astutely. 'Nothing to tell him, sweetheart? Did Richard admit to having known Mistress Linkinhorne?'

'Yes. He even admitted to being the man she was seen talking to on the last morning of her life – or, at least, on what I presume to have been her last morning – but vehemently denied any involvement in her killing.'

Adela opened her eyes wide and gave a short

309

laugh. 'My dear, what else did you expect? What else *could* you expect?'

'Nothing,' I agreed glumly. I swallowed another spoonful of broth and went on, 'I'm going to tell Mayor Foster, when I see him after dinner, that there is no more I can do to find Isabella Linkinhorne's murderer. One of her three former swains is probably lying, but there is no way I can prove which one after all this time.'

My wife sighed, but went straight to the heart of the matter. 'In that case, we must try to repay Mayor Foster the money he gave you. It would be only right.'

'I know.' I continued spooning broth into my mouth, but it suddenly tasted like river water. 'It's all my fault,' I apologized. 'I should never have agreed to take it in the first place, then I would have carried on working as I usually do, whilst trying to find an answer to the mystery.'

Adela nodded. 'Much of it's gone, I'm afraid. But we have a few savings put by. We'll use that to reimburse him. We'll manage somehow.'

Her brave words, uttered without any reproach to me, suddenly engulfed me in a wave of guilt. I got up from my stool, went round the table, pulled her to her feet and enveloped her in a heartfelt embrace.

'You're a wife in a thousand,' I muttered thickly, and kissed her again, to the great delight of Adam, who thumped on the tabletop with his little fists and shouted, 'Kiss, kiss!' at the top of his voice. Nicholas and Elizabeth dissolved into fits of laughter as they mimicked him.

'Kiss, kiss! Kiss, kiss!'

When she was finally able to speak, Adela, straightening her cap and smoothing down her skirts, demanded to know what she had done to deserve this unexpected bussing.

'I...I just wanted you to know that...that...' My voice petered out lamely.

'That you love me?' my wife suggested dryly.

It was my turn to nod, feeling suddenly foolish. Adela smiled understandingly and advised me to finish my broth before it got cold. But I also thought that there was a certain suspicion in her glance, then decided it was only my guilty conscience firing my imagination.

I resumed my seat, saying hopefully, 'Mayor Foster may well refuse to accept the money.'

'You must make him take it,' Adela insisted. 'Either that, or you must continue with your efforts to discover Isabella Linkinhorne's murderer.'

I laid down the spoon I had just picked up, shaking my head miserably.

'It goes against the grain to admit defeat,' I muttered, 'but I can't see any possibility of sorting truth from lies in this instance. It's all too long ago.'

'The affair, last year, at Bellknapp Manor, was in the past, yet you found the answer to that.'

'It was only six years in the past, and there was the more recent murder to help me. This is two decades gone.'

'Have you prayed to the Virgin and Saints to help you?'

'I've prayed to every Saint in Heaven,' I retorted snappishly, 'but so far, I've received no help to speak of.'

This wasn't, of course, quite true. My inspiration about the three sets of identical initials had surely been God-given, as had been my discovery, seemingly by chance, of the link between Robert Moresby and Ralph Mynott. But now, these hints and nudges appeared to have dried up and I was on my own. Floundering.

Adela said gently, 'Before you present yourself at Mayor Foster's house, you could visit Saint Giles's or Saint Werburgh's or even All Saints' Church and ask again for assistance.'

I took her advice and went to beg Saint Giles for guidance. My customary (and secret) heretical practice was to ignore the Saints and go straight to God, demanding His help as the price of doing His work of righting wrongs or bringing the guilty to justice. But today, with my own burden of guilt weighing me down, plus the nagging suspicion that God was perhaps not best pleased with me, I felt that intercession on my behalf was a necessity.

The church was quiet and almost empty at that hour of the morning. Kneeling on the rush-strewn floor, in the shelter of a pillar, I recalled the story that no less a personage than the great Charlemagne himself had, on one occasion, sent for Giles to hear his confession, but had told the saint that one of the sins on his conscience was too shameful for him to admit to. Giles, however, had later learned in a vision what the king's sin was – although alas, for the curiosity of the rest of us, he never revealed it – and, from henceforth, took Charlemagne under his especial protection. Well, I thought, if Giles could condone a sin of such proportions, perhaps my solitary infidelity may not appear so terrible in his eyes and he might be able to persuade God to overlook it, just this once. (But there was the rub. Would it be for just that once? I had to convince both the Saint and myself that it was.)

So it was in a sober and chastened frame of mind that I continued walking up Small Street until I reached Mayor Foster's house, and was admitted to the hall by the little maid who had brought the message. To my utter astonishment, I discovered that another visitor was there before me. Richard Manifold.

'What are you doing here?' I demanded rudely.

'I've been sent for. Why are you here?'

'I've also been sent for. The message was delivered to Adela while I was with you, earlier this morning.'

He grunted. 'My summons arrived just after you'd left.' We eyed one another uneasily. 'Why do you think Mayor Foster wants to see us both?'

I had no more idea than he had, but one thing was clear: I could postpone my declaration of failure until another occasion. Similarly, my offer to repay John Foster the money he had given me could also be delayed.

Our host did not keep us waiting long, but came downstairs in full mayoral robes and insignia a minute or so after my arrival. He was plainly on his way to a meeting of the Council, so, I guessed, would not wish to keep us long.

Whatever he had to say to Richard and myself would be brief. We bowed and waited for him to speak.

Horses and I have never got on.

To me, they are creatures with a leg at each corner and wild, staring eyes that mean nothing but mischief. Probably they sense my nervousness and despise me for it. Certainly the one I was riding, hired for me from the livery stables in Bell Lane, was not the docile animal I had been led to believe by the groom. It sidled and bucked unnervingly whenever it had the chance to do so, and made heavy going over every patch of rough ground.

My companion, who sat upon a horse with greater ease, and handled the beast with greater skill than I would have expected, laughed openly at my attempts to quieten my mount.

'We should be at Hambrook Manor well before suppertime,' Richard consoled me, 'and home again before dark.'

'I cannot see why I should have been asked to accompany you,' I complained petulantly. 'I'm not an officer of the law. Why not Jack Gload or Pete Littleman?'

Richard shrugged, turning his head to look at the city now far below us as we reached the open spaces of the downs.

'You heard what Mayor Foster said. He and other members of the Council feel that Lady Claypole should be warned about her possession of this bed of hers – or at least made aware that it is no longer her secret. *You* know which bed it is. There need be no searching of the house should she choose to deny its existence. Indeed, she would be foolish to do so with you standing beside me.'

I felt angry. This woman had tried to kill me; or if that had not been her intention (and I was inclined to give her the benefit of the doubt) at least to give me a nasty fright. I had realized by now of course, that she had been afraid of my investigations leading me to her brother, Ralph Mynott – which suggested that she either knew something that could implicate him in Isabella's murder or else that she was unsure of his innocence; most probably the latter. But what angered me was that she was not to be charged with trying to harm a respectable citizen going about his lawful business, but instead to be warned politely that, in future, any strange disappearances in the vicinity of Hambrook Manor would bring her under immediate sus-picion. Had she been poor or without the protec-tion of a title, I doubted if she would have been treated with such consideration.

I said as much to Dick Manifold, but he told me not to be such a fool: it was the way of the world. This I knew already. But injustice was something I found difficult to reconcile myself to with any degree of equanimity. However, I said no more on the subject and we rode on in silence. I wondered if Richard were thinking of Isabella, remembering his meetings with her, here on the uplands, desolate in winter but beautiful, as now, in late spring with the trees and shrubs of burgeoning green.

Hambrook Manor eventually came into view as we trotted over a rise and began to descend a slight declivity set with brakes of foaming hawthorn blossom. Another brief canter and we were approaching the outer gate, where the porter let us in without demur, obviously impressed by Richard's air of authority and his badge of office. We were handed over to the Steward, who gave me a leery glance, but again put no rub in our way, merely remarking that he would ascertain if his mistress would be pleased to receive us.

He returned within a very few minutes and bade us both follow him to my lady's solar. As we mounted the shallow flight of stairs leading to this room, Richard hissed in my ear, 'Leave the talking to me. Don't speak unless you're spoken to.'

I felt my gorge rising and made no answer, but my anger was short-lived. As we entered the solar, it became apparent that Lady Claypole was not alone. At the sight of me, Juliette Gerrish rose to her feet and, ignoring Richard, came towards me, holding out both her hands.

'Roger!' she exclaimed, smiling broadly. 'How very unexpected, but how very nice to see you again.'

Nineteen

'Your visit to my uncle reminded him of obligations to an old friend,' Juliette said. 'It made him feel guilty that he had allowed so much time to elapse without seeking word of someone he once knew so well. But as he himself has been sick again these past few days, he requested me to come and obtain news of Lady Claypole for him.' She smiled that engaging smile of hers. 'So here I am.'

Lady Claypole had admitted frankly to her possession of the collapsing bed – her husband, the late Sir Peter, had brought it back with him after a tour to the Rhineland and remoter parts of Europe, further east, towards Muscovy – but apart from some pranks played on very close friends soon after his return (which, of course, she hadn't approved of) the bed had never been used, as far as she knew. What had happened to me, she insisted, was totally unaccountable; a servant must have accidentally touched a hidden switch, or perhaps the mechanism was now so old and rusty that it had set itself off. Whatever the reason, my unfortunate experience had nothing to do with her, nor, intentionally, with any member of her household, I could be certain of that. However, it accounted for my hitherto inexplicable nocturnal flight, and she tendered me her heartfelt apologies.

I have no idea if Richard believed her or not. I know I didn't. But he had achieved the object of his mission – to let our reluctant hostess know that Authority knew of the bed's existence – without any need to search the house or unpleasantness of any kind. Indeed, we had both been invited to stay to supper with my lady and to remain for the night.

'And you can be sure that this time your bed will not try to swallow you,' Lady Claypole had added with a thin-lipped smile that seemed to me to cost her something of an effort. But maybe I was mistaken. 'And,' she added, addressing me in particular, 'Mistress Gerrish has also agreed to give me her company until tomorrow. She still has a lot to tell me about my old friend, Robert.'

But Lady Claypole's anxiety to hear news of Master Moresby was not great enough to keep Juliette beside her while she talked to Richard Manifold. And her simpering looks when she spoke to him made me realize, with a sudden stab of jealousy, that he was in fact a handsomer man than I ever gave him credit for. Our hostess plainly found him more attractive than she found me. (But, I consoled myself, he was somewhat nearer to her in age.)

'I'll see that the horses have been stabled,' I offered, and left the house, only to be followed almost immediately by Juliette.

She grinned a little ruefully at the wary expression on my face.

'It's all right, Roger,' she said, linking an arm

through one of mine. 'I promise I won't seduce you again.' And it was then she told me how she came to be at Hambrook Manor. 'My uncle confessed the whole thing to me,' she finished. 'The reason you went to see him was not simply to apprise him of the death of a woman he had once loved, but because you suspected that he might have been her killer.' She added, suddenly sharp and withdrawing her hand from my arm, 'I'm not so sure I'd have let you make love to me if I'd known you thought my uncle capable of murder.'

'As a matter of fact,' I retorted, equally sharp, 'I could have sworn that it was you who made love to me.'

We had reached the stables by this time and I left her outside while I assured myself that our horses – Richard's and mine – were being look- ed after. I need not have worried, of course. Lady Claypole's servants might be an odd-looking bunch, but they knew their jobs well enough. I rejoined my companion and began walking back towards the house.

'Do you still suspect Uncle Robert of murder?' Juliette asked, pointedly ignoring our previous subject of conversation and once again tucking her hand into the crook of my elbow.

'I don't suppose we shall ever know the truth about the death of Isabella Linkinhorne,' I answered snappishly. 'There are two other suspects besides Master Moresby, and I doubt if after all these years anything can be proved against any of them.' I didn't mention that one of those other two men was now sitting with our hostess. I didn't think it necessary.

There was silence for a moment, then the pressure of my companion's fingers brought me to a standstill. Her face was troubled.

'My uncle didn't, it seems, tell you the whole truth, Roger. He admitted as much to me when we were discussing the matter after you had left.'

'What is the whole truth, then?' I asked, resisting a sudden urge to kiss her.

'That day – the day he waited for this woman here, at Hambrook Manor – he did, apparently, leave the house on one occasion and ride towards Westbury to look for her.'

'Lady Claypole didn't mention that when I asked her. She confirmed that Master Moresby remained with her and Sir Peter throughout.'

Juliette shrugged. 'Perhaps she's forgotten, or else she didn't know. It's so long ago.' I wondered how many more times I would hear variations of that phrase. 'Anyway,' she went on, 'Uncle Robert confessed to me that he saw Isabella talking to another man near the village. He didn't know who it was, didn't recognize him, but I imagine from what he said – my uncle that is – that there was something about the pair that gave him pause. And there was something else, too, that suddenly made him doubt Isabella's intentions towards himself. A silly thing, so trivial that in the end he dismissed it and rode back here without approaching the couple, convincing himself that Isabella had merely met a friend, an acquaintance, while on her way to him, to whom she had stopped to speak.'

'Why did Master Moresby not approach Mistress Linkinhorne?'

Juliette smiled faintly. 'Exactly what I asked Uncle Robert myself.'

'And? What was his answer?'

'That she had an uncertain temper and would have accused him of spying on her. My feeling is that he was a little afraid of her. He was most certainly afraid of losing her.'

'Except that he never had her,' I replied grimly. 'No one did.'

My companion sighed. 'I think he knows that now. I think it's that knowledge that has made him ill in recent days.'

'I'm sorry to have been the cause of his sickness. Perhaps, after all, the past is better left alone.'

'It's not really your fault.' She put up a hand and lightly brushed my cheek. 'Your Mayor, I think you told me, is the searcher after truth.'

I caught the errant hand in mine and held it fast to prevent any further assaults on my strength of purpose.

'What was this other thing your uncle noticed about Isabella? This something that suddenly made him doubt her intentions towards him? Something so trivial, you said, that he later dismissed it as absurd.'

'Oh, that.' Juliette made no attempt to free her hand. 'Now, what was it? What did Uncle Robert say?' She considered for a moment, her fingers clinging to mine, prolonging the moment, her thoughts plainly not on what she was saying. Then she seemed to make an effort to pull herself together. 'Yes, I remember. It seems that while my uncle was watching, the wind – it was, apparently, a very wet and windy day – the wind tore at Isabella's cloak and he caught a glimpse of the dress she was wearing underneath. He recognized it as an old one, he said, somewhat patched and darned, which she wore simply for riding. It occurred to him that she would have been decked out in her finery if she was going to run away with him. There! He said it was a trivial reason to doubt her, and of course it was. For my own part, I feel sure his suspicions arose more from the way in which she and the man were talking together. He recognized an intimacy that he didn't wish to believe in.'

'Why are you telling me this?' I asked abruptly. 'You didn't have to, and you must see that your uncle having lied to me makes him more of a suspect than he was.'

She shook her head. 'I don't really know. But by your own admission there are two other men who have incurred your suspicion. It seems only fair to you and to them that you should know the exact truth.' She added, suddenly anxious, 'You don't really believe Uncle Robert could have murdered this woman, do you?'

I sighed, looking down into the troubled brown eyes. 'I don't know what to believe,' I admitted. Foolishly, and almost without being aware of my action, I stooped and kissed her gently between the eyes. Next moment, she had raised herself on tiptoe, both arms clasped about my neck, and returned my kiss full on the lips.

Badly shaken, I released myself and stepped

back a pace. She grimaced and echoed my sigh.

'Still the married man, Roger?' she asked.

I nodded. 'I...I think we'd better go in.'

She made no demur, merely giving me a saucy grin that, nevertheless, struck me as a little lop-sided. But she behaved herself impeccably throughout supper and afterwards, when, in order to while away the time until the hour for bed, we played some games of chance and hazard; although with Lady Claypole presiding over the boards and counters, there was small opportunity for even the slightest dalliance on Juliette's part. Or on mine.

Richard and I took our leave of both ladies before we retired for the night, saying that we should rise betimes and be gone from Hambrook Manor no doubt before they were up and about. Our hostess bore the news well and said that she would give instructions to her Steward to see that we were fed before we left. Juliette blew me a kiss when she thought no one else was looking and, aloud, begged me to visit her if I ever again found myself in Gloucester. I promised to do so, secretly vowing to give the town a wide berth in future. Whether or not my resolution would hold good, only time would tell.

Richard and I had been allotted a handsome chamber at the front of the house with a wide, comfortable bed for our slumbers. We were both dog-tired and wasted no time in idle chatter, simply stripping off our clothes and tumbling between the sheets with no other conversation than the mutually expressed hope that the other didn't snore. But we were both asleep within minutes. At least, I know I was.

My rest, however, was disturbed by dreams. Most had no shape or sequence, being merely a muddle of things that had happened to me over the past few weeks. But then, suddenly, the general confusion resolved itself into a scene where I was standing above the great gorge, on the very edge of Saint Vincent's rocks, teetering on the brink and striving to keep my balance. I could see no one, hear nothing – all around me was an eerie silence, devoid even of birdsong – but uneasily aware that I was not alone. Then, with a clarity that made me start, the hermit's voice said in my ear, 'Red stockings! I ask you! With that gown!'

I plunged forward, but not into the treacherous water of the River Avon far below me. As is the fashion with dreams, the scene had changed abruptly to the ruined Linkinhorne house, and I was falling from the smoke-blackened stairs into the riot of vegetation forcing its way up towards the expanse of sky visible through the long-since vanished roof. The iron, copper-banded chest lay on its side on the ground, the contents already spilling out without any help from me or my cudgel. Hercules appeared and I could see that he was barking frantically, except that he was making no sound...

I was sitting up in bed, sweat pouring from my body, every nerve jangling, peering through the darkness of an unfamiliar room. Beside me, Richard Manifold slept peacefully, his steady breathing punctuated every now and then with a

324

sort of gurgling snore. I took a few deep breaths to calm myself and still the ragged beating of my heart before lying down again, staring up at the embroidered underside of the bed canopy, with its dimly seen pattern of fabulous beasts prowling through an exotic wilderness of flowers.

Of course! Of course, I thought. I was sure now who had murdered Isabella Linkinhorne. Well, almost. There might still be a doubt.

All the same, 'Thank You, Lord,' I whispered into the darkness.

With the early start we had promised ourselves, and with refreshed and reinvigorated steeds, Richard and I reached Bristol in time for dinner the following morning. I left my companion to return our horses to the livery stables and to seek out Mayor Foster to report the success of our mission, and went home to find Adela.

She was, as she always seemed to be, in the kitchen, struggling with a recalcitrant fire that appeared reluctant to burn to heat the pot of stew hanging from the hook of the trivet. (Being Friday, there was more than a whiff of fish in the air.) The hornbooks and styli of the two elder children lay abandoned at one end of the scrubbed wooden table, where my wife had been teaching them their lessons, while Adam had obviously worn himself out because he was curled up on Hercules's flea-infested straw bed fast asleep. Women, I reflected, not for the first time, were the losers in the game of life; the thankless drudges who smoothed the paths of their men. With a sudden access of guilt, I swung her round and kissed her soundly.

'Roger! You startled me! I didn't hear you come in.' Adela took my face between her hands and studied it closely. 'Something's happened. You're looking cheerful,' she commented shrewdly.

I squeezed her waist until she could hardly breathe and kissed her again.

'I believe I know who murdered Isabella Linkinhorne,' I said.

Her eyes widened. 'Who?' she demanded eagerly. Then a worried frown creased her brow. 'Not...not Richard?' she stammered.

I slackened my hold. 'Would that matter to you?'

Her gaze didn't waver. 'Of course it would. It would matter to me if it were anyone I knew.'

I renewed my grip on her, smiling apologetically.

'A foolish question. No, sweetheart, it's not Richard, but –' I pressed a finger to her lips – 'don't ask me yet for a name. I have to convince myself first that I'm right. There are questions I must ask – or, rather, ask again in order to confirm the answers. But I promise you that today or tomorrow should see an end to this business.'

She was content with that assurance. Adela was never a woman to demand explanations beyond those I was willing to give.

'You must be tired,' was all she said now. 'Come and sit down and eat your dinner.'

As soon as the meal was over – during which my

326

two elder children had forcibly expressed their disgust that I had returned home without bringing them each a gift – I set out at once for Steep Street, Hercules trotting at my heels. I was again particularly careful to make obeisance before the statue of the Virgin, set in the garden wall of the Carmelite Friary, in case Our Blessed Lady had been the source of the information now in my possession. One can never be too careful in placating the hierarchy of Heaven.

Hercules and I reached the top of the street to find that the site of the old graveyard had at last been cleared and that only Hob Jarrett was still working there, loading a few remaining stones and trails of bramble into the cart, where it stood, together with the patient donkey, at the edge of the track.

'Finished at last, then,' I remarked affably.

'What's that supposed to mean?' Hob demanded, regarding me belligerently from beneath the thick eyebrows that formed an almost straight line across his broken nose.

'Just an observation. No insult intended.'

He snorted in disbelief. 'What d'you want?'

'You were the man who found Isabella Linkinhorne's body four weeks ago.'

'Four weeks ago come next Thursday,' he agreed, his manner thawing a little. 'Why?'

'When the body was first exposed, there was a strip of material, some remnant of what she had been wearing, in the grave with her.'

Hob nodded. 'That's right. Green stuff, silk or velvet maybe. It crumbled into dust so fast I didn't properly see. And there was a shoe.' He shuddered. 'And some strands of hair sticking to the scalp. Black hair. Gave me a turn, I can tell you.'

'There was the jewellery, too,' I reminded him, but he saw fit to take exception to this remark.

'What are you implying?' He thrust out his underlip.

'Nothing, on my life! You're very touchy today.'

'Ah, well...' He shrugged. 'My goody's ill, the children need new shoes, and you never know, when one job ends, when the next will come along. Still, I s'pose I can always go back to tenting.'

I thanked him for his help, at which he looked surprised and muttered something that I didn't quite catch before stooping and heaving another stone into the cart. Meantime, I started back down the hill, detaching Hercules from his interested snuffling around the donkey's hooves and before that long-suffering animal could retaliate with a hearty kick. The dog looked up at me enquiringly.

'We're going for a long walk,' I told him. 'We're going to visit our old friend, the hermit at the great gorge. Try not to upset him this time.'

The morning had turned warm and drowsy, as May days sometimes do, and as we climbed free of the city and the houses that scrambled up the hillside beyond its walls, both Hercules and I slackened our pace somewhat, stopping every now and then to exchange greetings with fellow travellers on the road. There was little news to be gleaned, although a fellow pedlar, who had made his way from London by a circuitous route, said that the Duke of Gloucester had been in the capital recently and that, if rumour were true, there was likely to be war with the Scots before the summer was out. This information chimed with what I had witnessed in Gloucester and what Juliette Gerrish had told me, but I hurriedly put the thought of her out of my mind (or tried to) and proceeded on my way.

As we approached the edge of the gorge and the narrow path leading to the hermitage, I picked up Hercules and settled him firmly beneath my left arm. The chapel of Saint Vincent brooded silently on its cliff top, and the descent to the river below looked even more perilous than it had done last night in my dream.

The hermit was at home, having just returned, if the basket of berries and leaves was anything to judge by, from his daily forage for food. He was as little pleased to see me as on the previous occasion, but seemed resigned, this time, to the presence of the dog.

'You again,' he grunted. 'What do you want?'

'It's not our day for being welcome,' I informed Hercules. 'Is it that we smell, do you think?'

'It could be that you're simply a nuisance,' the hermit suggested sourly, probably aware that he smelled a good deal worse than we did. Not that he would regard it. Men of God were not supposed to waste their time with washing. 'So? Why have you come to see me? If it's about Isabella Linkinhorne again...'

'It is,' I said. 'There's something I need to ask you. Something I need to get clear.'

'And what's that then?'

'You told me, when I was last here, that you saw Isabella the day she disappeared, riding along the village street. It was a wet and windy day – everyone I've spoken to agrees on that – and the wind blew back her cloak and also whipped up her skirt, revealing her legs...'

'That's right,' he interrupted. 'In red silk stockings and green garters.' He gave a fastidious shudder which didn't deceive me for an instant. This man, I was ready to swear, had always had a prurient interest in women, their bodies and what they wore beneath their gowns. After twenty years, that sighting of Isabella was as fresh in his memory as if it had happened yesterday.

Which was fortunate for me.

'So you told me the other day,' I said. 'You also added, "With that gown!" Now why did you say that?'

'Because she was wearing a purple gown, that's why. Red stockings and green garters with purple! An unhappy choice of colours, I'm sure you'll agree.'

I grimaced. 'I don't think it would have occurred to me. However, the lady in question probably *would* have agreed with you. Her former maid remembers that Isabella had snagged her stockings on a chair in the parlour and was very annoyed that the only other pair she had ready to put on were red ones. Perhaps she, like you, Master Hermit, had a nice eye for colour.' If he sensed the sarcasm in my tone, he didn't respond. I continued, soothing Hercules, who

330

was beginning to get restless. 'I also seem to recollect your saying that you saw Isabella around mid-afternoon. Are you certain that she was just setting out? At that time of day – and on such a day – could she not have been returning home?'

The hermit, who had automatically opened his mouth to refute whatever I had to say, shut it again, a suddenly arrested expression on his thin, ascetic-looking face.

'Returning home,' he repeated. 'Well, now you come to mention it... Ye-es, I suppose she could have been.'

'Which way along the village street was she riding?' I asked, leaning forward in my urgency and squashing Hercules against my side. He let out an indignant bark. I hushed him impatiently.

The hermit furrowed his brow.

'In the direction of the open downs or towards her father's house?' My heart was thumping, willing him to give me the answer I wanted.

Time seemed to stretch endlessly – a long, shining thread that might snap at any moment, once more leaving me floundering – before my companion reluctantly acknowledged, 'Now I come to picture it again in my mind... Yes, I believe you might be right. Yes... Yes...' There was another protracted pause, but, finally, the hermit gave a decisive nod of his head. 'She was riding home.'

'You're sure of that? You're certain?'

'Positive.' He regarded me with sudden respect. 'Funny, but I've never given it a thought before. Not once in all these years. It just stuck in my mind that she was going for one of her madcap gallops across the downs. I should have realized, of course, that at that time of year the days were short and when I saw her it was already growing dusk. And then, as now, the downlands were a haunt for robbers and poachers and all manner of other rogues after dark.'

I let out my pent-up breath in a gasping sigh and thanked him far more profusely than the circumstances warranted. He eyed me suspiciously, trying to work out what he had said that had pleased me so much, and whether or not he had unintentionally incriminated himself.

I gave him what I trusted was a beaming, reassuring smile, once more expressed my thanks and, to his and Hercules's relief, took my leave.

Hercules was delighted to find himself once more back in the ruined house, a happy hunting ground which he set out to re-explore, bounding up and down the shattered staircase, leaping from one dangerous tread to the other just to show me that he could. But when he realized that I was looking for something among the clumps of purple loosestrife and general vegetation, he abandoned his own games to help me search.

I had a rough recollection of where I had found the chest two weeks ago, and made my way towards an eyeless window set high in the ground floor wall. And there it was, just underneath, the lock that I had broken with my cudgel hanging drunkenly from the iron-bound lid. The dog capered around me, barking excitedly.

'Hush!' I ordered him.

The lid creaked in protest as I lifted it for the second time and peered inside.

The contents were exactly the same: two undershifts, a pair of brown leather shoes and a gown of moth-eaten purple wool. It must, in days long gone, have contained much more in the way of a young girl's finery, but over the years since Isabella's death, it had gradually been reduced to these few articles, the other things either given away or taken by housemaids who knew where the key to the chest was kept, and who considered it a crying shame to let rot garments that they could put to better use...

A sudden, unnerving thought struck me. I had made an unwarranted assumption that the chest and its contents had once belonged to Isabella. But suppose it had been the property of her mother, Amorette Linkinhorne. What then?

With hands that shook slightly, I pulled out the fur-trimmed gown and held it up to the light. It was cut on very slender lines, a young woman's garment, not that of an elderly matron, and it was woollen – a gown for cold weather. Moreover, it was purple and the skirt had been darned as well as patched. It had to be the same dress that both the hermit and Robert Moresby had seen Isabella wearing that day; the day of her disappearance.

The sun, on its passage across the sky, suddenly shone full through the empty window, showing up a dark stain near the neck of the dress. I drew a sharp, hissing breath that caused

Hercules to stop barking and look at me enquiringly, head cocked to one side. I examined
the stain more closely.

It was difficult to be sure after twenty years,
but there was a rusty tinge to it even now.

I felt certain it had been made by blood.

Twenty

'You killed her,' I said. 'You or your wife.
Isabella came home that day, soaking wet from
her long gallop across the downs, hours spent in
the wind and rain, so the first thing she did was
to change her gown. She took off the old patched
and darned purple dress she used for riding and
changed it for one of green silk or velvet. After
that... Well, only you, Master Linkinhorne, can
tell me what happened next.'

It was the following day. I had waited until
after dinner before setting out for the Gaunts'
Hospital, in order to make certain that its inmates would be up and about, and that the early
morning round of the apothecary and the
almoner would be over. I had spent an uneasy
night, my – and Adela's – rest periodically
broken by the need to review the facts in my
mind and reassure myself that my conclusion
was the correct one. Adela, as always a source of
comfort, did her best to convince me that, with
the evidence at my disposal, I had reached the

right conclusion.

'It has to be Jonathan or Amorette Linkin-horne. But will you be able to make him admit it? Master Linkinhorne has only to deny every-thing, and to maintain that denial, to make matters awkward. Both the Clifton hermit and Master Moresby would have to be called on for their testimony, and I doubt if either would be prepared to swear to what they've told you. Not after all these years and not against a man of eighty-five summers who's old and frail. If Mayor Foster is hoping for a plain, straightfor-ward conviction, based on irrefutable evidence, he will be disappointed.'

I could do nothing but agree with her: Adela's assessment of the situation chimed so exactly with my own. But my instinct was to be defen-sive, too. What could John Foster reasonably expect after a score of years? I had done better than anyone had a right to anticipate after such a length of time.

Adela had soothed me in the same gentle tone of voice she used to smooth away the children's troubles. And it had occurred to me, as it had done more than once or twice before, to wonder if she saw me as the eldest and perhaps the most troublesome of those children. As ever, I put the thought from me and allowed myself to be lulled to sleep eventually in her loving arms.

We had the remainder of yesterday's fish stew for dinner and, when I protested, my wife reminded me that, after today, the rest of Mayor Foster's money must be returned to him.

'And until you get back on the road again,

Roger, we have very little left of our own.'

So it was with mixed feelings that, after dinner, I walked out of the Frome Gate and along the Backs to the hospital, set against the cloud of apple blossom that was, at present, its orchard. The cooing of the pigeons from the pigeon loft sounded loudly on the soft morning air.

Before I could state my business to anyone in authority, however, I was waylaid by that ever vigilant pair, Miles Huckbody and Henry Dando.

'Saw you coming,' announced the latter triumphantly, his rheumy blue eyes screwed up against the sunlight shafting in through the open doorway behind me.

'That's right,' confirmed his friend, his seamed and wrinkled face – the face of a much older man than Miles Huckbody really was – expressing equal smugness. 'Keeps our eyes and ears open, we do. There's not much we misses.'

'If it's old Jonathan Linkinhorne you'm lookin' for,' Henry Dando cut in, 'he's in the infirmary. Taken there this mornin' after breakfast.'

'What's the matter with him?' I asked anxiously, but neither of my informants seemed to know (or care particularly, if it came to that).

I sought out one of the chaplains, who reassured me that there was no cause for alarm.

'Just the general malaise of old age. Fatigue and boredom. I daresay he'll be glad to have a visitor.'

I doubted it, not one who confronted him with what I had to say. I hesitated momentarily, won-

336

dering if I should retreat and return another day, but then decided that if the thing were to be done at all, it would be better to do it quickly and get it over with. The chaplain reaffirmed that the patient's indisposition was not serious and conducted me into the long, narrow, whitewashed dormitory that was the hospital infirmary.

It so happened that Master Linkinhorne was the sole occupant, much to my great relief. He was propped up against pillows on a palliasse at the far end of the room and glanced towards the door as I came in with my guide. As we approached and he recognized me, I saw his eyes widen in – what? Apprehension? Alarm? But the next moment, they were shuttered by his lids, and when he opened them again, they were devoid of all expression.

'Someone to see you, Jonathan,' the chaplain said.

I sat down tentatively on the edge of the mattress. Here and there, bits of straw stuck through the thin ticking, irritating my legs and making me thankful that I was not an inmate of the hospital, especially a sick one.

'What do you want?' Jonathan Linkinhorne grunted at last, after a silence during which I debated how to explain the reason for my presence; an accusation of murder is hardly the easiest of subjects to broach.

In the end, I decided that the direct approach was the best, probably the only, one to take, so I came straight out with it – and waited for him to refute my words with a storm of anger and indignation. He did indeed lift a hand as though to ward off what I was saying, and, to begin with, I saw both shock and denial in the faded blue eyes. The slack flesh around the jawline quivered for a moment before he suddenly heaved a great sigh and let his head fall forward in acquiescence.

'I killed her,' he said. 'I had to. Isabella had attacked my wife with a knife. It was Amorette's life or hers.' He drew a deep breath. 'It wasn't the first time she had done so. Once before, Isabella tried to stab her mother while in a towering passion.'

'What provoked her rage on that day?' I asked, wondering if I were being told the truth or not. And yet, after all I had learned about Isabella, it had the ring of authenticity about it.

As though reading my thoughts, my companion raised his head and stared defiantly at me, the eyes, in which blindness was steadily and surely taking a hold, sparking with anger.

'You may believe me or not, as you please, but what happened, happened exactly as I shall relate it to you. Everything is as clear in my memory as if it had occurred only yesterday.' A great sob was wrenched out of him, but he had his emotions under control again almost at once. 'It would be a wonder if it were not. There's not a single day has passed in the last twenty years when I haven't gone over those dreadful events in my mind and wondered if they could have been avoided. To kill one's own child must be the most heinous crime before God and man.'

'Tell me how it came about,' I suggested gently. I found myself beginning to feel sorry for

338

the old man.

Jonathan nodded. He was calmer now, breathing easily, an expression of relief smoothing out his features. The dreadful secret, suppressed for so long, was at last going to be shared with another.

'Isabella had been out riding all day; a day of terrible wind and rain. In the morning, after breakfast, my wife had pleaded with her not to leave the house; to forgo her exercise just for once. Isabella was suffering from the flux and my wife considered it unwise for her to ride at all in the circumstances, but especially in such weather. I added my voice, begging our daughter not to be so foolish. Begging is perhaps not the right word. Ordering would be a better one.'

'To which Isabella took exception,' I hazarded. Although from what I knew of her, it was more a statement of fact than a guess.

Master Linkinhorne pulled down the corners of his mouth. 'She had long outgrown our control.' He shrugged. 'You think me weak, I've no doubt. Most fathers would have taken a strap to her, put her under lock and key, but somehow I could never bring myself to do so. She was the child of our old age, Master Chapman; the child Amorette and I had given up hope of having when the Lord saw fit to send her to us. We lavished love upon her from her birth; no child could have been more cherished. And how did she repay us? With contumely, with vituperation, with...with... I must say it, with hatred.' There was a pause, then he grimaced ruefully. 'But I think, if memory serves me right, I told you all this when you came to see me three weeks ago. You must forgive me if I repeat myself. It is, unfortunately, a habit of old age.'

'No matter. But you were telling me about the day of the murder,' I prompted.

He visibly flinched at the last word, and said nothing further for a moment or two. Then he took another deep breath and continued.

'Ah, yes. The murder. Although I must confess that I've never thought of it as such.' A further pause, and then he shook his head vigorously as if renouncing something.

'That's not quite the truth, though, is it? If I hadn't considered it to be murder, I wouldn't have concealed what happened – even to the extent of sending out the servants next day to make enquiries as to Isabella's whereabouts and who might have seen her.'

I frowned. 'But not very urgent enquiries. Nor did you pursue them for any length of time. Once I began to suspect you, your apparent indifference to what might have become of your daughter, the ease with which you seemed to accept her disappearance, only added, in my estimation, to the weight of evidence against you. But you still haven't told me precisely what happened that day she returned from riding.'

Once more, he lifted his frail shoulders and dropped them. 'As I've said, it was a dreadful day. When Isabella came home not long before suppertime, she was soaked to the skin. She went straight up to her chamber and changed her gown from the old purple one she had put on that morning – one she kept for dirty and muddy days – to the green silk one my wife had made for her a few months earlier. Then she joined us in the solar where Amorette was doing her embroidery, seated at her frame, and I was idling away an hour before the evening meal. I asked her – Isabella that is – where she had been and what she had been doing in such weather. My attitude, my tone of voice were moderate enough, I can assure you, even though my wife and I had both been extremely worried for our daughter's safety. They certainly didn't warrant the unrestrained outburst of fury with which my question was greeted. (Although, in all honesty, I have to admit that the flux always made Isabella even more ill-tempered and intractable than she normally was.) For some reason – women's reasons again, perhaps – our daughter's insolence infuriated Amorette. She got to her feet in such a rage that she was almost speechless and did what I had never seen her do in her life before. She slapped Isabella full across the face with such force that Isabella was sent staggering back against the wall, cutting her bottom lip on one of her teeth.

'Amorette and I had been eating fruit; some of the previous autumn's apples taken out of winter store. There was a knife, lying on the plate along with the cores and peel. Before I realized what was happening, Isabella had seized it and was attacking her mother in a frenzy. My wife was fending her off as best she could and calling to me for help. I tried to drag Isabella away, but she was like a woman possessed, lending her the strength of ten. Within seconds, I was bleeding from a cut to my hand.'

'So you hit her with something. Something heavy,' I said, as once again Jonathan Linkinhorne paused.

'Yes.' The monosyllable fell flatly between us, heavy as lead, before he went on, 'There was a pewter vase in a niche in the wall. I hit my daughter over the back of her head with it.' Tears welled up suddenly in his eyes, furrowing his cheeks; great sobs racked him, the more shocking and poignant because they were silent. 'I didn't mean to kill her,' he rasped after a moment, 'just to stop her killing Amorette. She fell where she stood, but when we turned her over, to pick her up, we found Isabella was dead.'

The voice faded and became suspended, and the old man's chest heaved as though he could barely breathe.

'I'll call the Infirmarer,' I said anxiously, getting to my feet.

'No!' Jonathan gasped, reaching up and plucking at my sleeve. 'I'll be all right in a moment or two. I'll tell you the rest. It will be a relief to unburden my conscience after all these years.'

So I sat down again on the edge of the mattress and waited for the spasm to pass. When it had I asked, 'Did none of the servants hear anything of this quarrel?'

He shook his head. 'They had all gone home. The only two who might have done were both out of the house. Emilia Virgoe, Isabella's old nurse, and her maid, Jane Honeychurch, were both absent that day. I forget why.'

'Mistress Virgoe told me that she was staying with her sick sister in Bristol. You had given her leave of absence to do so. As for Jane Honeychurch – Goody Purefoy as she is now – she said...' My voice tailed off as memory came flooding back and I recollected exactly what it was that Jane Purefoy had said.

The old reprobate on the bed gazed limpidly back at me, but a tic suddenly appeared in one of his cheeks. 'What did she say?' But the question was tentative.

'That she had gone into Bristol to visit her foster mother. That your wife, who was visiting a friend there, had taken her in the covered waggon. That Mistress Linkinhorne also brought her home again, after dark. That, by then, Isabella had already disappeared.' During the ensuing silence, Jonathan Linkinhorne and I stared each other out, but his gaze was the first to drop. I went on remorselessly, 'Isabella didn't attack your wife, did she? She had done so once, but not on that occasion. Suppose now you tell me what really happened.'

I thought, by the way he compressed his lips, that he would refuse to say anything more. There was, after all, nothing I could do to force him to speak. He was a sick old man and there were no witnesses to the conversation we had just had. But in the end I think, as he had said, the need to unburden himself was genuine. Reluctantly, he abandoned his former story.

'All right,' he admitted. 'I didn't kill Isabella. She wasn't attacking my wife. As you've discovered, Amorette wasn't even there. But my cousin was.'

'You mean Sister Walburga?' I interrupted.

Jonathan nodded. 'Yes, Jeanette. She'd entered the Magdalen nunnery as a postulant some few days before and had come to take formal leave of me. It isn't a retired order, but she knew that we wouldn't see much of one another in future, and she wanted my blessing. My approval, I suppose, of what she was doing; of the step she had taken. And it was while she was with me that Isabella came home.' He heaved himself up a little in the bed. 'What I told you just now wasn't altogether a lie. Parts of it were true. But it was Jeanette and I who were in the solar when Isabella came in after changing her gown. I did ask Isabella where she'd been and she did fly into a rage, but it was me she attacked with the fruit knife...' His voice became suspended.

'And it was Sister Walburga who hit her with the vase,' I finished for him.

'Yes. I didn't want to implicate her unless I had to.'

'So what did you do when you realized that your daughter was dead?' I asked, although I could guess at least part of the answer.

'It was getting dark. I had promised Jeanette some vegetables to take back with her for the nuns, and they'd been dug up earlier by one of the men before he went home, and loaded into the cart we used for market. She said I must help her put Isabella's body into the cart as well, and drive back with her to the nunnery. It's outside the city walls, like this place, so curfew didn't matter. She said a grave had been dug in the nuns' graveyard for one of the Sisters who was very sick and had been expected to die, but who, in my cousin's opinion, was more likely to recover. I asked what would happen if she didn't, but Jeanette said it was a chance we had to take. And if she did get better, my cousin said it would be an easy enough matter to plant the idea of a miracle in the minds of the other two nuns.'

'Which she successfully did, according to Sister Apollonia,' I said. 'But go on.'

My companion shifted restlessly. 'There's not much more to tell. We had the house to ourselves: the hands we employed, the two girls and the men, all had homes in the village. We couldn't afford to feed them more than their dinners. Only Emilia and Jane Honeychurch lived with us. So we put Isabella's body in the cart, I drove it to the graveyard, we buried Isabella in the vacant grave, I left Jeanette at the nunnery door, together with the sack of vegetables, and returned here. I turned Isabella's horse loose and lived in dread for the next few days that it would make its way back again. But it never did. It was a valuable animal and some-one no doubt found it wandering and thought his luck was in.'

'Your wife?' I queried. 'Did you tell her the truth?'

'Oh, yes. I had to.' The rheumy eyes clouded over. 'It hit her hard, but in the end, she agreed that we had to protect Jeanette because she had only been protecting me. We made a pretence of searching for Isabella, but of course we knew we would never find her. We knew where she was all the time. But the knowledge was too much for Amorette to bear. The following year she drowned herself in the Avon. Of course, most people thought it was an accident, and there was no proof to the contrary. Even I couldn't swear it was suicide, although naturally I had my doubts...'

'You told me, when we spoke before, that you sent that day to Emilia Virgoe's cottage to ask if Isabella were there, yet you knew she wasn't at home.'

'God's fingernails, man!' Jonathan thumped his coverlet in exasperation. 'As far as I knew then, what I told you didn't matter. I didn't think you were going to ferret out the truth and disturb my peace.' He began to breathe heavily again. 'And you can't be sure that what I've told you now is really the truth, can you?' He gave a wheezing laugh that stuck in his throat and threatened to choke him.

He was right, of course. He had told me two different stories within a very short space of time, adapting the second to fit the information I had gathered for myself.

Jonathan gave a throaty chuckle which rapidly degenerated into a spasm of coughing. When, finally, he could speak, he wheezed, 'Jeanette, if you question her, will deny everything.' I wondered how he knew that. 'And then you won't know who to believe, now will you?'

'I know Isabella was killed at home by you or whoever was with you.'

'I'll deny everything I've told you. I'll swear

you're making it up.'

I hesitated. I knew that such evidence as I had was flimsy. A lawyer who knew his trade – and which of them doesn't? – could easily bemuse Hob Jarrett and his two cronies into doubting the evidence of their eyes; into doubting even that there was a piece of Isabella's gown still in the grave, let alone that it had been green. Silk or velvet? They had described it as both at one time and another. And Robert Moresby's evidence, relayed to me by Juliette? On reflection, no colour of the gown Isabella was wearing had been mentioned, nor, as Adela had guessed, would Master Moresby wish to get involved. No, I might have solved the mystery, but I would never prove my case. It was true, what Jonathan Linkinhorne and everyone else had said from the beginning: it was all too long ago. Raking over such cold and dead ashes was a profitless pastime, a wasted effort.

'What will you do now?' Jonathan asked. His voice, in the last few moments, had grown fainter.

I glanced at him in concern, but he waved his hand at me impatiently, a dismissive movement as if he understood that there was nothing left for me to stay for.

I got to my feet. 'I'll tell Mayor Foster what I've learned. The rest is up to him.'

My companion smiled weakly, but his tone, when he spoke, was a little stronger.

'He won't do anything. At least, not if he's wise. Warn him, if you have to, that I'll refute everything I've told you.' He was seized by another bout of violent coughing before adding faintly, 'I intend to end my days, whatever their number, here and die in my bed. And if His Worship has any intention of visiting me himself, with the mistaken notion that he can wrest the truth from me, tell him to spare himself the trouble.' He sketched a ghastly smile. 'I may even do that for him.'

Jonathan Linkinhorne was certainly a sicker man than the chaplain believed him to be.

I said again, 'I'll fetch the Infirmarer.'

He shook his head. 'Nothing he can do. Won't let him. Won't take his potions. Leave me be. Just go.'

I went.

John Foster bit his lip.

'So you really think there's nothing we can do? No accusation we can bring?' As I shook my head, he added sadly, 'I had hoped for better than this.'

I felt a flare of annoyance, almost of anger – unusual in my dealings with this man.

I had waited until Monday before seeking out the Mayor, catching him early, just after breakfast, at home, too soon for him to have started the working day. I had told him everything I knew, the evidence I had for believing Isabella was killed in the Linkinhorne house, how I had come by it, and finally repeating Saturday's conversation with Jonathan himself. But I had also advised that to pursue the accusation could do no good.

'You should have had a witness to your talk

with Master Linkinhorne,' the Mayor said fretfully. 'Surely you should have thought of this?'

I took a deep breath and waited until I had slowly unclenched my hands.

'It would have done no good, Your Worship. With a witness, he wouldn't have said anything; he wouldn't have admitted to the truth at all.'

'Whatever the real truth is.' John Foster sighed, then his features, previously set in unwontedly stern and aggrieved lines, gradually relaxed. 'Forgive me, Master Chapman. I realize you did your best and it is, as you say, all a very long time ago. Well, well! I shall say nothing of what you've told me. There would be no purpose in doing so. But the ground must be re-consecrated, of course.'

'You intend to go ahead, then, with your plan to build your chapel and almshouses on that plot?'

'Certainly.' He looked somewhat surprised that I should ask such a question.

'And to dedicate the chapel to the Three Kings of Cologne?'

He smiled. 'Even that. It would have been nice, of course –' his tone was still faintly reproachful – 'to have earned my peers' approval by solving for them a mystery which has interested them more than a little. However, it was not to be, and I'm not the man to be discouraged by small setbacks. Besides,' he added with a comical grimace, his good humour now quite restored, 'if the building progresses at the same rate as clearing the graveyard ground has done, it might be some time yet before I need make my intentions fully known. And by then – who can tell? – our disagreements with members of the Hanseatic League may be over.' But he spoke like a man with no confidence in such a prediction.

'I'm sorry,' I said, preparing to take my leave of him, 'that I was unable to fulfil all your hopes of me.' I proffered a leather bag, the same drawstring purse he had given me a few weeks earlier, but which now jingled rather less than it had done then. 'The rest of your money, sir. My wife is a careful housekeeper.'

He was affronted. 'No, no, Master Chapman! I won't take it! Of course, I won't! You've earned every penny of it. If I've been churlish in my thanks, then please forgive me. It was reprehensible of me. You have achieved a great deal.'

I argued a little more, but soon saw that I was giving offence where none was intended, and so took my leave, walking down the street to my own home.

Adela grabbed the purse, when I explained what had happened, and put it away. As the person whose task it was to put food on the table and attend to her family's wants, she was less scrupulous than I when it came to accepting gifts of money. And who could blame her? I was never going to make her a rich woman, not if we both lived to be a hundred.

'You're disgruntled,' she said, putting her arms around me. 'And yet you solved this mystery, as you've solved all the others.'

'But not as satisfactorily,' I argued. 'No one's

been brought to book for the crime.'

'It was a very long time ago,' Adela protested, words seared into my brain. 'Twenty years. And from all that you've ever told me, there have been other occasions when the guilty person has apparently gone free. But God, my love, moves in His own mysterious way. It's not our place to question His wisdom. You've done all you can. That should be enough.'

But somehow, it didn't seem enough. I was beginning to wonder if my God-given powers were deserting me; if it wasn't time I settled down and became nothing more than a pedlar. (Richard Manifold would have said that that was all I was, in any case.) Perhaps God had no further use for me.

It was a sobering thought.

AOK

ALFIE